Blood Relations

Michelle McGriff

URBAN
Renaissance

www.urbanbooks.net

Urban Books, LLC
78 East Industry Court
Deer Park, NY 11729

ISBN 13: 978-1-60162-348-5
ISBN 10: 1-60162-348-8

First Mass Market Printing May 2012
First Trade Printing December 2009
Printed in the United States of America

10 9 8 7 6 5 4 3 2 1

This is a work of fiction. Any references or similarities to actual events, real people, living, or dead, or to real locales are intended to give the novel a sense of reality. Any similarity in other names, characters, places, and incidents is entirely coincidental.

Distr
Subm
Kens
C/O
Atten
405
East
Phon
Fax:

Dedication

To all those who have and keep family secrets

Acknowledgments

Blood Relations was written because *Obsession 101* was so intriguing to some of my readers. They got into the characters from that book and wanted to see the saga of Rashawn Ams through to completion.

Although this particular storyline is now complete, the family is so intricately woven into the Palemos (my fictitious community) that their story—their family will continue to cameo many books to come.

Even though I currently live in Portland, Oregon, my heart belongs to the San Francisco Bay Area. Being a native Californian and growing up in the Bay Area, I wanted to offer rich urban stories for those of us on the West Coast to enjoy.

The Palemos is an area in the Bay Area right around Palo Alto that I created in order to give my characters a home base that was familiar to me. I wanted to use a fictitious place in order to take city life in the Bay Area a little further over the top with the use of literary license. I say this because some readers want very strict realistic lines draw up when the writer uses their city or town—and I try to do that but at the same time, allow for imagination to flow. So I will include many familiar sights and sounds—the Bay Area Rapid Transit system—BART, The Golden Gate Bridge and a few small coves that only natives know about. I hope this will bring a satisfied smile to the Bay Area reader's faces.

While living a "sort of" dual residency, I get to meet many different "types" of people. The cultural difference between Oregon and California (both northern and southern) lend me much fodder and willing muses for writing as well as opening my mental doors for rich characters to come through. I believe the West Coast as an entirety has a gold mine of stories to be told.

I want to thank those who have offered their lives, laughter, and love as inspiration to my work. These people have stuck by me for many years now and have seen me grow as a writer. Some are new, but have come right in line as a true fans and I love that. I do miss Candace Cottrell and her wonderful book covers but I'm sure she's doing big things and wowing other's with her talent. Gayle Jackson-Sloan, I know what you told me . . . but still, I believe there is another book in there! Thank you

Shelia M. Goss for always being there to yak with, you always seem to know when I need a mental break from writing and vice versa. It's been great being friends.

There are so many people I want to name by name but I can't, these pages are only allotted so much space in a novel. You do all know who you are though. I can see you all now, "she knows she shoulda put my name in those acknowledgement pages." Consider it done!

Can you imagine a novel of thanks . . . hmmm sounds like a best seller. Remember, best sellers are not written they are bought so yes, a list the names of all those who have helped me along the years would be bought by millions!!!

I want to thank those with Internet radio shows who have interviewed me over the years. Those shows really do help, so keep it up! Oh and call me, I'd love to come back! (smile).

The Internet has been a wonderful place to find support groups (Online bookclubs, offline book clubs like Kindred Spirit, Face Book friends, Myspace friends, as well as old high school friends realize I 'still' write) and I want to thank all of those people who have come on board with me in the support area.

Colored Summer made Black Expressions Top 100 in 2009 and I just want to say I'm so thrilled about that. I can only hope that this notoriety will soon have me on other lists such as *Essence Best Seller*, *Publisher's Weekly* and ultimately the *New York Times*. With the continued support of Maxine Thompson (www.maxinethompson.com) and her literary agency, Carl Weber and his imprint getting me in print, Natalie Weber's great choices in editorial staffing, Jan's reading, Terry's critiquing, Joanne's logic and good sense oh & legal know-what, Mary, Terrill and Heather's allowing me to vent, Denise and Butu's making me smile, and Mr. C.'s sweet reminders that all I need is a love to keep going—I believe I'm actually on the road to big things!

My author friends and I support one another wholeheartedly and push for the success of each other—now that's a family connection. But I do want to thank my blood relations as well for continuing to support me in my writing and educational endeavors.

I hope you all enjoy *Blood Relations* and add it to your "WOW" list.

Prologue

Craven's long legs uncrossed as she jutted forward in her swivel office chair. "I said, I don't have a good feeling about this."

"I think you're being a prude. I mean how many times and chances would a person like you have an opportunity like this?"

"Person like meee?" Her voice reached a defensive shrill.

He raised his hands in surrender. "I didn't mean it like that."

"It doesn't matter how you meant it, get outta my office!" she barked. "We're through talking." She pointed her long, slender, well-manicured fingernail toward the door.

"You're being a fool. Tell me you weren't immediately intrigued and seduced by this opportunity!"

"Yes. No!" she yelped, covering her ears. Craven had to admit within her heart of hearts that yes, she had been intrigued by the opportunity—

initially. But "seduced" by the opportunity . . . no. Something other than the opportunity had seduced her. But since the visit she'd had from that odd visitor the other day, she'd been less than trusting of the seductive philanthropist backing this project. What her odd visitor had told her had made her uncomfortable, fearful of the philanthropist actually, and fear was something—much like anything not carrying a designer label—she didn't wear well. She now regretted having shared the prospects of this project with her partner, Hap Washburn, before really checking the whole thing out and making a final—*final*—decision.

"Why would you give up a chance to make medical history?"

Craven glared at Hap. "This isn't medical history. This is about money. This is murder!"

"This isn't some kid's game, Craven; sometimes there are sacrifices. Haven't you read his work? Don't you see and understand the big picture?"

"You're not . . . you're not making any sense!" She shook her head violently, interrupting his diatribe. Of course she'd read his supposedly hypothetical work; she had her doubts on all of it, and him. He seemed really close to the border with ethics and sanity as far as she was concerned. But she knew Hap admired the man—more than a little bit. It was ridiculous. He wasn't a god. He was just a man. And she knew that first hand. "Hap! He's talking about killing an innocent . . ." Craven fanned out her hand emphatically, "child . . . A boy. His own flesh and—"

"I'm not looking at it that way."

"Apparently!" Craven slammed her hands on her hips. "Look," she said, tightening her lips and, in a nervous mannerism, moving her hair behind her ear, "I have to be honest, when I first saw those numbers I was almost caught up, but . . ."

"But what?" His expression became pensive.

"I've been thinking about this. And I just don't think it's right. He's crazy. His work is unethical and . . ."

Hap's eyes burrowed into hers now. If silence could make a sound, the growing silence between them would be deafening. "You trying to cut me outta this?"

"No! Of course not," Craven lied. She wanted not only him out, but maybe herself too. True, she'd taken the first payment without telling him, but . . .

She swallowed hard, unconsciously allowing guilt to ride across her forehead as quickly as a bobsled racer at his best downhill speed. Hap went for her throat just as quickly. Her reflexes were catlike, but not fast enough. "You're lying.

Damn you!" he growled, closing his large hand around her throat. "You are so selfish!"

Slamming her stiletto heel onto his foot, she used her other foot to kick his shin hard, before headbutting him. He cried out in pain, losing his grip just enough for her to get away from him.

"You're crazy!" she screamed, charging for the office door.

Statuesque at nearly six feet tall, her stride was long, and she'd almost made her escape before he tackled her to the floor, rolling her over and sitting on her hips, again taking her by the throat, this time with both hands. Hap was a lanky man, around her height. He'd apparently been bigger at one time, as his clothes often bagged on him—despite his efforts to look "in style." That often bugged Craven, but once he was out of those rags, he was a true contender. Unfortunately, not here, not now—right now she was quickly becoming a victim.

"Craven, we are supposed to be a team. We were supposed to do this together. But no, you always do this," he growled.

"Whyyy, why are you trying to kill me?"

"I'm not trying . . . trust me," he said, evil peeking out from under his tongue.

"You don't have to do this."

Her strength was not enough to match his, although she tried, wriggling under his weight as he straddled her. "You have to die, Craven. You just do! Nothing can stand in my way. If you aren't with me, you become the enemy. You must understand that. He wrote that in his book, too," Hap explained, sounding almost excited to have remembered that little tidbit. Her movement under him seemed to excite him as well, although this was no love play—no repeat of that morning's activity, of this she was certain.

"I thought you loved me," she said, hoping to make him remember what they'd shared that morning, what they'd had over the last couple of months. "I'm your girl," she simpered. "You're not my killer. You're my soulmate."

"Soulmate," he chuckled wickedly. "Then I guess I'll be joining you in hell one day."

Craven thought about his words. The thought of eternity with Hap Washburn had never crossed her mind; especially not in such a place as terrible as hell.

"Hap! Hap, don't get crazy. I'm sorry. I'm sorry," she begged. Hap stared into her eyes. She could see regret backstroking in his soft brown pools. He smiled, showing blood at the corner of his mouth. He'd apparently bitten his tongue when she headbutted him.

"I came to show you this," he said, pulling a syringe from his lab coat.

Her eyes widened at the sight of it. She knew what was in it and what would happen if she was injected. "No, Hap," she gasped, tightening her grip on his hand.

"You look really hot when you're scared." He grinned.

"Well, then I must look like fire then because I'm scared as hell right now," she admitted.

Laying his body weight on her, and stretching himself, prone, over her, she realized then that his plan to kill her had been diverted. Slipping the syringe back in his lab coat she felt him, within the same motion, unzipping his trousers. "I'll kill you when I'm done," he purred. Maybe it was her thong that gave the impression she was open for business, but she wasn't. He entered her without permission. Believing his intent was to murder her within the next three to four minutes did nothing for her sexual ardor. Neither of them climaxed. It was the weirdest thing.

Before Craven died she felt a kind of nick one feels when shaving already smooth legs in the shower. The pain, increasing to a burn, was like the slight heat one might feel when using a cheap razor to line up one's brow.

Chapter 1

It was the freakiest thing. His friend's neighbor was found dead yesterday morning. "Heart attack," Reggie said, explaining it again to his stepbrother. His friend had called and was telling him about how his "hot and sexy" neighbor, whom he'd often enjoyed watching undress through the window (*perv*) was just *dead*.

"Wow," Junior said excitedly. "Are the cops looking into it?"

"No, fool. Cops don't look into heart attacks. Sheesh." Reggie hated when Junior got in his personal space this way. He was talking on the phone and here Junior was—eavesdropping. *Why does he feel he has the inside scoop like that? We ain't pawdnas . . . joined at the hip and all that,* Reggie pondered in growing irritation. Sure, Reggie's mother was married to Junior's father, but still, it wasn't as if Junior was "truly" a part of this family—not according to the things he'd overheard when his parents argued. And they argued a lot. A lot of the arguments were about old stuff—that was obvious—because Junior's mother was at the root of it all, and clearly what had gone on between Reggie's stepfather, Chance, and Junior's mother, Juanita, was old news. At least that was Chance's end of the argument. *Why can't Ma just let it go,* Reggie wondered now, thinking of his always stressed-out mother and pushing the front door open. The warmth and good home-cooked smells hit his face.

"So his totally healthy neighbor just dropped dead, just like that, and nobody asked any questions. Nobody suspects foul play," Junior babbled on.

And then there's the always-there Junior. Maybe that's why my mom can't let it go, because he's always here, Reggie realized, groaning slightly at the sound of Junior's voice.

"Mom's not here. She said don't snack it up either, because we're having a big dinner since she's leaving in a coupla days," Rainey, his half sister, said in passing, her head not coming up from her textbook, or her feet from the floor as she shuffled into her bedroom. Now, Rainey was another story; she was the daughter of his mother and Chance. She fit in. She even looked like Chance. Fair skin, freckles, light-colored eyes, not too tall. Yeah, she looked just like him. Junior didn't look like Chance or his mother, Juanita. Junior was big—not fat—but tall, taller than Chance, and darker, too. Even Juanita's complexion was more of a honey brown. But Junior's was dark—more like his own complexion, and Reggie knew he took after his mother in that regard. For all Reggie knew, he took after his mother in all regards—because he didn't know who his father was.

"Big dinner—sweet—because I'm starving," Junior said, dropping his books on Chance's favorite large recliner.

"When are you going home?" Reggie asked, not caring if the question was rude. He'd ended his conversation and was about to start another.

Junior just smiled as if he didn't care either. "I am home, broman."

"You wish," Reggie mumbled, lugging his heavy backpack into his room and closing the door behind him, as if that were enough to keep Junior out. He was tired of Junior—or maybe it was his life he was frustrated with. It was always the same: drama, arguments, bad feelings and vibes. He was looking forward to this break, this getaway. He was going to Eugene, Oregon to look at the college there. His mother was against him going out of state. She wanted him to attend the local college where she and Chance worked. "H to the no," he huffed.

He glanced at his clock and wondered where his stepfather was. Then, through the door, he heard Chance talking to Junior. For an instant Reggie felt a little jealous, but shook it off. He was the one who really needed to talk to a father right now. He had some major decisions to make with his life. But no, he was reduced to talking to his buddies or counselors at school. *Whatever*. When he was gone, Chance and Rainey would have all the time they needed with their father. "Since I'm the one who really doesn't belong in this family," he mumbled. Sometimes he wished he knew who his real father was.

Just then his phone rang. The return number was blocked. He hesitated, but then answered it.

"Is this Reggie Ams?

"Yeah."

"Well, young man, this is a very exciting day for you."

Chapter 2

Rashawn looked again at her calendar. Really soon, she would be taking off on vacation. "No kids, no husband, and best of all, no . . ." She thought about Juanita, Chance's ex-wife. That woman was the bane of her existence. Every day it was something new. If she didn't know any better, she'd believe Juanita was a threat to her marriage, but there was no way Chance was still into that crazy woman. He'd sworn off Juanita when they got married. Before then, however, Juanita had tried everything, even getting pregnant and putting that child on Chance. Anybody with eyes could see that Junior was no more his son than Reggie was. But Chance had refused to get a blood test—sometimes Rashawn wondered about that. "Too late now, fifteen years is just way too late to worry about that." Maybe it was just sour grapes that Rashawn felt. It wasn't as if she'd given him a son—no. But she had given him a beautiful daughter, one he could have had by himself, as strong as the resemblances were.

Fifteen years had indeed been a long time to worry about a lot of things. Glancing from her window out over the campus, she wondered if in fact she'd actually stopped worrying or just put the memories away. In the last few years she had moved up the career ladder, taking one promotion after the next until she was dean. She'd not had time to worry about what she couldn't change . . . like the past. Nonetheless, she'd started dreaming about the past again. Painful dreams that woke her in a sweat. She tried talking to Chance about them but he wasn't having it. He wasn't about to take that trip down horror avenue.

She'd been raped on this campus, and to this day she wasn't sure she'd recovered. She'd surely challenged the memories by staying on this campus this long—working here as if to say, "Bring it on, I got a handle on it." But even now, sometimes she found herself on the wrong end of the campus or parking lot and again the panic would wave over her.

Chance is probably right. It has been long enough to let the past go, Rashawn reasoned as she ran her hand over the red leather of her wing back chair. The knock at her door brought her back from her reverie instantly. It was a light tap followed by the door opening. Renee, her secretary, stuck her head in and grinned. Renee was a young black woman, maybe around thirty, but she had an old soul, that Rashawn knew. Renee reminded Rashawn a lot of her baby sister, Shelby.

Shelby was barely forty, but since retiring from a pro basketball career a few years back, she acted like a senior citizen most of the time. Perhaps it was the word "retire" that had gotten to her, or maybe it was the life she was living with her husband and daughter in Eugene, Oregon, where her husband coached at the junior college. It was a quiet life, Shelby had told her. Rashawn wondered if her own life could ever get so subdued, what with a house full of teenagers all the time. *Thanks, Juanita, for the extra kid,* Rashawn balked internally.

Yeah, Juanita was an old-school home wrecker, still playing the same old games and up to the same ol' tricks. It was a constant battle to keep Juanita out of her life while helping Chance do his part as a father to her son. Yes, Rashawn would say her life was rockin' most of the time.

"I was going to head on home if you don't have anything else for me to do," Renee said. Rashawn wasn't used to having a secretary, and over the last few months since taking the position as dean, she'd not really used Renee to the fullest.

Never had Rashawn thought her job as a teacher would end her here one day—dean of an esteemed private school in northern California. Years ago, however, this very same school, Moorman University, had been the source of great agony and trauma in her life. Here on this very campus, she worked alongside a rapist and the father of her son, Reggie. However, Moorman University had been redeemed for its blame in her pain, for here within these hallowed halls, she'd met her husband— Chance Davis—and had been, literally, given another chance at life, love, and happiness. Chance was a good man. He'd raised Reggie as his own, along with a daughter they shared, Rainey. He'd been a good father to Chance Jr., too, despite her vote still being out on that paternity test result. Sometimes Rashawn wondered if her life and brain weren't still suffering from the effects of the date rape drug she'd been subjected to during yet another attack by a demented terrorist, Allen Roman. Sometimes Rashawn noticed how obsessed she was with the same thoughts rolling around her head, over and over, replaying the same scenes in her mind.

"So are you all packed?"

"You bet. I can't wait to get away. I need a change of scenery. My brain is stuck seriously on stupid I think."

Renee chuckled. "I just love retreats. I've never heard of a literary retreat though."

"Oh, it's one my sister is involved with. She moved out to Arizona to write novels and there's a woman there who hosts these retreats for book clubs every now and then. I've gone before. They're wonderful—good food, laughs, and you get to meet some really fascinating people who write really good books."

"Really, now why didn't I know your sister was a novelist?"

"I don't know, she's pretty good. She writes mysteries."

Renee twisted her lip. "Oh, that's why . . . fiction. I never read fiction. It's so far from real life."

Rashawn chuckled. "You can say that again. But I read them. After all, she is my sister. Besides, sometimes you need that little step outside reality."

"Now that's sisterhood. Me and my sister are just not close. It's almost as if we have different parents. It gets crazy sometimes."

"Well, Reggie is the same way. You'd think I wasn't his mother sometimes, the way he fights me on things. Like this college thing. He is insistent on going to some out-of-state university instead of Moorman. Can you imagine? But that's not going to happen."

"Oh my gosh, Reggie? It's already that time? It seems just yesterday he was a toddler and—"

Just as if his ear may have been burning, Rashawn's office phone rang with his new cell number blinking. "It's him. I just got him a new BlackBerry. He must be playing with it."

As Rashawn answered the phone, Renee pointed at the clock and then to the door to indicate that she was leaving. Rashawn nodded. As Renee backed out of the door, she looked almost as if any second she would curtsy. Renee was a precious sort.

"Hi, baby, what's up?" Rashawn said into the phone.

"I got a call from U of O. They want me to come visit this weekend!"

"What?" she asked. The air was suddenly quiet, as if the imagined soft, soothing elevator music of her mind stopped with the zip of a needle over vinyl. The silence snapped her mind back into reality. "The University of Oregon?" Her voice peaked on a high note. "In Oregon?"

"Yeah, Mom, we talked about this already. My college plans? We agreed they were like, my plans. We talked about them."

"Well, yes, but—"

"And, well, I wanna go up and see the campus. *They* want *me* to come see the campus. Do you know what that means? I could end up playing for the Ducks." Reggie was excited, and Rashawn fought hard to keep up with what he was saying.

"Wait, wait. I'm going on vacation this weekend and—"

"Mom, this is about me, okay? It has nothing to do with your vacation."

"I didn't say it did." Rashawn didn't like what he was implying. "Have you spoken with your dad?"

"Chance? Puh-lease, he's not gonna want to go. He hates the train, and—"

"No, I mean have you . . . The train? And what have I told you about calling him Chance."

"Mom, it's all worked out. Me and some of my buddies are gonna train it up there this weekend and stay over winter break. They say it's already snowing up there. It's gonna be the shhh . . . er, mad fun," he corrected.

Rashawn's lip curled. "Mmhmm. We'll talk about this later."

"Oookay. But talk about what?"

"Everything, Reggie. University of Oregon was not the school I had in mind for you. Plus, young man, lately your attitude has been pretty . . . stank."

"Yeah, okay, well, we'll talk later, Mom." Reggie took on a manly tone. "But right now I'm about to call my pawdnas so we can get our plans straight . . . if you don't mind." She hated that tone. He reminded her of his biological father when he would take on that patronizing air, that correcting tone. Considering Reggie had no idea who he was, he was a lot like him sometimes.

Allen Roman, a distinguished professor, a scholar, a genius—a crazed lunatic who broke the law in the name of science, using human subjects in an mind-control experiment gone very, very wrong—he was Reggie's biological father. The memory instantly chilled her bones. He'd been deported shortly after all he had done had been revealed. Instead of making a name for himself in the world of science, he selfishly used his genius to further his own interests. He had drugged her repeatedly, raping her over a period of months. He had driven his brother insane, causing an alter ego to burst forth from his subconscious, a violent and menacing, murderous personality who referred to himself ironically as Doc. Doc, in his confusion, believed that he was in love with Rashawn and needed to protect her from Roman who, he knew, was raping her. He began stalking her, which caused her to believe he had been the one to rape her. The night Doc viciously attacked Chance in a jealous rage, Rashawn shot him— killing him. She was cleared of murder and in the end Roman was deported.

Just a few years later they'd gotten the report that Roman, too, was dead. The nightmare had finally ended. Rashawn dreamed about all of it for a long time, but soon the dreams ended. However, lately, they had started up again, and seeing the resemblances of that madman, Roman, in Reggie didn't help.

Chapter 3

Ovan was on the case. He was never far from it, actually. But now it was official, thanks to friends in low places; he'd been assigned. The thought of being the one to put a stop to the sick and crazed Allen Roman had kept him awake at night with excitement. While everyone else thought they were safe, believing that Roman had died, Ovan knew it wasn't true. Allen Roman had not died in Jamaica where he'd been banished to many years ago.

For the last few years, Roman had been in London raising hell under a new identity—that of Dr. Seymour Lipton. Ovan, too, had settled there, following his every elusive move, waiting for the chance to get assigned to the case. Although Ovan's home base was South Africa, where he was born, he made a living traipsing the world in search of law breakers who could not seem to be captured by the standard means of law enforcement. He loved his work and his partners,

Maravel and Julia. Both women were geniuses with computers and masters of disguise—never short on ideas and identities. So when news of the "mad scientist" hit the airwaves, Ovan knew immediately he wanted to be on the case. Personal reasons more than logical ones pushed him forward. Ovan wanted to put a stop to Allen Roman.

A few months ago, apparently feeling the heat of Ovan's chase, Roman faked his death again. It had taken all of his creativity, but Ovan had the body exhumed. To the shock of everyone around, the body in the casket was not the black man, Allen Roman, but that of the real Dr. Seymour Lipton—a Caucasian man. It took all but an act of Parliament to get an autopsy, since Dr. Lipton had no living family. Nonetheless, it was completed, and proved that Seymour had died from heart failure. *As does everyone, sooner or later,* Ovan thought to himself at the time.

"They weren't looking hard enough," Ovan pondered aloud. "I know Roman killed him."

What he didn't want them to find in the body of Dr. Lipton, Ovan wasn't sure. But he knew in his heart that it was only a matter of time before something would link Roman with more than just fraud . . . It would link him with murder. *There is no way Dr. Lipton died of natural causes.*

With time, Roman's reasons for murdering the good doctor would reveal a renewed mission of Roman's own design—of this Ovan was sure. Ovan had plans to stop Roman before he carried any of it out. Like the chase of cat and mouse, this case had Ovan globetrotting in pursuit.

Allen Roman: the phantom so many wanted to believe was not a threat to international security. *Poppycock! People need to stop believing he's so bloody powerful and maybe he'll stop being so. International—yes. Threat . . . only if you let him be.*

Ovan kept his eyes open—wide—and today he'd hit pay dirt. Dr. Craven Michaels was pronounced DOA— heart attack. Normally it would have gone unnoticed, except he knew firsthand that Craven was in no danger of dying of a heart attack. *Heck, she nearly gave me one on our encounter. The women had the endurance of a mule!* Just the thought of her thick thighs, and beautiful brown eyes closed from reasons other than sexual satiation made him sad—no, it pissed him off. He knew who was responsible for Craven Michaels's death. It was none other than Allen Roman. Although the police had only seen the obvious, the crime scene had Roman's name written all over it. Her being healthy one moment and dead the next, and having all but confessed to have been working with Allen Roman . . . Well, the coincidence was just a little too great for his taste. *And everyone thinks I'm crazy.*

No, Ovan wasn't grasping at straws here. Craven had told him about the strange proposition requesting the use of her surgical expertise. She had brought her partner on board, and now regretted it. Why she regretted it, she hadn't fully explained . . . well, not in a way Ovan completely understood. Talking to Craven was difficult at best. "Who performs private surgeries?" he asked, smoothing back his soft waves in the mirror. He was exhausted but trying to play it off. Yes, she was a healthy woman indeed.

"I just love your accent. Who'da thought London would produce someone as exciting as you," she purred. "Mmm, yeah," she moaned from where she lay, still writhing from the pleasure-filled hour she'd just had while he . . . drilled her . . . for answers.

Ovan turned from her vanity and adjusted the towel around his tight abs. He was small set but very well put together with a nicely defined musculature—and not to mention healthy libido. Just the sight of Craven was arousing him, but he had to leave. He had to get back to work (well, she'd been a work out, but he meant real work).

He'd gotten plenty of information out of her . . . plenty to work with. If nothing else, he knew Allen Roman was in the city.

She licked her lips, noticing his thick manhood rising. She curled her finger for him to come to her, to please her again. But he stood his ground. He needed just a few more answers, first. "Fine." she acquiesced. "Yes, sometimes I work for cash—such as in this case. It was a lot of cash, so I said, 'Yes, I'll perform the transplant outside my hospital's insurance network.' Sure, it's kinda . . ." she wavered her hand side to side, "unethical, but, I am licensed so—"

"Where? I mean where would you do this 'unethical' stuff? You can't possibly find hospitals to let you . . ." Ovan stopped speaking at the sight of her stalking toward him on all fours, like a cat. Her large breast dangled, swaying hypnotically back and forth. He gulped air.

"No. I have a cabin, in Oregon. It's set up—"

"You perform procedures as complicated as organ transplants in your cabin?" he asked, fighting the two brains—one that ruled each of his heads.

"Sometimes. I have a partner, but sometimes it's just better to work . . . how should I put it?" She put her finger to her lip and then grinned, sitting up on the edge of the bed. "Alone. Cash and carry. My cabin is out in the middle of nowhere, so yeah, we do surgeries there." Craven's smile resembled a naughty teenage girl caught in the bathroom with a cigarette. "I guess it's illegal but whose gonna tell? You? It doesn't really seem like you're the type of law man who sticks real close to the book. Besides, I do what I do when someone needs me to do it and I do it well—no complaints. Like now, I know you need me to perform an emergency procedure on that right there. It looks painful." She pointed at his lower anatomy. "And I'm ready, willing, and able to take care of that . . . no charge." She winked.

"What about your partner? What's his take on this whole thing?"

"Honey, my partner wouldn't enjoy this as much as I would. Trust me, he ain't hap-hap-happnin' like you are," she giggled.

"I didn't mean this . . ." Ovan stammered. "I meant . . . never mind. You're one wicked woman. What's his name?" Ovan said, fighting the pull of her eyes.

"Now, come on, Ovan, you want to know too much. First you wanted to know who's paying me. Now you want to know my partner's name. It's just too much. Next you'll want to know where I put the money that dude gave me as a retainer and directions to the cabin. Besides, I just told you my partner's name—you were not listening," she whined, rising to her knees and wriggling her tight body, giving her breasts and hair a hearty shake while running her hands over her flat stomach, as if she was growing uncomfortable in her own skin. Craven looked Ovan over from head to toe and took in air deeply, wantonly. She was getting antsy now. She was done talking business. Ovan was not too tall, lean, and rather wiry, which came in handy at times like this. Many people were taller than him and therefore underestimated him, especially women. Some said he looked a lot like the performer Prince, which he often used to his advantage—his large bedroom eyes and long lashes gave him a look of innocence that was sorely misinterpreted. He was far from innocent, and as far as any other resemblances to Prince, well, he wasn't that vocally talented either.

Craven had gotten out of bed and shook her thick hair wildly again, seductively, before placing her hand on her hip and again curling her finger back into her direction.

"Just give me one name," Ovan asked, taking only one step, battling the draw of her seduction. "Your partner or your benefactor."

She stepped closer, noticing his manhood tenting the towel wrapped around him. "I'll tell you after."

He moved forward, the peak of the towel standing between them now. "Is one named Allen Roman?"

"I said I would tell you after," she growled, biting playfully at his bottom lip. She was taller than him by a couple of inches, but nothing seemed to be a problem for the limber woman.

"You wouldn't lie to me, would you?" he asked, pinching her pointed nipples.

"I'd never lie to the FBI," she said before dropping to a squat and taking his towel with her.

"We'll have a copy of Michaels's autopsy report as soon as I can get through all this blinkin' red tape and archaic encryption. I guess it's been proven again, you can't always have a body when you want it," Maravel remarked smartly, bringing Ovan's mind back. Her tone was implicative and dripping with sarcasm. He felt his eyebrow rise slowly while giving her the "I can't believe you just put my business out there like that" look. She winked ever-so-covertly and turned back to the computer monitor where she was trying to build a report for lifted files from secure data bases. It was her forte. "I did, however, finally manage to get a copy of the autopsy on Dr. Lipton—London's faxing it over."

"How in the world did you manage that? Finally. God, that took forever. They are always a bugga to deal with. Why is that? You'd think their files would be more accessible."

"Right, I'm sure they are to someone with authorization to use them." Maravel chuckled, seemingly ignoring his close presence as he leaned over her shoulder to get a closer look at her data—and get a nose full of her perfume. She'd been right about one thing: her body was one he had never been able to get his hands on. Those were the rules . . . well, sort of. He'd broken them only once with their other partner, Julia. But then again, rules are only rules when one of the parties objects—like Maravel.

Chapter 4

Juanita stretched. Her afternoon nap was filled with delicious dreams of Chance Davis, her ex-husband. Even after all these years she had a warm spot in her heart for him. Or maybe it wasn't her heart, maybe it was just her bed. She would always have a place waiting for him there. Unfortunately, getting him away from that wife of his was a serious quest, a never-ending and, so far, unsuccessful challenge—but even after all these years she still had to regularly try. Getting Chance back had put a damper on everything else she used to find fun, including sex with other people. Maybe she was obsessed—who cared. Rashawn had something that belonged to her and she wanted it back! That wasn't obsession, that was the difference between right and wrong. And Rashawn was wrong for coming between her and her Chia Pet—Chance.

That Rashawn Ams had been a formidable opponent when she snagged Chance all those years ago, putting her fatherless son in his face, playing on her and that boy's needs for some emotional stability. Oh sure, Rashawn had been stalked and nearly killed by that psychopath Doc, "Until she shot him all to pieces *phhhst.*" Juanita blew a raspberry while thinking of the situation that had stayed on the front page for days: *College professor claims self-defense after shooting security guard nine times at close range.* "Right, I was convinced it was self-defense all right," Juanita lied. She saw Rashawn as underhanded and sneaky for having played on Chance's emotions and his soft nature. "Heffa almost got my Chancy Wancy killed over her mess. I'll never forgive her for that."

She smacked her cute, heart-shaped lips. "He wasn't ready for all those drama bags she was carrying. Putting some kid on him whose father she didn't know. It was not fair the way she trapped him. He was not ready to be a stepfather," Juanita said with a huff. "He was ready to be a real father. I had his only child and our son needed him. But then . . ." Juanita thought about Rainey, the beautiful, fair-skinned child Chance and Rashawn had together. "Okay, fine, so he has her. Damn that Rashawn, she even took that from me," Juanita grumbled. Junior was dark skinned, tall, and husky, kinda like Reggie, Rashawn's son. But in Reggie's case, the dark complexion made sense considering that Rashawn was damn near the color of mahogany wood, even though she had those crazy gold-colored eyes. But he didn't have her eyes. Maybe it was Reggie's biological father who had dark eyes, for Reggie's were just off the color of onyx stone. He was a beautiful specimen of a black man and when he grew up, he'd break many hearts.

Juanita understood Reggie's dark tones, but then here comes Rainey with her fair skin and light eyes. Chance musta put ugly on that one, because she looked just like him. She was Chance's pride and joy—looking just like his mother. Rainey was a beautiful child and Juanita could tell he favored her over Chance Jr. "Yeah, well. . ." Juanita sighed heavily, glancing over at the picture of her son on the nightstand. "Just not right." Chance Jr. was tall and dark skinned, with a head full of loose curly hair. Even at only fifteen, Juanita could see "basketball star" all over him. He was gonna be athletic, just like Rashawn's son. "So why is everyone acting like Reggie is all that? He's not, not with Chance's own star on the bench just waiting his turn." Again, Juanita looked at Chance Jr.'s, picture, wishing he looked more like Rainey. But he didn't.

She kissed the picture and stroked it lovingly. "Doesn't matter, baby. Mama loves you."

Juanita knew that Rashawn hated that she'd named her son after Chance. It was a constant reminder that she had been able to seduce Chance to her bed while the two of them were dating. And still Juanita raised suspicion that they "got it on" once in a while now—as much as she wanted it to be true. She wanted Chance back. Despite all her cheating and crazy acting, she wanted Chance back in her life. Besides, who else would love her?

Juanita was diagnosed a sex addict and borderline bipolar a few years back. It forced her to leave her practice, what with everyone joking that there was more "psycho" in her psychotherapy than should be. "To hell with 'em. Damned haters," Juanita huffed, thinking about her life and how Chance had always been there for her. Maybe in his own way, he still was. He surely must still love her.

Chance just allowed the games to play. *He's such a pacifist,* Juanita thought, smacking her lips at his less-than-passionate lust for drama. Even when Rashawn was screaming paternity suit, Chance just took the whole thing with a yawn and responded with, "I don't want to take everyone through it, haven't we been through enough?" Yes, Chance had been through it. He'd nearly been killed and never once had Rashawn really thanked him for his efforts.

Juanita continued to paint the masterpiece in her mind—Rashawn, the heartless, selfish bitch who cared about no one but herself. Juanita sometimes didn't believe she really even loved her son the way a mother should. "Shouldn't matter who his daddy is," she said, lying back on the bed, resting, on her chest, the picture of her son standing with Chance. Then she tossed it aside and reached for the phone. She called Chance's cell, her mood shifting suddenly. She needed to speak with him today. She needed money—today. Christmas was just around the corner and Junior wanted things. Sure, Chance had paid his support for the month, but how far did he expect twelve hundred dollars to go?

Back when she agreed with the court-ordered support, Juanita had a thriving practice. She didn't need Chance's little handouts, but the years had crept by and Junior grew tall and demanding. He ate like a horse. He wanted to wear trendy clothes and hang out with his friends drinking expensive coffee drinks and smoothies every-day—all the things that a working mother could afford, but then, Juanita wasn't a working mother anymore now, was she? Unlike Rashawn who worked constantly, ambitiously trying to prove something to everyone—bitching about how tired she was all the damned time, especially when Juanita needed some downtime and alone time, and especially when Juanita had requested that Chance Jr. stay over a few days beyond the weekend.

"Actin' like the kids shouldn't get close," Juanita went on, still building on the fantasy that Rashawn was the true bad guy here. "That's her problem. She's jealous of me being a stay-at-home mom. Well, too bad! I need more money."

And yes, Rashawn bitched about that, too.

Juanita sighed heavily at the thought of her rival. True, Rashawn had proven herself to be a worthy adversary. Sometimes Juanita felt ashamed at all the lies she had told to keep drama going, but then other times, like now, when she was so broke, and so lonely, she didn't give a damn.

"Put your stepfather on the phone," she said gruffly, speaking to Reggie as if he were the only stepchild in the joint.

Chapter 5

"Dad, it's Nita on the phone," Reggie called on his way out the door. He was headed out to practice. The team sucked as a whole, but he loved playing with his friends and they loved having him on the team. With Reggie on board, at least they got touchdowns during the game. Reggie was the MVP, no questions asked, and he enjoyed being the star. Reggie really had his heart set on playing college football, and not in Moorman U's colors.

"So does being the MVP of a team that loses all the time really count?" Chance had asked once while signing the permission slip that would allow Reggie to play out of town. Reggie just chuckled.

"It counts," he huffed, puffing up slightly, strangely and suddenly resembling a man Chance would forever be working on forgetting. With his chiseled jaw line and broad shoulders, Reggie looked a lot like him sometimes. Although Doc's skin was that of a white man, he was Allen Roman's half brother. He was half black, with a heart darker than any skin tone could be. Blain, aka Doc, had a charm that women found irresistible for the most part, and maybe Rashawn had gotten caught up a little bit. Chance would never know for sure how Doc had ended up getting so close to her he had access to her home as easily as his crazy brother Allen Roman did. But none of that mattered now. Chance shook his head, erasing the memories as quickly as they came.

The memory of the big monster of a man breaking him into as many pieces as possible without killing him—*death might have been preferable at that moment*—brought a chill over him. Chance shuddered slightly as he remembered the moment he saw his life flashing before his eyes. He'd nearly died that day because of his love for Rashawn and Reggie—and he'd do it again in a heartbeat. He loved his family and would fight for them to the death if he had to. Minor though it all seemed, in comparison there were things worse than what he'd been through, in Chance's mind. For instance, Reggie calling him by his first name whenever he could get away with it, pushing the rules to a breaking point—Chance had to put the hammer down on those seemingly small things. Reggie would never understand why life and the rules seemed so out of whack, but it was okay. He didn't need to understand. Chance just needed to be a good father and he knew he would always be.

Chance took time with Reggie as well as his own daughter, Rainey; helping them with homework and extracurricular activities, and even taking them on camping trips and to amusement parks and such. He even stretched further and included his "other Chance" in many of the activities. All of the children got along; *they are keeping me young*, he would force himself to think. Of course, Rashawn and Juanita were another story, in Chance's mind. Their bickering, bitching, and plain old crazy actin' was surely driving him to an early grave.

Year after year, the two women in his life went at it. Sure, he took good care of his body, keeping himself in shape. He would run for miles sometimes—more for his own peace of mind than anything—but still. Sometimes when he looked in the mirror he would simply shake his head in wonder. "You'd think I was Denzel Washington or somebody . . ." Chance would say to the aging reflection.

Chance also enjoyed his work. He was a remedial math teacher at Moorman University. He'd taught there for more than fifteen years now. But since Rashawn's aggressive climb to dean began, he had dropped to part-time in order to give the children more attention where she was coming up short. It was a choice they both made and it had worked out. Chance was better with the kids anyway, in his opinion. As he picked up the grocery list on his way to the phone, he thought about Rashawn's domestic skills. She was great housekeeper, planner, wife, and woman. It wasn't as if Rashawn had ever really planned to be a mother—let alone a mother of two-and-ahalf active teenagers. Being dean of a university offered her a better fit.

Glancing at the grocery list now, it was clear that the kids had added things, intermingled within Rashawn's balanced nutritional pyramid. Along the way up the list, he notice items with tell tale signs of balance invasion:

Whole wheat rolls. Oreos. Soy Dream. Polish Dog w/cheese. Tofu . . . yeah right.

This position as dean was her calling. Of course, this promotion also meant that he was now going to have to increase his duties around the house, like shopping and cooking. That thought and this whacked-out grocery list nearly caused him to forget who was on the phone.

"Helleeerrrooo," he sang nonchalantly into the receiver.

"Chance . . . hi, ummm, I was wondering if Junior could stay over 'til the weekend," Juanita led, as was her style. Chance was immediately brought back into focus, his mood dropping several degrees.

He answered while looking over the grocery list. "I'll pick him up on Saturday, Nita. He comes here after school. You pick him up. I get him every other weekend. Why are you always trying to change up stuff?"

"But, Chance . . ." she began. He knew this was coming. Juanita never wanted Junior to extend his visit without ulterior motives. She'd made their son an unwitting accomplice to her job, that being to both bug the hell out of Rashawn as well as milk him for funds. As for Junior, he'd be a great corporate man when the time came. The training he was gaining from his mother was priceless. What a piece of work Juanita was.

And to think I once loved her, Chance thought, his brain drifting to her bed. She was a wild cat, seductive as hell. He was crazy about Rashawn, true, but nobody had it on Juanita—she was a sexual pro. No, it wasn't love—not in the purest sense—it was lust, greed, and insatiable need that kept them together and kept him going back after they broke up. To be truthful, it was only by pure resistance that he hadn't gone back since he and Rashawn married, because Juanita hadn't stopped trying. As a matter of fact, over the last few months it seemed as though she must be in a dry spell, as her attempts had become less than covert. Chance was going to have to up his defense for sure. He didn't feel guilty about his feelings; he was human. And Juanita was—sex crazed.

". . . and he needs . . ." Chance heard Juanita say, as he once again tuned into her voice. It didn't really matter what she was saying. In the end, of course Junior would extend his stay through the weekend, and probably stay over the entire winter break. And Chance would purchase whatever the boy needed . . . *It's only right.*

Junior was his son.

Well, as much as Reggie is.

Chance wasn't stupid. He was barely five ten and Juanita was a half a minute taller than five feet even, and already, at barely fifteen years old, Junior was eye to eye with him and nowhere near finished growing. In addition, with Juanita's eyes being grey in color and his own being brown—albeit on the light side, closer to hazel—Junior's onyx pools just didn't fit the DNA profile. Suffice it to say, there was very little about Chance's namesake that he could claim, as claiming blood relation was something that, in his heart, he was not be able to do.

Paternity test? What was the point at this late date? Chance knew he was the only father Reggie or Junior had, and would ever have. Juanita was a sexually charged woman—who knew who Junior's father was. Back then, "no" was not part of her vocabulary when it came to sex—his either, for that matter. Chance felt that he was in the running just as easily as any other man.

That was half of the attraction, and that she'd actually agreed to marry him, to settle down with him considering how many men wanted her. Back then it had been flattering. But faithful was something Juanita could never be. Even while she was married to her last husband, Dennis, Chance often revisited his comfort spot between her thighs. Shameful as it was, he'd even slept with Juanita on a regular basis while dating Rashawn. They weren't committed at the time, so Rashawn forgave him for the indiscretion, but only with the promise that he had truly recovered from his disease—The Juanitas. He'd worked hard to recover, and now believed in his heart that he had. Anytime he felt as if he would slip back into darkness, Junior was there as a bright, reminding light. Just knowing— or worse yet, not knowing—the truth had set Chance free of her spell. But not for Juanita's lack of applying the juju. And, truth be told, Juanita was looking kinda good these days, too. *Not that I'm really looking all that hard,* Chance told himself.

Chance knew who Reggie's father was, but Chance Jr. didn't stand a chance of ever being related to anyone beside Juanita. Besides, being a father to both boys hadn't put a dent in anything he had going on, and his daughter, Rainey, was enjoying actually having two big brothers. It was probably the best thing for her. Chance enjoyed having sons; he'd always wanted sons. So it was working out, at least for him and the kids.

". . . and you promised that spring break Junior was gonna stay with you and you didn't keep your word then, either—that's all water under the bridge, I know, but this is Christmas. It's bad enough I have to spend it alone, but don't do this to Junior. Or maybe it's Rashawn who's making you neglect yo' chile," Juanita went on.

It was time to stop her now. She was bringing Rashawn needlessly into the mix. There was one thing that would turn him off quicker than anything, and that was Juanita's jabs at Rashawn. Chance had to admit that Rashawn had all but stopped commenting on Juanita and her little nasty remarks. There were so many other things to be busying her mind with: her job, her responsibilities, and lest he forget, Rashawn's crazy sisters. She had five of them, and with the holiday season they were coming out the woodwork, and would soon be converging on him full force.

"Nita, that's enough," Chance answered. "I'm bringing him home," he continued, barely getting in a good-bye before hanging up.

He heard her cursing as the receiver headed quickly toward the cradle.

Chapter 6

At the police station, Detective Lawrence Miller watched as the strange guy he'd never seen before stood looking through one of the older files, flipping it over from front to back, as if there were extra notes expected there; more information than the weak report held. Finally he looked up. "So is this all you've got?" Ovan asked.

Lawrence shrugged his shoulders. "I wasn't on the case. I wasn't even a detective back then."

"Yeah, but damn, this case was a biggie. It made the news and all that. I mean, good cops were killed. Hell, one of the killers was a cop! It was big news and you don't remember it? Right here in your precinct and you don't remember—"

"It wasn't my case—I told you that. I wouldn't know. And at the time this was not my precinct. I told you that, too. It's an ancient case, closed case. Why you here bringing up old stuff?" Lawrence sighed heavily. This third degree was not his thing. He could dish it out, but surely taking it was another story—one he wasn't interested in. And this guy didn't seem to be too overly serious about things. He was acting like it was playtime—yuckin' it up with the chief and all that before coming out here to the pit, acting like he owned the joint. Chief just came out of her office smiling like a teenager and said, "Let him see the file." That wasn't like her to just give someone free reign at a file—a closed one at that. Lawrence was speechless.

Lawrence wanted to get rid of him. Hell, he wasn't even sure who this cat was. If Jim were here, he'd know how to get to the bottom of this. Jim was Lawrence's partner and loved working homicide. He was kinda like this guy—full of fun all the damned time, but Jim knew when to do his job, and he was hella good at it. Lawrence wasn't about fun, not at all. He was too serious for that kind of silliness. Besides, homicide had never been fun, and if and when they actually closed a case, he preferred it stayed closed.

"Who are you with again?" asked Lawrence, noticing the dude's minute size (about five six or seven), British accent, and his pretty-darn-persistent attitude. The uptight, albeit expensive looking, suit, sharply edged facial hair, and diamond stud in his ear hadn't impressed Lawrence much either. This little white-looking guy was like a cross between James Bond, Prince, and the Hulk. Well, minus the green face and height . . . and bulk. Okay, so maybe not the Hulk . . . Maybe the blond dude on that old TV show, *The Man from U.N.C.L.E.*

"I'm Ovan Dominguez. I'm working a special task force for the British government—I told your boss all that. I even showed her my," the little Napoleon began, answering one of Lawrence's many questions and looking devilish all the while, ". . . badge," he said after a dramatic pause that left Lawrence feeling a little uneasy.

"So you're like the Euro version of the FBI? What's going on that our closed cases deserve a once-over from you kinda guys?"

"We think one of your closed cases might be open again."

"Had a bad feeling you were going to say that. Do you realize that this is homicide? We don't like hearing that people who are dead aren't as dead as we thought. Kinda scary . . . yadamean?"

"What soooo." Ovan pointed at him, still balancing the open file on one of his palms. He was standing, and had been since Lawrence had made it known that Jim's desk was not available for him to sit. Sure Jim was on vacation for a couple more days, but still. "It's not that simple, but I feel your sentiments on that 'dead back to life thing,' surely

I hate when that happens," Ovan joked. "But since it has . . ."

"Why do I get the crazy feeling you're about to ask me for some help? Why do I get the funky feeling that I'm not gonna want to do it? Why—"

Ovan looked around and lowered his voice. "Look, Detective Miller, this case is A-1 classified and—"

"And how did I know you were going to say that?"

Ovan smiled wickedly, forcing Lawrence to accept the reluctant bond of understanding, despite his misgivings and note to himself to make a few phone calls after this guy left his office. Since the chief looked all twitterpatted and flush, when she came out of the office after talking to him—now that Lawrence thought about it—he had a feeling he might be alone in his suspicions. He shook his head of the thoughts connecting the chief and Ovan, and what could have possibly put that flush on her face. *No, wait, that kinda thing happens in vice. This is homicide,* he reasoned. *What did happen in there! Lawrence would have to give Jim a call as well.*

Ovan Dominguez, the British equivalent of the FBI (or so he said) standing in front of his desk on a Wednesday evening. Yeah, this guy looked as shady as a summer lawn of a large plantation home in Atlanta—the kind his mama said she grew up in. Lawrence all but expected Mr. Dominguez to pull out his dark shades and stun gun before leaving— the kind they had in that movie. The one that made the person forget what they were thinkin'. Yeah, this Dominguez cat was up to something major. Lawrence could smell it.

"So, Mr. Euro, what do we know that you guys don't know that has you looking for a haunt? And, more importantly, whose haunting the halls—Dominguez?" Lawrence wanted to say his name again, too. Britain and the name Dominguez just didn't play the same tune in his mind.

"Someone who is a one- or two-time killer, Detective Miller, and if I'm right, he's going to kill again."

"Is that right. And you know this how?"

"Because he's never stopped killing."

"Your killer got a name?"

"Yes . . . he does," Ovan answered. He was toying with Lawrence now, and Lawrence was not too cool with that.

"Speaking of names, where did a guy like you get a name like Dominguez?"

"My father, I suppose. Look here, Detective Miller, before we become best friends I need to know I have your support on this case. Your superior assured me your cooperation."

"Really. She did that, huh? Well, she shoulda checked my calendar."

"Fine, then what I'm really asking, I guess, is that you don't get in my way."

Lawrence burst into laughter. "Me in your way . . . doubt that."

"Good. Then we have an understanding."

Lawrence was now sure he'd be seeing more of this guy, and he wasn't looking forward to it.

Chapter 7

Flexing in the mirror, Reggie stood tall and handsome. He looked much older than most kids his age, but he knew it to be because of his height and probably his features, too. Dark eyes and sharp, chiseled jaw, thick neck and big hands, he looked very different from most of his family. His mother was tall but had really light eyes, almost gold colored, and her features were soft and pretty. He didn't have any uncles, so he really didn't know what the Ams men looked like, short of a photo of his grandfather—the one he was named after, and that Reginald Ams wasn't all that big. But none of that mattered; Reggie was destined for greatness. He knew this. He was gonna play ball—pro ball. At first he thought it might be a dream, but not since getting that call from the athletic department of University of Oregon. "Inviting me to take a look at their team! Me!" he told his reflection. "How many people get invited personally to a school to look it over— specifically their athletic department—without that being an unsaid promise of making the team? How many?" He smiled broadly and again wondered if he maybe looked like his father. It wasn't as if he knew who his father was. His mother had apparently been a wildcat back in the day—sleeping with men she didn't know. *Go figure.* Considering how uptight she was now—*can't imagine it.* But, she was old now, Chance was old now—Juanita was old now too, despite how she acted. They were all old and fulla farts. And it was time for him to blow this stank joint.

Just then there was a banging on the bathroom door. "God, Reg! I gotta pee fa real!" Rainey bellowed. He yanked open the door. His half sister was fourteen. She normally had a quiet nature—except when her bladder was full.

She looked and acted nothing like Junior, nothing like him. Funny, now that he thought about it, as strange as it seemed, he and Junior looked and acted more alike than Rainey did to either of them. It was almost as if she was the stepchild.

"If you were a boy you coulda just peed outside," Reggie teased, pushing her forehead tauntingly before brushing past her. She swung at him and missed before slamming into the bathroom.

"Gross!" she screamed from inside.

Chapter 8

Ovan left the station house. He'd made his point—and new enemies. That was fine. He'd rather work with people who didn't like him but respected him and what he was doing, than those who just carried on brainlessly following stupid rules they didn't understand. Lawrence wasn't a brainless follower—Ovan could tell. Behind that staunch demeanor was a cop who wanted justice. "And that's just the kind of guy I need on my side," he said aloud before patting his stomach, realizing his hunger. But he'd had a plenty of exercise today: a little flirting with a female precinct captain, a little dancing with the enemy (he had to view Lawrence that way until something dictated otherwise), and a full day of hunting the devil—Allen Roman. Tomorrow he'd head down another road. He needed something substantial to prove that Allen Roman was truly here in the city, and some stronger leads on him. He'd have to be living somewhere. Surely Roman would not be able to resist a scholarly environment too long. Perverted though it may seem, he could easily be drawn back to his own stomping ground: Moorman. Back to his old obsessions, like Rashawn Ams. The case made it clear Roman had a thing for her—in a big way. Roman never went anywhere without a purpose, and there was a reason he was here in California. "It won't hurt to see if Rashawn Ams has anything to do with his trip here. Craven all but admitted that he was in need of some big time surgical procedure—Maravel should have his medical records by now. After dinner I'll head over there. We'll see what's wrong with him . . . besides insanity." Ovan mumbled.

Stepping off the curb, Ovan noticed a dark sedan parked on the opposite side of the small park. He didn't know why the car drew his attention. It made his skin crawl and the hairs on the back of his neck rise. Dusk was falling and making it harder to see. He stood staring for a moment at the parked car in hopes of focusing on and making out the driver—no luck.

Crossing the street, he took his car keys from his pocket and headed for his car, thinking he'd just drive past the car and get the license number, or perhaps a better look through the eyes of a computer run on the plate. As he started his car, turned on the radio, fooled with the mirror, and primped just a tad, he hadn't noticed that the car had moved from its spot and, was slowly creeping around the park. Looking up, he saw the sedan coming toward him. The driver slowed down and lowered the window as he passed.

"The chase begins," was all Allen Roman said before speeding off. Stunned, and slightly in shock, Ovan spun a hard U-turn in the middle of the street, screeching his tires. His fancy Porsche with the specialty muffler, flow meter, and standard manifold replaced with custom headers set off car alarms for three blocks, gaining the attention of plenty of on-duty cops who immediately joined in the chase.

"Dammit!" Ovan roared, noticing that Roman didn't gain any attention in his plain car. He turned off the main drag they had been on. Sirens blasted and patrol cars were in chase of Ovan now as he lost the tail. Before he could turn the same corner as Roman, Ovan was cut off by a patrol car. Slamming on his breaks, his belt jerked him roughly back from the steering wheel. "You idiots!" he screeched.

"Get out of the car," the officer said, drawing his weapon. There was plenty of commotion with the sounds of the car alarms and people coming from their homes to shut them off.

"Why are you stopping me? Did you not see that I was in pursuit?"

"Duh! Put your hands up."

"I was in pursuit!"

"Of who?" the officer asked, pulling out his tablet.

"The sedan. I know you saw him speeding. I was chasing him." Ovan was attempting to gesture with one hand up.

"Nope, we didn't see anybody speeding but you." The officer patted Ovan down. Fortunately, he'd tucked his weapon under his seat earlier that day. He was free from an arrest—at least for the moment—unless they searched his car for some unknown reason.

Reaching for his wallet, Ovan fussed, "Can I at least give you my ID . . . Can I do that?" The officer nervously jutted the gun in his face. He handed the officer his ID.

"Is this legal in our country?" the officer asked his partner.

"Of course it is! Can one of you call Detective Lawrence Miller? Can you just do that so we can get on with our evening?"

"Oh, you know Miller? Does he know you?"

"Oh, good Lord!" Ovan sighed heavily.

The officer shrugged and reluctantly walked back to his vehicle while the other, the one holding the gun, stood with Ovan.

After a moment or two, the officer came back, laughing. "Lawrence said we should beat him up and then let him go," he joked. Both officers got a hearty laugh now. "Nah, he's okay I guess. Miller said he's some big shot FBI agent from England." The officer holding the gun finally holstered it. "I guess you're one of us—sort of. Sorry, about that."

"Sorry my arse! Bloody well cost me the entire case. Who knows if I'll see that guy again before he . . ." Ovan snatched his wallet back from the officer, cursing bitterly under his breath.

"Look here, you're in America now so you better get a clue how we do things around here. Get get this bucket fixed, or you're gonna be getting stopped often," the officer explained as Ovan climbed back behind the wheel. Out of spite Ovan sped off, revving the motor and setting of several more car alarms.

After a fruitless endeavor of cruising the streets a bit, Ovan headed back to his hotel. Entering his room, he saw the light on his phone blinking. He rushed over to hear the message. His gut was telling him, before he pushed the button, who the call was from. For the last year, since Roman had discovered that it was Ovan on his tail, he'd made sure he got as close as he could to him. It was as if they had established their own game rules. Ovan had broken many rules, though—and planned to break a few more before this was over. "Stay out of my way, Dominguez; this doesn't concern you." Allen Roman's voice was deep and distorted, as if spoken through a disguising device. He could only assume it was a device that would block the location of the call as well.

Roman was a maniac, but not an idiot. He had a reason for everything he did or said. "If it doesn't concern me then it must be personal to you! Thank you for answering my question about Rashawn Ams," Ovan laughed. Roman had covered his steps well, and although Ovan knew he was behind the killings of the doctors, he was still hoping to figure out the bigger reasoning behind the illegal experiments on human subjects as well. Because of Allen Roman, one too many lives had been destroyed. Tying those two crimes to Roman would give Ovan's mission some legitimacy. It was the least he could do before killing Roman for his own personal reasons. Ovan needed a bit of a cover-up for his own evil. Finding out why Roman was doing what he was doing was as good as any . . . At least, he hoped it would be a good enough reason to justify blowing his brains out. Yes, Ovan had a game plan too. It was all a game, one that was coming to an end. He picked up his phone to call Maravel.

"Ovan, what is it?" she asked, sounding as if she'd been breathlessly awaiting his call.

"Roman. I saw him today."

"My God."

"You say that like you're surprised. Like you didn't think I was right."

"No, Love, I knew you were right. I had just prayed you were wrong."

"So he is here, just as I thought, and now I think I know why. Get me some information on Rashawn Ams. Also, I hope you got those medical records."

"Yes, I did. It seems our Dr. Roman is a pretty sick man."

"How so?"

"Sick enough to be looking for a kidney donor."

"Interesting . . . Well, his brother's dead. Who else?"

"My guess is he has someone in mind."

Chapter 9

"Remember that Christmas we conceived Junior?" Juanita flirted, hanging tinsel on her tree. She had saved the duty until Chance arrived, bringing Junior home. It wasn't much of a tree anyway, just a little tabletop, but it was something. She started stringing the tinsel as soon as he had walked in. She hoped he'd catch on and give her a hand—or more.

"It wasn't Christmas, it was right after Thanksgiving."

"Oh, you remember," she said, purring just a little, feeling the heat rising up.

"Yeah, because me and Rashawn made our thing official right *after* that," Chance remarked, smiling wickedly.

"Why you gonna ruin the moment bringing her up?" Juanita choked. Tossing the tinsel at the tree any ol' kind of way, she realized now how this attempt to involve him wasn't working. He stood by the door with his hands in his pockets.

Why did he bother to even come in? He should have just waited in the car. But no, he always came in. It was his house, after all.

"I miss us," she said before rethinking the statement.

Chance's eyes widened in surprise as he looked in the direction Junior had gone. Sure, he had ear buds in place, but . . .

Chance pointed, whispering loudly, "He could have heard you. Are you nuts?"

"Call me crazy. I don't care." Juanita realized suddenly how good it felt to speak her heart. She'd been off her medication for a while and maybe it was starting to show. She had been on Zoloft for a while now—it wasn't working, not as far as she could see. But for the first time in months she was feeling more like herself again, so maybe it had been. She giggled at the thought.

Chance went for the doorknob. "I'm leaving, Nita." Juanita rushed over to stop him, making sure her body made contact. She was wearing his favorite perfume. She always made sure to spritz it on when she thought she might see him.

"I'm sorry, Chance. Don't go. Just stay with me for a minute. I'm sorry," she begged. She hadn't meant to scare him off. Maybe she had lost her touch—maybe the meds had messed her all up. Chance shook his head, and in his normal mannerism when nervous, pushed his glasses up higher on his nose with his middle finger.

"Man, there is nothing to eat here," Junior bellowed from the kitchen. "At least at Dad's there's major grub," he went on.

"Mother Hubbard's cupboards are bare, son!" she called back.

"You don't have food?" Chance asked, sounding serious.

"I didn't make it to the store," she answered nonchalantly before noticing the true concern on his face.

"Is that why you wanted Junior to stay with me?"

No, I just didn't make it to the store, Juanita thought, but didn't say, noting Chance's softness returning in his voice. She nodded slowly—playing it, baiting him. Chance sighed heavily.

"Nita, are you paying the bills?"

"Yes, Chance, I'm managing to keep *your* house." she said, emphasizing the dig. True, it was Chance's house and he had allowed her to live there. Even when she'd married Dennis they lived together in Chance's house. He'd worked hard to buy it, going as far as putting the home in his sister's name. He'd refused to give it up in the divorce or sell it to keep it out of litigation, so he just opted to let her live there.

Reaching in his pocket, he pulled out two twenties before glancing at his watch. "I don't have time to run to the Chinese Palace, so just call in."

"So you don't have time to eat with us, either, I gather."

"No, I don't," he answered.

Chinese food on the floor in front of the fireplace was such a turn-on for Chance—back in the day. Hell, everything was a turn on for Chance. He would put pieces of orange chicken between her tight breasts and then eat them out. He would pour sweet-and-sour sauce on her belly and dip his spring rolls. He would put sweet-and-sour sauce on his "roll" and she would suck it clean. Oh the fun they would have . . .

And they call me a sex addict, Juanita thought, trying to ignore the heat growing between her legs.

She made sure her hands touched his as she took the money from him. "Junior," she called loudly without taking her eyes off his.

"Ya!" he called back.

"Come get this money from your father and call CP to get us some grub," she said, grinning and putting on her most grateful face. "Make sure you order me some spring rolls with extra sauce."

"Oh, CP! Thanks, Pop," Junior said, snatching the money and rushing to the cordless that sat on the sofa. Juanita leaned up again, polluting him with her scent, kissing him lightly on the cheek, allowing her lips to maintain contact with his skin as she moved closer to his lips.

"Hey, while you're being generous and loving, I need a BlackBerry like Reg." Junior called out.

"Forget about it," Chance said, pulling back from Nita quickly, as if the spell had been suddenly broken by the sound of Junior's voice. Speaking over Nita's head, Chance added, "Gotta go," and quickly backed out through the door.

"Damn." Juanita groaned slightly.

"Aw, missed again," Junior said before bursting into laughter. Juanita realized then that Junior knew her well and recognized her game. So she just played along, snapping her finger and twisting her lip in mock disappointment.

"You're getting too old, my son. Up in grown folks' business," she added, patting his shoulder as she walked toward the kitchen to pour a glass of wine. "What was cookin' at ya dad's place?" she asked.

Chapter 10

"My my, Chance, you're still just as greedy as ever," he said, watching through the tinted window of the rented car. "I would have thought my Rashe would have been enough for you, but noooo, you still require a little Juanita on the side. I can't blame you of course; between the two they are such an irresistible pussy feast. But, under the circumstances, Rashawn is worth so much more to me right now. So since you've got two squaws, maybe I should Indian give and take my cunt back," he added, clearly showing his love for Rashawn had waned a bit. Never had he felt so much bitterness toward anyone as he had toward Rashawn Ams right now. "You took my son, Rashe. You turned on me, betrayed me by having another man's child, and now you think that all is forgiven because a few years have passed? I forgive nothing, and I'm taking my son back since I'm sure I need him more than you do."

Just then his phone rang; it was Reggie. He cleared his throat and answered the call, sounding as professional and academic as he could.

"Hello, Mr. Smith. I know you said I could call anytime. And I know you just called me but . . ."

"No nooo, Reggie my boy. What's up?"

"My parents . . . well, my mom. She's being kinda difficult about me coming out to Oregon this weekend. So I need to know how long this offer is good for."

"Well, time is running out. Perhaps you should just try the direct approach. I find that mothers like it when you show them that you're grown up. When you can prove to them that you're independent. Tell you what, I'll purchase the ticket. You just get on the train—"

"You're gonna buy my ticket?"

"Yeah. I mean, it's not a common practice and I'm sure your parents would get all crazy if they knew—"

"I won't say nothin' to nobody! I know the deal. You get me and you get a future money maker, so it's a write-off. I know the deal," Reggie said, trying to sound in the know. His uncle was an entertainment attorney, so he had heard about these kinds of tradeoffs before.

"Glad you do," he said, deepening his voice, taking a firm tone.

"Besides, my dad is all for it."

"Your dad?" Roman asked, trying not to show the instant wrath that burned in his belly. He tried hard to hide the jealousy he felt for Chance Davis.

"Well, my stepdad, but you know . . . Anyway, yeah, he's actually kinda for it so I'll work that angle. But I won't tell him about the ticket either. That way, he might give me some extra bread to work with while I'm there."

"You won't need that, either. It's on me, son," he assured.

"Wow. I'm glad I called you, man. You've renewed my excitement."

"I'm glad I could help. There's something special about you, Reggie, and I definitely want you on my team."

"You got me, Mr. Smith!"

The conversation ended. Roman held the phone in his hand for a long time, staring at its face. "I know I do, because I always get what I need."

Chapter 11

Rashawn's sleep was restless. Of all dreams that could be had, Rashawn, in her deepest unconscious state, revisited the night Reggie was conceived. The violent night she lost her pride, her dignity, and her fight against a rapist: Allen Roman, Reggie's biological father. She could almost feel the gravel against her face, smell the oil from the cars that had parked there previously. She could feel him inside her, filling her to the brim, ripping and tearing at her tender inner linings as if she weren't even human. She could remember him threatening her life, "Don't fight me or I'll kill you." Little did he know a little part of her died that night, and she wasn't sure she had ever been able to bring it back to life.

How many more children of his perversions were out there, Rashawn didn't know, but surely there had to be others, for as time went on, Rashawn had found out that Allen Roman had involved many unknowing women in his madness. Sometimes she would get letters or e-mails from women who suspected perhaps they too had been victims of his crime, yet none claimed to have mothered his child.

Allen Roman had an obsession with his own sexuality. He thought he was a god, of that Rashawn was certain. Maybe he had chosen her to be his queen. In his last letter to her, he implied his intent to impregnate her upon the initial attack, and his plans to impregnate her again upon the subsequent violations. When he drugged her, invading her while she lay vulnerable and unconscious, he had planned to give her another child.

Roman would never know he had succeeded, because Rashawn had a miscarriage with the second pregnancy he'd caused. No one but her sisters knew of that pregnancy and they had kept the secret locked tight—along with the knowledge that Allen Roman was Reggie's father. They all allowed her to lie to her son, and risk appearing as a loose woman, not wanting him to know the animal his father was. There was no way in hell they wanted Rashawn's son to know the creature who had caused his existence. All Rashawn wanted Reggie to know was that she had worked hard to develop and nurture a true motherly love for him . . . despite it all. She knew she should do better in that area, but it was just hard, and the older he got and the more he resembled Allen Roman, the harder it got.

"You okay?" Chance asked, noticing how she had tossed and turned violently, awaking now with a start.

"Bad dream I guess," she answered.

Chance ran his finger through her thick hair—freed from the scarf by her tossing and turning. "I thought angels only had sweet dreams."

Rashawn sniveled and smiled weakly. "Yeah. Gonna check on Reggie," she said, throwing back the covers.

Chance tugged at her gown. "You know, you're gonna have to stop worrying about that boy. You still check on him like he's a baby." Rashawn's eyes welled up with tears. Chance noticed and pulled her into an embrace. "Wow, sweetie, he's seventeen, you have to let—"

"I had a dream about Roman. I . . ." Rashawn confessed, breaking their rule of many years: "Never say his name in this house!"

"Oh, baby," Chance sighed. "All that's over. Long over! Blain . . . or Doc . . . whoever the hell he was . . . Roman . . . they are all burning in hell right now. It's over. Now, we can talk about it, but what good is it going to do? We agreed it's never going to be worth the air we put out discussing it." Chance climbed out of bed. "Nobody is ever going to hurt my family again."

Rashawn could tell that just the mention of that name brought back painful memories for him as well. Chance had fought hard to save her life that night, but Doc— Roman's half brother— nearly killed him. He still limped slightly from the bones broken by that beast of a man.

"Now, I don't want to talk about it. I know you can't control dreams but you need to put your head in a better place," Chance said, scowling, standing beside the bed and looking at her.

Rashawn lay back on her pillow, quickly drying her tears that came despite the fight to stave them off. Working even harder now, she pulled her emotions together. Chance was an understanding man, but apparently she had pushed him to where he just didn't feel like going tonight. When he returned from the bathroom he slid into bed, turning his back on her.

Chapter 12

Juanita tossed her large bag in the back seat of her car. "Come on!" she bellowed. She was furious. Junior had made her late this morning. Sometimes the arrangement wasn't as convenient as she would like, but she wasn't about to take Junior out of the school that Reggie attended. No way was she going to build on the family bridge that Rashawn was trying to create—adding more distance between her family and Chance's. No way. This coming summer Reggie would graduate, and right after that Rainey would start her freshman year, so yeah, Junior was staying in this school. Now if only she could get Junior to realize how important it was for him to stick with the program! "Being all late, actin' like I don't have other plans," she barked, thinking about her Thursday morning belly dancing class. "God!" she screeched, running back into the house. "Junior, please come on!" she called up the stairs. Junior descended the staircase slowly. His head was buried in a book and his ear buds were no doubt, tightly in place. He looked up at her, his dark eyes piercing. For just a second, Juanita had to do a double take, for the resemblance to someone other than Chance Sr. was almost frightening. She shook her head free of the thought. Surely one time with a lunatic didn't deserve a haunt like this, she reasoned.

There would be no way she would accept anyone other than Chance Davis as the father of her son. Even Dennis, her ex-husband whom she was married to at the time, was put out of the running years ago. And there was no way she would even consider the man who had briefly crossed her path via her therapy couch—the madman, crazy nut that Chance Jr. looked like right now.

"Come on!" she fussed, motioning for him to follow her out to the car, jingling the keys hurriedly as if he really couldn't hear instead of just choosing not to. She forcefully emptied her head of all thoughts other than how much she needed a trip to the spa, and climbed behind the wheel of her Toyota Cressida. The engine sounded terrible.

This business of being broke all the time is for the birds.

Now she would have to find a way to get Chance to pay for the work on her car.

As if I don't have enough going on in my life.

Her mind wandered as she jumped on and quickly off the freeway toward the Palemos, where Chance and Rashawn lived. It was a small, "up from down" area between and just east of Milbrea and Daly City. It was an old area and in need of some redevelopment. They had rebuilt Palo Alto—turning it from a drug-infested slum into a bustling and expensive community—that's where she lived. *So how come they can't do that to the Palemos?* she thought, turning onto the block where Chance and Rashawn lived.

Suddenly, she slammed to a halt at Junior's shriek and the sickening sound of metal crunching. "Shit!" she screamed, realizing that she'd run right into the back of some dude's expensive looking imported sports car. "Why now?" she bellowed, smacking her forehead against the steering wheel.

She quickly looked around for witnesses, or maybe some do-gooder cop too busy filling his quota to be interested in seeing what had really happened. This wasn't at all what it probably looked like. The immediate area was empty. This fool who had caused this accident was moving at about ten miles per hour as if he didn't know where he was going . . . or else just didn't know how to drive.

Jumping out of the car, she was about to give him a serious piece of her mind. Bracelets and coins dangled everywhere on her getup, showing from under her coat, and clanging as she slammed her hands on her hips. "The speed limit is thirty-five, moron!" she yelled while quickly approaching the car from behind. Sometimes Juanita could be fearless.

The man behind the wheel stepped from the car, and her eyes scanned the full length of him—which didn't require her to even look up. They stared at each other nearly eye to eye. He had broad shoulders, a thick neck, and a fabulous smile. He was small, sure, but truly compact and fully equipped with all the features—of that she was certain. She wanted to see his eyes; she could only imagine the color. But he didn't lower his dark shades. However, the muscles in his arms could be seen under the thin cotton of his crisp, white shirt, and that was enough to hold her interest for the moment. His skin was the color of an arctic sunset, smooth and beautiful—exotic. Juanita felt her mouth drop open.

"You hit me," he said, his voice deep and rumbling, as though from the halls of Buckingham Palace. She found her hand on her bare belly, as if the vibration from it could be felt from the inside out.

"Yes . . . um, well, you were driving too slowly, and you even put your brakes on too suddenly, sooo . . . this was all your fault."

"But you hit me from behind, so that puts you at fault no matter what. Isn't that the rule in this backward country," he explained simply, his voice soft but determined.

"No, now, that's not all together true, young man," she began, putting on an air of maturity.

"Young man?" He smiled. His teeth were bright, but it was his eyes that lit up his entire face when he pulled the shades away and looked out over her head. If was as if he wanted to laugh, but felt his laughter was only meant for friends to share, and she was a stranger. But not for long, not if she could help it. His green eyes cried out for her friendship. "You say that like you're old enough to be me mum." His head was cocked slightly to the side. He was sexy, and Juanita was fighting the urge to pour on the charm. It had been a long time since a man had affected her this way. She had been good for a long time—concentrating only on Chance and his married playing-hard-to-get ass. But now this man, this man could make her go bad—real bad. "I'd dare say you are probably young enough to be my kid sister," he said.

Was he flirting? Surely, he was flirting. Well, in that case . . . "Get outta here," Juanita retorted, a giggle chasing her words. "You're just trying to get out of admitting that you are at fault here. Let me see your paperwork. You know the drill: ID, insurance, and all that stuff. I mean, we need to exchange information," she said, trying to keep on mark yet show him a little interest at the same time. And he was interested, she could tell the way he was eying her costume. She moved her jacket to make sure he could get an eyeful, too. "And I guess we should call the authorities," she added reluctantly.

"No need, ma'am, you're looking at 'em," he said, pulling out his badge. Juanita's heart sank to her toes, staring at the badge and ID of Ovan Dominguez—Cop. The sight nearly turned her stomach.

"Mom!" Junior called from the car.

Juanita froze. She had forgotten just that quickly that Junior was in the car watching her make her move on this handsome man—this handsome cop. Juanita noticed Officer Dominguez looking around her toward the sound of Junior's voice. She watched his eyes as they studied Junior and then returned to meet hers.

"Your brotha?" he asked.

"Uhhh no . . . my son," she admitted, almost choking on the words.

Her emotions covered her face in the form of a light blush. Ovan apparently noticed, as he smiled warmly before retrieving a pen out of his car's visor to give her his personal information. "But, yeah, back to this, you're right. I'm at fault here. I was looking for an address and wasn't paying attention to what I was doing. Tell you what. Call me . . . uh, with the estimates and the agency will take care of it or whatever—I'm in somewhat of a hurry," he said, handing Juanita his card.

She looked at it closely; the words all scrambled around but still came back to three that meant the most at this moment. Ovan Dominguez—COP. It was as if that part jumped out at her more than anything.

"Do you want my number?" she asked, right before Junior bellowed again. "Junior! Please!" she yelped before her eyes crossed and then closed slowly to keep from rolling in her head. When she opened them, he was staring deeply at her . . . through her.

"No, you call my secretary if you want me to take care of things. There will no problem taking care of this here," he said, fanning his hand over the front of her car. Juanita strained to hear a double meaning. She so wanted there to be one. She'd not even considered the fact that he had a secretary. Since when did gumshoes get secretaries these days?

They shared an awkward moment before she smoothed back her wild hair. "I know this neighborhood well. It's the Palemos. My ex and his wife live here . . ." She paused before pointing at Junior. ". . . and I was taking him to. . . ." She suddenly realized that she was rambling. "Who were you looking for?" she asked him after clearing her throat.

"Juanita, come on!" Junior yelled out, sounding rude and disrespectful. He was begging for a grounding, but she would have to hold that off because for two weeks he was going to be staying at Rashawn's house—whether they liked it or not. Ovan looked around her again and then back at her, his face bursting into a full-on grin.

"It doesn't matter anymore . . . because I found you," he answered. Yes, he was indeed flirting. No mistake.

Chapter 13

Breakfast was quiet. Sometimes things were livelier when Junior was there, Rashawn had to admit that. "So, I'm surprised Junior didn't make here for breakfast," Rashawn said, breaking the silence.

"Well, I think Nita is trying to lay low considering she asked me yesterday if Junior could stay the entire winter break," Chance said.

"What?" both Reggie and Rashawn asked at the same time.

Chance looked at them. "And I haven't given her an answer yet, but—"

"I'm leaving, Chance. Why would you tell her yes? I won't be here for the first few days."

"And what difference does that make?" Chance retorted, not meaning to sound rude.

Rashawn dropped her fork loudly on her plate. "Well, excuse the hell outta me."

"That's not what I meant . . ."

"He's gonna be here all winter break? That's so not cool. I have plans," Reggie griped.

"And what difference does that make?" Chance asked Reggie, this time the question having intended meaning.

"I don't care if he's here," Rainey mumbled under her breath while picking around on her plate with her fork.

"Of course you don't," Reggie said with a sneer.

"Why does everyone act like that toward me?" Rainey whined.

"Nobody is acting any kind of way," Rashawn jumped in. "It's just I'm not going to be here and it's a lot of work for Daddy to have all you guys by himself."

"Rashawn, that's not true. I do it all the time."

"Yeah, Mommy, you're hardly ever here anymore," Rainey said, her innocence showing.

"Yeah, Mommy," Reggie added, without a drop of anything innocent showing anywhere.

"Look. I'm working hard to—" Rashawn began, but quickly stopped speaking. Reggie's phone rang. "Shut that off at the table!" Reggie quickly grabbed the phone. It was a rule—no phones at the table. At that open show of blatant disrespect, Rashawn stood from the table and gathered her plate and juice glass. The phone now vibrated against the glass Reggie had laid it next to. Rashawn held out her hand. Reluctantly, Reggie handed the phone over. She continued into the kitchen to set her plate in the sink after shoving the phone into her pocket. "Now, do whatever is it you people do—decide whatever it is you need to decide. Since, you know, I'm not really a factor in your little family decisions." She was pouting, but didn't care.

"Stop it, Rashawn. You're blowing things outta proportion," Chance said without getting up to comfort her. She noticed that. He just sat there finishing his breakfast. "Nita just asked me to extend Junior's visit and I think I will. I mean, she could use the break, and—"

"What?" That did it. Now Chance was defending Juanita. When he came in last night from taking Junior home he was acting funny. Of that Rashawn was sure. He didn't even give her a kiss, but instead went in and changed his shirt before dinner. All she noticed at the time was that Junior was not there. Maybe she should have noticed more.

Glancing at his watch, Chance stood. "Come on, guys, I'll drop you off on my way to work."

"I thought we were riding in together. I'm leaving tomorrow. I had hoped we'd spend time together and . . ." Rashawn went on. The kids gathered their books quickly and rushed toward the door. A ride to school was not a common thing–it only happened when she and Chance fought during breakfast. Okay, so it happened a lot.

"I'll swing by your office for lunch. How's that, baby?" he said before heading out the door, not waiting for an answer.

"Peachy," she said aloud to herself looking at the messy table that she had only moments to clean. Just then, Reggie's cell phone went off in her pocket. She hesitated, but pulled it out enough to glance at the number. The number was blocked. Picking up the fancy gadget, she pushed talk and put it her to ear. "Hello?" she said.

There was only silence before the caller hung up. "Whatever! I don't care if nobody ever wants to talk to me again!" she yelled, shoving the phone in back into her pocket. She emptied the table quickly before she too found herself running out the door as if on fire. She was late.

Chapter 14

"My life depends on this being kept secret," he said, rolling down his sleeve after securing the bandage.

Hap Washburn was a new surgeon—a hungry, eager one. Hap's girlfriend had died suddenly and he hadn't so much as mentioned it. He hadn't mentioned the money that Craven Michael had secured, either—money that Hap probably stole when he found out she was dead. Hap was hungry or, better yet, greedy. Roman could see it all over his face when he was attempting to explain why Craven not being in this plan was a "better idea, easier," he had said. "Less complicated," he had pointed out. Not an ounce of grief . . .

Roman was impressed, but on the other hand, he wasn't sure if he could trust such a desperate man. But if nothing else he'd shown his avaricious side, and Roman knew, with that, as long as he offered Hap what seemed like a little fame and notoriety, Hap would be loyal. "I understand that. My career depends on this being kept quiet as well."

Apparently, the thought of a surgery like this one made his juices marinade, and being the only surgeon on the case made it all the juicer. Sure, this surgery was as illegal and unethical as hell, but if successful he would make medical history for sure. And for a black doctor, even in this day and age, making history was where it was at! He was down for this, as the young people often said. Roman enjoyed young people. He had enjoyed being young—for the most part. There were portions of his young life that he hated to remember; one part in particular was being raised with his half brother, Blain. He hated Blain like no other person on earth, and was glad when Rashawn Aims killed him. Sure, Blain was killed for something of which he was innocent, but no matter.

Roman had been trying for years to find a way to kill his brother. Maybe it was a violent way to get what he wanted, but violence was in his blood. How could he not be affected? He'd only known that way of life. As a boy, he'd watched his own father commit the most violent of crimes, just to get what he wanted—his life back, taken from him through betrayal. His father was a genius and didn't deserve to be executed the way he was, not for killing a traitor. Call it revenge, call it a revisit; now Roman wanted only the same thing as his father. But he would not be treated as a common criminal in the end. For one, he was much too brilliant to be caught. His father allowed emotion to cloud his reason, but Roman had no such emotions. Roman's father was betrayed by a man who had claimed to be a servant of God. Roman had no weaknesses where God was concerned—maybe because he felt rather godlike most of the time.

"So it seems Reggie was easy to persuade."

"Persuade? What do you mean?" Roman asked.

"I'm thinking, all you had to do was offer him a chance to play ball for a bunch of ducks." Both men chuckled at the funny sound of the team's name. "At just the promise of fame, he jumped at the chance."

"What makes you think I had to trick him? He's my son; he should be more than ready to help me."

"Right, letting you kill him in the name of science. If you think I'm just gonna believe that he went for that deal without a fight . . . phhhst." Hap snickered.

"It's all in how you approach people," Roman said before bringing up Craven. Hap looked at him as if knowing what he was implying even before he said her name.

"Craven and I had our differences, but, yes, it was unfortunate what happened," he said.

"Yes, it was. By the way, she didn't happen to mention anything about . . . some extra money I'd given her? You know, before she . . . died." Roman emphasized the word.

"Extra money?"

"Yes, I had given her a bonus before I realized she had gone against my instructions—bringing you on board without my permission." Roman smiled wickedly. "I'm sure you knew about it. I'm sure she told you about it."

"She didn't tell me about any money," Hap fibbed. She'd promised some, but had not delivered yet—nor told him she'd had it already. She claimed she hadn't gotten it yet from Roman. *Lying bitch.*

"That's too bad. Well, I guess she was faithful about keeping that little secret—it's just unfortunate that she didn't follow the rest of my instructions. Oh well, good thing she didn't die in any pain."

"What?"

"I said," Roman paused dramatically as if Hap really could not understand what he was saying, "I'm glad I didn't cause her any pain. Actually, she was quite . . . relaxed," Roman smiled wickedly, "by the time I gave her the injection."

"You bastard!"

"So I've heard. But listen to me, Hap," Roman said, as if tasting the name in his mouth and rolling the bitterness around. "Craven jeopardized my entire operation. She brought you on board without my approval, promising to pay you with my money—which is the only reason you're not dead. I figure I might as well use you. I've paid you—of course, it's up to you to find where she put your share. Anyway, just so you know, I hate when people don't follow instructions."

Hap's face was covered with all sorts of mixed emotions now. Gone was his look of confidence. "She didn't give me anyth—"

"Save it," Roman said. "You were a fool to trust a woman—especially one who's willing to sleep with the boss. Now, about Reggie, I need you to make sure the plan goes as I have designed. You're not quite as seductive as Craven," Roman said, smiling wickedly, "but surely you can find some way to get a young man to follow you to a cabin in the middle of nowhere."

Hap stammered slightly before getting his question out. "Where will you be?"

"I've got some unfinished business to tend to before I join you all."

"I thought you said you would be there before us," Hap screeched. "I'm not in this to babysit!"

"I'm not asking you to. I'm asking you to do what Craven is no longer alive to do. I'll be there within a day or two . . . no worries."

"None of this sets well. Not at all. You act as though Craven's murder is not going to be noticed at all."

"Well that's your problem, Hap, since you're the one who acted foolishly, not dotting all your 'i's and crossing all your 't's. As far as anyone knows, you were the last person to see her alive, and her autopsy will show you were the last person to 'visit her'—can't believe you had sex with her without a condom. Are you crazy?" Roman shook his head in disgust. "Me, on the other hand . . . No one will ever know how deep our love went . . ." Now Roman was laughing.

"What the hell do you mean?"

Allen Roman smacked his lips and shook his head. "You're the one who decided to rough her up and rape her within hours of her death—which, at the moment, no one suspects is murder, but don't count on them being in the dark for long. I have reason to believe that your little tumble won't go unnoticed by forensics. However, if you do your job you won't go to jail for murder."

Hap took in a full chest of air as if clearing his head of the information he'd just been given. "I don't intend to go to jail."

"Then I guess you better watch your step," Roman said, draping his jacket over his arm and heading for the door. Hap, as if suddenly realizing the full impact of what he'd gotten into, felt his blood chill, to an icy temperature.

Chapter 15

Back at the station, Ovan reviewed the morning's events as well as the court file he'd managed to get his hands on, among other things.

The file reviewed in detail the state's position on the civil and criminal cases involving the "get ass" epidemic. That was what they had named the date rape drug that Blain Tollome and his team of campus security cops peddled around the school. Many girls up and down the peninsula had been raped as a result of ingesting the drug. Juanita Duncan's name had come up in several instances, but one stood out: Yvette Furhman. She had been murdered after the discovery that she had become pregnant by one of security cops working for Blain Tollome. Notes from the therapist, Juanita Duncan, indicated that she suspected Allen Roman (who was addicted to the exotic island drug to alleviate pain he suffered due to bad kidneys and a failing liver) of murdering the young girl, although all evidence pointed to Blain Tollome. Juanita Duncan had been one of the University's therapists during that time, along with Allen Roman. "So they were colleagues.

Interesting," Ovan mumbled. *Yes, this Dr. Duncan is probably a good place to go for some inside information on Roman,* Ovan thought.

Although the file did not connect the dots to Allen Roman as directly as he had first imagined it would, there was a lot of information concerning the hypno/psychotherapist Juanita Duncan that demanded his further, detailed investigation. That was his justification for borrowing the file that morning from the DA's office. It wasn't the "borrowing" of the file, however, that had him in a rush to leave. He also had found himself in a precarious situation with the deputy DA that made lingering around awkward.

That deputy DA was a hot blonde. Feisty and full of, apparently, pent-up, raging hormones. It always amazed him what a heightened yet underused libido would make a woman do. But there was no way he had intended to shag that woman.

It wasn't as if she wasn't lovely, the way she sat on the corner of her desk, crossing her legs so that he caught sight of plenty of thigh. But he truly had come there to work. Despite his reputation, he really was a serious agent.

Making up a story, he told her he was an attorney working a civil case dealing with one of the date rape victims, who now felt that because of this rape she couldn't have an orgasm in her married life. The DA seemed more than willing to help. "Anything for an orgasm," she joked. Inappropriate though it was, Ovan read through the veneer and into the woman's true feelings.

"Well, they are very important to some people," he said, glancing quickly through the pages of the file, realizing only then he'd hit a mother lode of information on Blain Tollome and the case surrounding the date rape drug. There was too much to memorize and much more than he'd have time to read there, in her presence. She was all but breaking a sweat as it was. So he skimmed for more connections to Allen Roman. She noticed his intensity—apparently it aroused her.

"I know my office is small, but do you mind if I close the door," she said, bringing his attention back, pulling it away from the file. She'd pulled her long, blond mane from its tight bun and allowed it to fall freely around her shoulders. She also unbuttoned the top two buttons of her crisp white blouse.

Sex. What a phenomenon, he thought, wondering what he had done or said to make this woman want it right at that particular moment.

Within a moment or two—allowing for the removal of panty hose—she was bent over her desk with her hand holding down the photo of her smiling husband and two kids. Ovan worked over her back side. She was hungry; he could tell because of the way she violently twisted her hips, hoping to find the spot that would offer release of her pent-up tension. Feeling her desperate need, he pulled from her. She turned to him, red-faced and highly agitated. "No. I didn't . . . yet," she began, out of breath and overheated. Ovan shushed her calmly.

"I know," he whispered.

Changing his condom—he always carried two—he instructed her to turn back toward the desk and squat. Following her down the floor, Ovan entered her slowly while reaching around her waist, using his middle finger to plow through her thick pubic hair until he found her magic button. It was ready and waiting, pulsating like mad and nearly too hot to touch. Gently he stroked it, calming it, making love to it manually while stoking her inner fire with his hardened manhood. It was a technique he knew well, and used often on desperate housewives. Within moments her knuckles whitened from the grip she had on her desk's edge, while she gave into what was probably the best orgasm she'd ever had in her life, if not her first "real" one. Deep guttural moans escaped her lips as he slowly moved his hips in a circular motion, while stimulating her clit, which grew slippery with her juices. From the outside of her, while rubbing gently on deeper inner lips, he could feel himself stroking inside her and he knew he was hitting the right spots. "Tighten yourself around me," he whispered in her ear, feeling her muscle contracting instantly. With that, her vagina began to convulse while her mound grew and her lower lips swelled with sexual fever. His hands were soon drenched in her fluids as she came repeatedly, spreading her knees wide to take him all in, gasping for air as she did. Her belly sucked in tight as he now grabbed at her mound, using the palm of his hand and fingers to create suction.

"Oh my God," she breathed, "I've never . . . you're so . . ."

"I know," he whispered in her ear, nibbling lightly on her lobe.

There was a knock on the door, but she only opened and closed her mouth, too weak to answer, which was fine by Ovan as he was in no position to receive guests. He was concentrating on her pleasure. Her smile grew broad with her lips flinching every now and then as he would hit new spots—possibly ones she never knew she had.

Just watching her ecstasy was exciting to him, and, accepting that she was satisfied, he thrust deep into her core, finally coming.

He pulled from her, then carefully removed the soggy condom and tossed it into the trash. He slid back into his pants and, without her noticing, eased the file inside his coat, which he threw over his arm while she lingered prostrate in front of her desk, hanging on to the edge of it. If anyone were to see her now, they would surely think she was drunk. "Pull yourself together, love. You've got work to do," he said into her ear as he bent over. She nodded slowly with her eyes closed, licking her lips as if having just enjoyed something delicious.

He tiptoed out, making sure the coast was clear before relocking her door and making his way to his car. He was whipped, but he knew he still had plenty of work to do today. Reaching his car, he realized he'd not had a moment to wash his hands. Taking a sniff, he smiled at the memory.

His mind left the pleasant memory and came back to the smelly precinct. "Juanita. Why does that name sound so familiar?" He flipped through more pages in the file. He'd have to drop by and pay her a visit later, since his visit to Ms. Ams-Davis's home was stymied by that crazy woman running into the back of his car that morning. That woman who hit his car . . . She was crazy, true, but cute enough to eat, or at least lick on a bit. Ovan allowed a wicked smile to curve his lips, as was his unconscious mannerism when thinking about sex—which was all the time! He'd had breakfast with the DA, and thinking of the woman who hit his car had him ready for an afternoon snack.

Lawrence noticed his expression. "I have no idea," he mumbled. He was showing continued annoyance at Ovan Dominguez's presence at his desk again today. He'd made it clear yesterday that even though his partner, Jim Beem, was on vacation, his seat was not "empty."

"No problem. I'll stand—again," Ovan had responded this morning, and even now he had been doing just that for at least an hour.

"Well, I need to get to her office and speak with her."

"What about? Rashawn Ams?" Lawrence asked. Ovan was surprised that Lawrence had been curious enough to actually give glance through the file and remember any part of it.

"Yes. Your file, as I mentioned, was disappointingly limited. The DA's file, needless to say, filled in many gaps. I knew there was a stronger connection between her and Allen Roman. Sure, she's connected to Blain Tollome—which was not my ambition here. I'm on the trail of Allen Roman. Did you know he's ill? Kidney problems. He's not on dialysis—too easy to trace I suppose."

"But he'd have to be treating himself somehow," Lawrence added.

"My thoughts exactly. He is a doctor of sorts . . ."

"Mad scientist from what I've heard."

"Ahhh, you've been listening." Ovan smiled. Lawrence reluctantly returned the nicety, but shook his head as if to say "But that still doesn't make us friends."

"My partner has led me to believe that Mr. Roman is in need of a transplant. That leads me to think he's looking for a donor on his own—willing or not—and a doctor to perform the surgery . . . legally or not."

"Exactly, why would a man like that want to wait in line like everybody else?"

Ovan looked sincerely at Lawrence. "I'm trying not to alarm Ms. Ams, although after reading the report I stole— I mean, borrowed from the DA's office, I do believe that Roman isn't far from her doorstep."

Lawrence smirked at what seemed to be a wild, off-the-wall and far-stretched connection between Rashawn Ams and Allen Roman. "And why would that be? She have a kidney he might want?"

"As a matter of fact, yes. She's got his son."

Lawrence couldn't help but reach for the file Ovan had—the "borrowed" one he'd refused to touch earlier, claiming that he wanted no part of such ill-gained information. "I thought of just bogarting over there earlier but changed my mind entirely—that's definitely not the way to do this," Ovan admitted.

"But what you're really saying is that you still have no proof that this Roman cat is really alive, and didn't want to get stuff started for no reason."

"Oh, I know he's alive. Remember, I'm the one who tried to apprehend him yesterday evening, but nooo, your over-eager beavers stopped me."

Lawrence rolled his eyes.

"He's taunting me, you know . . . begging for me to enter his game," Ovan said, pointing his finger at Lawrence, who now had his head buried in the file.

"The game?"

"Yes, international cat and mouse. He's leaving trails, everywhere he goes, like breadcrumbs the size of dead bodies . . . dead doctors, two so far: one in Jamaica, one in London, both dying of heart attacks after dealing with him. There's plenty of proof that he's up to something maniacal beyond just murder.

"Right, right . . . maybe," Lawrence mumbled, not really listening.

"I'm just waiting to hear back concerning Craven Michaels's autopsy, but if what I suspect is true and there's a connection between how these surgeons died and what Roman is up to . . . Sure, they all had heart attacks, I get that, but I'm saying if those heart attacks were . . ."

"Were not natural . . ."

"Exactly! That's my thought. Then I just need to know what they did to cheese him off. I know what you're thinking, that I can't prove to you that Allen Roman is even alive—but he is. I chased him, nearly had him my clutches."

Lawrence again sighed and swooned at Ovan's dramatic speech.

"Fine, disbeliever, you're just going to have to trust me. Oh, I know what you're thinking: 'Well, Ovan, how is he *killing* people who are having heart attacks, aren't the heart attacks killing them?' "Do the math." Ovan went on.

"Take Craven, for example. I really don't think a healthy woman of thirty-five is gonna just drop dead that way. And trust me, she was pretty healthy, if you know what I'm saying." Ovan snickered wickedly without saying what would probably either come out wrong or be taken wrong. He didn't know Lawrence well enough to let him in on everything that rolled around in his mind that was even slightly off police work. He'd even avoided fully disclosing how he got the file from the office of the DA.

But apparently Lawrence had caught on, slapping his head in disgust. "You and my partner! What's with the view you two have of women? Just because a woman has a nice body or fat ass, that doesn't mean healthy in the biological sense. It doesn't mean anything—"

Ovan held up his hand to stop Lawrence's diatribe before it got too far. "Trust me, it was more than a fat ass that told me that about Craven," he said, allowing his sexually charged chauvinistic attitude to come through now. "I know healthy when I . . ." Suddenly his mind clicked and his finger snapped. "Juanita! Yes. The fat-assed woman who ran into the back of my car this morning! Yes . . ."

"Excuse me?" Lawrence said, trying to follow his thought pattern. Jim often jumped around too when following a hunch.

"She hit me."

"With her car?"

"I was snooping about in the Ams's 'hood,' " he said, "trying to decide on my approach, when all of a sudden—bloody hell! Half naked belly dancer rammed me from behind. Feisty little gypsy. Damned sexy as hell, too." Ovan reached into his pocket, hoping her card would appear. No such luck. "Damn, that's right. I gave her my card so that she could call my partner with the charges to her car. Maravel is so much better at paperwork than I am," he rambled.

"You took the blame?"

"Wouldn't you? Beautiful, half naked woman with the promise of a great shag in her eyes," Ovan swooned slightly, leaning on the table as if starting to daydream and needing the support.

"Hell no! My rates would go through the roof. Crazy foo'."

"Yes, I'm a big fool because now I don't know where to find her. Damn it all straight to hell! And I bet this Juanita," he said, holding up the file, "is the same woman from this morning. Ex-wife of Chance Davis—I bet she is. Juanita Duncan is the ex-wife of Chance Davis. This woman was on her way to her ex's home, a home that was in the same hood as Rashawn Ams. Yes, it's got to be the same woman. And her name was Juanita as well—how many of those could there be. Of course. This has really been my lucky day!"

Lawrence shook his head at the eccentric little man. Ovan knew Lawrence saw when him. It was clear Lawrence was still undecided about whether he liked Ovan. "Let me get her address for you. I'm done talking to you right now anyway—I need a break from you. Besides, none of this has to do with Allen Roman being alive," Lawrence huffed, shaking his head in disgust while taking the file over to the clerk to get an address for Juanita Duncan.

"You'll see, ol' boy," Ovan mumbled, watching the obviously lonely man make his way over to the clerk. Lawrence wasn't bad looking nor in bad shape. He was big, true, but he actually was pretty buff—and Ovan was not like most men who can't tell the difference between a muscle and blubber. Ovan couldn't stand those guys who called their fat "buff." Ovan took extraordinary care of his body, and it disturbed him to no end to see other men just letting themselves go and then wondering why they turned women off.

It wouldn't be his concern, except for the fact that they were always asking him, "Gee, man, howdja shag that one?"

Ovan decided then that he would have to take Lawrence out for a few drinks before all this was over, loosen him up a bit. But first he was going to take another look around Craven's place, stop in on the good Dr. Duncan, and then see what he ended up with. Maybe he'd have another run-in with Allen Roman along the way. Maybe he'd get in a clear shot this time—kill the bastard. If anyone knew his personal involvement in the case he would have been taken off a long time ago. It was amazing how having a handy computer geek for a partner could enhance the changing of one's identity. No one would ever be able to trace his real name.

Chapter 16

The day was a long one for Chance. Too long. It had given him too many opportunities to think about his life. He tried not to do that often. It wasn't as if anything was wrong with his life, but not too much was right, either. Maybe he was just bored. He'd been hanging out with his sister-in-law and her husband a little bit lately, getting their advice on this whole Reggie situation. He felt guilty, as if rushing Reggie out of the house. That wasn't it. It was just that Rashawn needed to let him go. Let him grow up. Chance knew he had no ulterior motives for wanting Reggie to go to school out of state. But with Reggie around, Rashawn was having a harder and harder time letting go of the past. It was almost as if now that Reggie was growing up the wounds were reopening. "Maybe because he looks like that guy so much," Rita, Rashawn's sister, said, offering Chance a possible solution. "I know if I were raped and my child started looking like the rapist it would be hard for me. We've all pretended that Reggie only looks like us, but you know he doesn't. He barely looks like Rashawn and she's his mother, so he sure as heck doesn't look like the rest of us."

"But it's just time to let go. Maybe it's not even all that deep, maybe it's just that she needs to let go. I'm going to want Nita to do the same thing with Junior in just a couple of years. These boys have got to grow up," Chance had said to Rita.

"Hell, yeah. If they don't go, them Negros will eat you outta house and home," Rita's husband chimed in. They had two sets of teenage twin sons and one daughter. "Hell, I wish my kids were smarter so the younger ones could have skipped some grades, and all of them could have just up and gone to some college outta state together. Yeah, I wish they were geniuses like . . . who's the kid on that show . . . Dooky Howser."

"Doogy, baby, Doogy," Rita corrected, rubbing her head in disgust at his comment. She then turned to Chance. "Crazy man, you know he don't want all his kids outta state 'cause then he'd have to deal with me every day. Anyway . . . Chance, you've been a great father. You deserve an award . . . seriously. And you're right; Reggie should be allowed to go away to school. But you have to see Rashawn's point, too."

"I don't though. She doesn't treat Rainey the way she treats Reggie, or Junior. I know, I know, Junior isn't her son, but sometimes I think she doesn't care about anybody but Reggie."

"Well, you know that's not true," Rita interjected quickly.

"And they fight all the time, she and Reggie. And . . . and she's been having nightmares again," Chance finally confessed. "About Roman."

"He's dead!" Terrell again jumped in.

"We know this, T." Rita smacked her lips and rolled her eyes. Chance smiled. Rita and Terrell argued all the time and fought with their kids constantly. But love was thick in their house. They were what Chance always considered to be a real family. Rashawn called them "a mess."

"Then why is she dreaming about a dead man—that's what I wanna know," Terrell asked, heading back into his office. He was an attorney who worked out of their home.

"You just have to be patient with my sister. This turning fifty has not been good to her," Rita told him—as if he would understand what that meant.

Rethinking that visit with Rita and her husband, Chance looked out the window now. He watched as Rainey walked toward the house. She was laughing with her friends—one boy, one girl.

The boy suddenly tugged at her hair, and the girlfriend reached around Rainey and slugged him. Rainey was laughing. They all were. Just the thought of that boy hurting his daughter for real . . . the thought of anybody hurting her, the way Allen Roman had hurt Rashawn, tightened Chance's belly. No, fifteen years would not be near long enough for him to get over it. "Nobody is ever going to hurt my kids," he said under his breath.

"Hey, what's cookin'?" Reggie asked, lifting the lid off of Chance's pot. He turned back toward the kitchen. Rainey walked in.

"Soup. My specialty," Chance answered.

"Oh yeah, I'm down," Reggie slurped greedily. "I gather Mom is still pissed and this is make up food?"

"Smells good in here," Rainey said as soon as she cleared the door.

"Your mother is leaving tomorrow, so I wanted her to have a good going away dinner. And, no, this isn't a make up meal."

"Mmhmm . . ." Reggie winked. "Scared she won't come back, eh?"

"Oh, she'll come back. She can't survive without me," Rainey teased.

Looking around now as if he'd missed something, Reggie asked, "Where's Junior? He wasn't at school today."

"He's home, I guess," Chance answered, stirring his pot.

Rainey looked at her father and then at her stepbrother. "God, you guys are horrible. You don't even know if he's home sick. I'm sure he wants to say good-bye to Mom too. Call him."

"You are so cornball and stupid," Reggie barked.

"No, she's not, and it's a good idea," Chance spoke up.

"I have a better one . . . giving me back my BlackBerry. Now, that is a good idea," Reggie grumbled, heading back to his room.

Chance reached for the wall phone and started dialing Juanita's number. "Shoulda had it at the table."

Chapter 17

Juanita pulled into the driveway with Junior. It was obvious that Rashawn wasn't home. Junior jumped out of the car quickly. She always had mixed feelings about how excited he was to be at this house. But then again, their day at home together had been far from fun-filled. After the fender bender, Juanita detoured to the car dealership to get estimates. She got a flat on the way and had to call AAA. Of course, her membership was suspended due to her being behind in the payments. It wasn't as if she could change the tire in her costume, so she and Junior caught the city bus home. Robbing Peter to pay Paul, so to speak, she floated money from one account to another to pay her AAA insurance premium, then arranged for them to tow the car, which they did to the tune of a one-hundred-dollar deductable—ugh. Breaking down and using money from her "stash," she paid the tow guys, who then fixed the flat that, by now, she could have changed herself. By then,

Junior was way too late for school, so he spent the day playing video games and she spent the day cussing and fussing at wasting so much time and money on a stupid flat that, again, was Ovan Dominguez's fault!

Junior turned the knob and walked in. Rashawn wasn't home, so Juanita took advantage of the opportunity to make herself at home by following him inside. The house was quiet except for the sounds of the TV coming from the den. The lingering smell of popcorn was in the air, as well as the wonderful aroma of Chance's favorite recipe, homemade minestrone soup.

"Hey!" Chance said, coming from the den and dusting the salt from his hands. Juanita frowned, thinking about his blood pressure. "I was just . . ." he began, sounding guilty.

"I know what you were doing. Eatin' something you have no business eating. Ya watchdog ain't even outta town yet and here you are already messin' up."

Chance's smile faded quickly. "Don't call my wife that."

Juanita immediately regretted her words. "I'm sorry . . . really. That came out wrong. What' cha cooking?" she asked, changing the subject.

"His specialty," Rainey answered, coming from her room. Junior had quickly disappeared into the den and had taken over Chance's seat and his bowl of buttery, salty popcorn. Chance noticed and sighed slightly–looking disappointed about losing his decadent treat more than anything. "You staying for dinner?" Rainey asked her. "It's Mom's going away dinner."

"Where is she going this time?" Juanita asked, realizing that apparently Chance didn't want her to know, or he would have told her.

Rainey lit up. She seemed to enjoy talking to her. Juanita liked her too. She reminded her so much of Chance, a sweet child indeed. "She's going to Arizona for two weeks! She's going to see her sister, the writer."

"And you know what they say: while the cat's away!" Junior yelled out from the den. "Parrrtay!"

"Noooo, none of that," Chance corrected, heading to his pot to give it a stir. Juanita followed him.

"So just you and the kids for two weeks?" she asked. Chance glared at her.

"I can handle it. Why do you and my wife think I can't handle it?"

"I didn't say anything remotely like that . . ." Juanita grinned.

"Yes, you did," he fussed playfully.

"No worries, he's got me," Rainey said. "I can handle these boys," she assured.

"I'm sure you can, baby." Juanita again noticed how pretty Rainey was. She felt immediately melancholy, imagining Rainey to be her own daughter—but, alas, she was Rashawn's daughter. She was the glue that held Chance by Rashawn's side. "You're more and more like your mama every day," Juanita said.

Chance looked at her as if unsure of what she would say next. "And that means?"

"Don't be so defensive. That means she's turning into a beautiful young lady." Juanita laughed and then whispered loudly and playfully to Rainey, "Willing to get in over your head, but then," she turned to Chance, "I'm sure that's the *you* in her," she added, bursting into laugher. Chance clearly couldn't resist and laughed too. Dipping the spoon in the pot, he tasted the soup.

"Yeah!" he exploded.

"Ohhh, let me taste it," she requested. It was a knee-jerk request but she was caught up. Warm house, warm laughter. . . . Yeah, she was caught up. And as soon as Chance raised that spoon to her lips, the door opened and Rashawn walked in. Yeah, she was caught up, or she would have been ready for that one.

"Well. Cozy," Rashawn said. Her tone cooled the room down by degrees. Surely it matched outside now. Chance quickly set down the spoon and hurried over to her, kissing her tenderly. Juanita felt her own mouth open slightly as if she had received the tenderness of his lips.

The moment was suddenly awkward. "Well," she began. "Junior. I'm going. If you need more stuff, just have your dad . . ." she glanced at Rashawn and Chance standing there, "or just come get it," she stumbled.

"Yeah," Junior answered, sounding as if his mouth was full.

Quickly, Juanita grabbed her purse and brushed past Rashawn, pausing only to whisper, "Have a nice trip," before rushing out the door.

Climbing behind the wheel, she noticed Rashawn's car parked on the street. She was parked in Rashawn's normal spot. She looked back toward the house and thought about the perfect family inside. She thought about how that family could have been hers if she hadn't cheated, schemed, and lied so much. "I'ma get back on my meds tomorrow," she promised herself.

Chapter 18

He didn't have time to wait for the local police to figure out that Craven had been murdered by Allen Roman. Somehow, someway, he was going to have to prove it to them. They were stuck in the "natural causes" groove and refused to move, according to Maravel. He'd been working with Lawrence Miller for a couple of days now, but still he'd not reached his sensibilities. He could tell. "Maybe if I were more forthcoming with the real deal . . ." he began. "Like that would really get me further," he admitted, picking the lock and slipping into Craven Michaels's house unnoticed. Lawrence Miller was a good cop, but even he hadn't been willing to just open the door and let him inside Craven's house to look around again. It could have been because British Intelligence hadn't heard of him. Lawrence had been quick about checking out his references.

"I'm on special assignment," Ovan had told Lawrence, hoping that would win his assistance, but no, Lawrence simply hung up the phone. "No matter, I don't hold it against you, big fella. I know what I do and why, and right now all I care about is getting into Craven's flat," Ovan reasoned, putting away his tools that had allowed him to break and enter without making a sound or a scratch. He'd been the agency's second-story man for years, so getting in here had been a piece of cake.

Heading straight for her home office, Ovan noticed that Craven had many books on surgical procedures pulled out on her desk. They were all open to renal issues. "Kidney failure," Ovan said aloud. "Right on. Nothing else can relieve your pain, so it's time to deal with it, eh, ol' boy? So, are we in the market for a new kidney?" Ovan asked while snooping around through her notes. He found the name "Roman" doodled on a notepad. "Seems to me that transplanting a kidney to a dead man would be a waste of a perfectly good kidney . . . unless, of course, he's not dead." Ovan quickly folded the page from her notes into his jacket. He'd show Lawrence; surely then he would be ready to believe the truth about Allen Roman.

Banking the information away, he continued to snoop—articles on transplants, transfusions. All the information boggled his mind, yet he filed away as much as he could for Maravel. She was better at deciphering riddles. After a little more snooping, he considered himself done for now. He tiptoed past Craven's bedroom, and for a second he reminisced about the time he'd spent with her there. The memory drew him inside and over to the bed. It was in a tussled state. "Hmm, looks like my girl might have entertained a little before her heart stopped," he said, noticing under the edge of the bed, nowhere near clear view, the minute edge of a torn condom package. With the edge of a pen that sat on the night stand, he scooped it into the plastic bag he pulled from the pocket of his jacket. "If nothing else, I'll see who your last partner was and who knows, maybe I'll trip up on a 'colleague'—or even better," he reasoned, thinking about Craven's sexual habit much the way he looked at his own. *Of course she'd sleep with a partner or colleague, I would. Hell, I'd shag in a heartbeat providing I have the time.* He wondered why he hadn't shagged Juanita Duncan yet—*oh yeah, I haven't met her.* He chuckled. The thought tickled him for only for a second, because he heard keys jingling in the lock of the front door. He quickly ducked out of sight.

"I mean, she already died for it," the intruder whispered, seemingly mindless as he stomped into her bedroom, immediately rummaging through her dresser drawer. "Where is the damn money," he mumbled, leaving her room and heading toward Craven's office, where her body had been discovered by her maid. Ovan moved quietly from his spot in order to get a better view of the man who, while in the office, slammed around a bit longer before stopping and looking around as if he felt himself being watched.

"Who's there?" he called out. Ovan ducked into the darkness. The man looked around again and then hurriedly rummaged through the desk, pulling out a small key. "Yeah! That's what I'm saying. Hello, Benjamins," he exclaimed, tucking the key into the pocket of his lab coat and starting for the front of the house. Ovan jumped out of his hiding place.

"What'cha got there?" he asked, taking a fighting stance. He didn't know who he was about to fight or what he was fighting for, but he knew he wanted what that man had in his pocket. It was a clue, a piece of evidence that would take him one step closer to Allen Roman.

"Who are you?" the man asked.

"The question is, my man, who the blazes are you? Perhaps a colleague of the late Dr. Michaels . . . or maybe her murderer!" The last comment hit a chord, Ovan could tell.

"He's not going to frame me like this," the man spat, angrily charging at him.

"Who is framing you? What are you and Allen Roman up to?" Ovan asked while tussling with the man, gaining the upper hand. At first speculation he figured the man for more of a scholar, less of a fighter, with his lanky, nerdy appearance. But he was wrong.

"I don't know Allen Roman," the man said before fists came to blows and Ovan had to rely on brute strength to get the man off of him.

"Of course you do. Craven did and you must be the partner she was talking about."

"And what of it!"

"Then you know Roman is alive too—ah ha! Framing you! Roman is framing you for Craven's murder!" Ovan hit the man hard, knocking him off his feet. "I just want some answers." Ovan spat after knocking the man to the floor. "Hand over what you pulled from the desk."

"What?" the man asked stupidly.

"What's in your pocket!" Ovan yelped, reaching down toward the pocket of man's jacket.

"You mean this!" The man then, instead of pulling out a gun, pulled out a syringe and stabbed Ovan in the arm.

"Bloody hell!" Ovan exclaimed. He stumbled backward as the drug took its immediate effect.

"Did you just kill me?" he asked, his double vision immediately beginning to cross his eyes.

"No, but you'll sleep awhile . . . at least until I call the police and report your intrusion in my girlfriend's house. Maybe I'll tell them you murdered her."

"Your girlfriend?" Ovan asked, struggling for consciousness.

Hap quickly put the syringe away before pulling a tissue from the box that sat on a small table and wiping the blood from his lip. "Yes. My girlfriend."

"Who . . ." Ovan was struggling to speak. He was going down. ". . . are you?"

"Wouldn't you like to know."

Chapter 19

Rashawn smoothed on the wrinkle cream. It was designed to search and destroy ahead of time, or so it promised. Her older sister had recommended it, along with Yam Cream and Cat's Claw tea and several other potions, poultices, and elixirs to ensure youth for many years to come.

Just then, from the mirror, she noticed Chance watching her from the bed. He wore a half-smile, an almost sarcastic smirk—if she wanted to go there in her mind.

"Thanks for the dinner, baby," she purred, avoiding all mention of Juanita getting the first taste. She was leaving tomorrow and the trip was all that was on her mind.

"Anything for you," Chance responded, climbing from the bed and walking up behind where she sat facing her vanity mirror. He ran his hands over her shoulders and kissed the top of her head, before moving her hair and kissing down the back of her neck.

"You smell like a pie," he teased. "All these fruity greases and creams," he joked on, looking at the labels of her miracle mixes.

"Stop, Chance," Rashawn mumbled, hiding her humiliation. It was nothing Chance had said in particular to embarrass her; she was just feeling . . . *that way*.

Just then, he slid his hands down the front of her robe and down under the top of her soft satin gown, cupping her full breasts, gently thumbing at the nipples. Rashawn looked at him in the reflection of the mirror. He looked at her. He wasn't wearing his glasses, so she could see his eyes clearly in the reflection. He wanted her. It had been a couple of weeks since they'd made love, and Rashawn had started to wonder if they had reached "that" point in their relationship. Her sister had warned her about letting the love wane: "Don't let it happen, girl," Carlotta, her oldest sister, had told her.

Arching upward, she accepted the nonverbal proposal, sighing heavily, giving into the quickly growing passion. Standing back from her, Chance dropped his shorts, exposing his readiness to her. Standing there in his undershirt, with his shorts around his ankles, the invite was surely awkward, but Rashawn wasn't about to decline it. Since their first time together, their sexual compatibility had improved a hundredfold.

Pulling her to him, he squeezed his engorged member teasingly between her thick thighs, flirting the promise of fulfillment and satisfaction, kissing her earlobes, whispering sweet "nasties" in her ear. Pulling off their remaining sleepwear, they quickly slid between the sheets so he could deliver on his proposal.

Rashawn covered her mouth to keep herself from screaming as Chance worked himself deep inside her pleasure cove. Deeper and deeper the probe went until finally he reached the pinnacle of her pleasure. She came quickly, but once was not going to be enough tonight. Normally there was more foreplay than this, but who had that kind of time? *Not me*, Rashawn thought, rolling Chance over and climbing on top. *I may be old, but this sista here still got this shit*. Rashawn growled while working Chance over, causing his eyes to roll back in his head. She bit at his lip playfully until he pulled at her hair and went for her neck. *Ohhh, Lawd, a monkey bite. How am I gonna explain this*, Rashawn thought, a giggle escaping her lips. Chance rolled her back under him and went at her sex with determination. His face was reddening and he'd even broken a sweat. Rashawn was tickled, opening her legs wide to allow him all she had. Since the day they made love the first time, Chance always showed his fortitude in bed, never giving up until she'd had enough. It was good then, and had since only gotten better. Sometimes Rashawn understood Juanita and her desire to get next to Chance, and to have him back in her life . . . like now.

But then again, why did she let him go?

Needing both her hands now to grab hold of the bedding, she gave way to the orgasm that rumbled up from deep within, burning at her thighs, and literally curling her toes. "Shhhitttt!" She opened her eyes and met Chance's light pools of passion. It had been a while since their session had gone longer than half an hour, like this one had.

Chance was not aware of his own prowess, and downright sexiness; of that fact, Rashawn was certain. He was too caring and gentle—caring enough to make sure that she was thoroughly pleased before pleasing himself. Sometimes he would even ask if she had had enough. "You feeling it?" he whispered now. She nodded in response, a response that brought renewed vigor as he now sought his own pleasure, taking the ride to a new height of excitement, giving way to a low volume of verbal appreciation of her body. She shushed him, softly stroking his smooth back, kissing him tenderly on the top of his balding head. He rose up, pulling her knees up to his chest, filling her to the core, swiveling his hips to make sure to hit her pleasure points with a mastered technique that again sent her into a quake of pleasure. It rattled her so that even Chance held her tight to control the convulsing. Together they came, with Chance freely releasing his emissions. Rashawn had long given up her birth control pills and condoms as her doctor had given the final confirmation of her menopause over a year ago.

"I'm not done," he whispered, inching down her body until he reached her heat. He'd not orally pleased her in ages. Urging him to get to business by pushing him lightly on his head, he took the hint and buried his tongue deep inside her before using it to toy with her clit. She purred and cooed in her joy. "I love you, Shawnie," he said before gently tonguing her love button that sat swollen and willing to respond once more to attention. Rashawn was excited and feeling refreshed. Sex was fun tonight and she was enjoying herself. All that was on her mind was gone. She almost wished she wasn't leaving. Finishing, Chance lay beside her folding his arms behind his head, smiling to himself, no doubt proud of his accomplishment. Rashawn noticed his manhood had not yet retired fully, so, still feeling a little frisky, she took it between her lips. In his surprise he gasped. It had been even longer since she'd pleased him this way. He was immediately stiff as she ran her teeth lightly along the shaft and around the head before doing all the things he liked her to do for him with her mouth. "Good golly, you're the best," he whispered after coming again. She moved up behind him in the bed like a spoon in a drawer, satisfied and tired.

Clinging to her, spooning with her, Chance showed his softer side awhile longer. He was ready to talk. It was funny, since often Rashawn would be the one to fall asleep on him, leaving him alone in the dark with his end of the conversation.

"So what do think of Reg's decision to check out U of O?" Chance asked.

Rashawn, barely holding on to consciousness, nodded. Then, realizing what she was agreeing to, she smacked her lips loudly. "I mean, no . . . I'm not happy." She giggled, drunk from the love.

"You gonna have to let Reggie go."

"Says who, Chance, you?"

"No, says Reggie. Says the cosmos. He's a man now. He can handle his own business."

Rashawn sat up and turned to him in the dim light from the vanity across the room. "Reggie doesn't have any business."

"Shawnie, come on now, he has to be allowed to make his own decisions. I'm talking as a man. I'm talking as his father."

"As his fa—" Rashawn held her tongue. Chance had never said that before. It touched her. It didn't change her mind, but it touched her. "Chance, I'm not ready for this. He can't just be going on 'trips,'" Rashawn said, making quotations around the word trips, "he's not even eighteen. By the time the first semester starts he still won't be eighteen."

"Rita said—"

Rashawn was sitting straight up now. "You've been talkin to Rita?"

"Honey, you've been busy and—"

"I'm not that busy. Who else have you been over this with besides me?" Her arms were folded. She was pissed.

"Nobody." Chance was lying. She could tell.

"So what did Carlotta say?" she asked, knowing he had gone over her head to Carlotta, her oldest sister.

"First let me tell you what Shelby said."

By now Rashawn was holding the sides of her head. "Oh my God . . . Shelby!"

"She said he could stay there if he decided to

go with U of O. She said he could stay there with her in Eugene."

"Oregon! Do you know how many people disappear in Oregon? It's like the state of the weirdo. Ted Bundy is from there!"

"Not Eugene. He's not from Eugene."

"The Unabomber . . ."

Chance was sitting up now as well. "Rashawn, your point? Your sister already said that Reggie could stay with her. He wants to play football. He stands a good chance of making the Ducks. He deserves this chance. Stop being so selfish!"

"Selfish!" Rashawn was screaming now. "I know you did not just call me that!"

"Yes, selfish. Lately it's been all about you. Your career. Your retreats! You! What about Rainey, Reggie, me . . . hell, even Junior is a part of this. You haven't even given him the time of day in weeks! He's a person too!"

"Look don't start bringing in outside people. Next you'll be saying I owe Juanita something. And what was that tender lovey dovey cozy shit I walked in on tonight? What's up with that? I don't owe her or her son anything!"

"He's my son too!"

"Oh, you don't know that!" Rashawn spat before catching the hateful words. Chance was slapped into silence harder than if she had used her hand. He threw back the covers and climbed out of the bed. Sliding into his shorts he headed into the bathroom without a further word.

Rashawn held her head as it grew heavy with regret and thoughts of how she would apologize. Lament left her mouth in the sound of a painful groan as she pulled her gown back over her head and shrugged into her robe. Only Soy Dream would fix this now—and maybe some cookies. She left the bedroom and headed for the kitchen.

Pulling back from the freezer, Rashawn felt the presence of someone. She slammed the door of the freezer, thinking, hoping, it was Chance so she could apologize, but no, it was worse . . . it was Junior. "Junior," she yelped in her surprise. Guilt had to have shown on her face because he cocked his head to the side, although he didn't remove the ear buds that seemed permanently attached to his head.

"Sorry, I was hungry. Is it okay for me to eat?" he asked. Rashawn nodded, still feeling shame at what she had said in the room. Watching him grin broadly—his crooked smile reminding her of her own son—softened her heart. She had a tender spot for Junior when the truth came out of her heart, making its way up to her brain. He had no way of accounting for his parents. It wasn't his fault he was here, and in reality he wasn't a bad kid. Junior adored Reggie and got along well with Rainey. He wasn't spoiled like many kids who were only children. Junior was friendly and funny and eager to please. He loved his tech toys and was actually more helpful around the house than Reggie, for the most part. "I missed getting a chance to eat this the other night. I mean, my dad's stew is great, but this roast is jammin', Shawnie," he said, using the pet name his father had given her. She didn't mind, and watching him prepare his sandwich, she cared even less who his father really was. Junior was soft and gentle like Chance, and, yes, she was fond of him. "Your ice cream is melting," he said, pointing at her small pint of dairy-free dessert.

"Oh yeah," she said, scooping out a big spoonful and filling her mouth. Junior began enjoying his food, licking his fingers after each hearty bite. "I wish I was going to look at a college in Oregon."

"Oh, Reggie told you about that?"

"Well, no, not really. Actually, I overheard him talking to his friend on the phone. I guess they're planning to really have some fun up there at the dorm and—"

"Oh really? He said he's planning to stay at the dorm?"

"Well, no, but he was gonna party at the dorms . . . or something like that. He's got this Internet buddy and well, he's in a frat and so Reggie said he wanted to check out the fraternities and stuff, see the college action—hell, why not? I mean, heck," Junior corrected.

Juanita had a filthy mouth, so Rashawn could only expect that Junior would pick up the habit. It was better than smoking or drinking for sure, so she didn't overreact; besides, he usually corrected himself. Heaven only knew what Reggie felt he could say now that he was smelling his own musk.

Rashawn nodded her understanding and sucked her teeth in growing irritation at Reggie's secret plan. This was not what she had in mind for Reggie's college plans— partying every night in a frat house. No. Way. "Fraternity?"

"Yeah, I mean if he's gonna play for the Ducks . . ."

"So he's already planning to . . ." Rashawn bit her lip and shook her head in irritation. The realization that Reggie had no plans on attending Moorman hit her hard. Junior must have noticed, as he suddenly stopped speaking. Maybe it was the way she sat there holding her spoon poised on the table while staring at him intensely, or perhaps it was the roast he'd filled his mouth with that had stopped his words, who knew, but right at that time Reggie appeared in the doorway of the kitchen, so neither of them was going to say another word.

"Mom," he yelped, causing Junior to jump as if startled.

"Hey there, Reg," Junior chuckled, choking slightly on the bite of meat. "I, uh, I was just getting ready to bring you some grub. Your mom was here talking to me and—"

"I see. And you were talking to her about . . . ?"

"Nothing," Junior lied, gathering up a couple more slices of bread and a slice or two more of the meat and rushing past him on his way out of the kitchen.

Reggie turned to follow him, but Rashawn stopped him dead in his tracks with just her voice. "Reggie, let's talk, son," she said.

"Maaaa, noooo," he groaned, throwing his head back before spinning on his heels to face her.

"Yeah, let's. So, tell me your plans . . . since you do indeed have 'plans,' " she said, bracketing the word "plans" with her index and middle fingers curling down in quotation marks in the air.

"Mom, I told you. I told you what I wanted to do."

"You told me no such thing. You said—"

"I want to go to U of O. I do. I want all the stuff that Junior was blabbing about in here. I want the fraternity. I want the Ducks, Mom. You just don't understand. I have star potential—Coach tells me every day and the scout . . . the scout, Mr. Smith, he called me personally! Mom, he called me personally to invite me."

"I understand that you want to go to college away so you can waste my time and money but Oregon? This is more than just a summer camp we're talking."

"I know this, Mom. It's four years and I'm ready. I'm gonna be eighteen soon and—"

"No, you just turned seventeen. I know how old you are. I don't think you do and I sure don't think you're ready for this."

"Mom, I do . . . and I am. I've been talking to the scout every day since he first called me—well, until you took my phone," Reggie added slyly. "Look, can we talk in the morning?"

"No, we can't. Because according to your brother you're planning to take this trip sooner than later. I'm leaving tomorrow, so we need to . . ."

Reggie leaned back and glared at her. His face twisted slightly. "My brother? I don't have a brother. Junior? He's not my brother. He's a pain my ass. He's—"

Rashawn rolled her eyes. "Look, it's just semantics; Junior is just as much your brother as Rainey is your sister."

"No, he's not, Mom. You've said it yourself. He's not my brother. He's Juanita's son. He just an inconvenience we are forced to accept."

"I never said that," Rashawn whispered, feeling shame growing from deep within. Had her thoughts come out? In the heat of her anger had she spoken some deeply buried ugliness? Had he eavesdropped during a wild, crazy, regrettable argument with Chance—had Junior overheard? When had she said that about Junior? "I've never said that."

"You've said it so many times . . . maybe not those exact words but you've implied it. I hear you and Chance fighting about it all the freakin' time!"

This was awful. What kind of mother had she become? What kind of woman allowed such vile thoughts to be heard from behind closed doors? "God . . ." Rashawn rubbed her forehead. "When did you hear me and Chance fighting?"

"I hear you and Chance fighting a lot. All the time lately. And you fight about everything and I'm sick of it. I'm sick of everything. I'm sick of being here. Junior is sick of it too. And who can blame him. Nobody wants to be where they are not wanted."

"Junior thinks I don't want him around?"

"He's not blind. Nobody is. You are always saying whatever you want—whenever you want—about him. Everybody is tired of your arguing and saying whatever rude thing you want to say. You say Juanita is bad. You take the cake. Big Chance is tired of your attitude too!"

"Oh really!" Now Rashawn would add hurt to her shame, the combination producing anger.

"Yeah, really," Reggie taunted, stretching his neck out far enough to receive a slap, if Rashawn gave into the feelings that were welling up in her right now. But she would not give him any more fuel for his fire tonight.

Instead she spoke calmly, coolly. "So you think by hurting my feelings you're gonna get your way?"

Reggie's expression changed suddenly. It was as if he didn't realize he was hurting her with his words . . . or better yet, that she would acknowledge that he was hurting her. "No, I—"

"Sure you do. But you know what, Mr. I'm So Sick of Shit? Check this out. You can go to Oregon."

"I can?"

"Oh yeah." Rashawn's lips tightened between her words and her neck began to jerk from side to side. "Yeah, and you can go with your brother, your sister, and y'alls daddy and Juanita for all I care and you all can just be sick of me together! You can stay in Oregon for the rest of your life!"

Rashawn threw the spoon in the sink and jerked open the freezer door, tossing the Soy Dream inside. She slammed the door shut and then without saying anything more, she headed toward Rainey's room. Right now she was sick of just about everybody too.

Chapter 20

Juanita was frustrated. She'd had absolutely no fun at the mall spa. Her favorite masseuse was out. Oh, how she needed the release. The tension was killing her.

So she went shopping, hoping to find a pair of orgasm-causing shoes . . . nothing. She hated using emotional substitutes—there was nothing better than the real thing. Even a good fantasy was better sometimes. The only saving grace had been her chance meeting with Ovan Dominguez. She'd thought about him all day. He was going to play the challenge game, she could tell. But then again, it wasn't as if she wasn't a professional at working with hard-to-get men. Chance had trained her well. So well that here she was now, standing in the middle of her kitchen in the middle of the night thinking about the mystery cop and what would be her next move to get him.

He'd gotten back in his car after the accident and drove off. He'd not even gone where he was headed. So she knew she had affected him—how much, she didn't know. She had his number, but it didn't look like a personal phone number. And, probably wasn't. "It'll probably ring at his desk," she said aloud, looking at the number again. She fought calling it all day but could no longer resist. She'd have to call. She knew she had affected him. Yes, she was refusing to admit how much he'd affected her. She dialed the number on the card. Yes, it was late, but what the hell, right? Suddenly her heart nearly stopped. It was a dead number, ringing only to a voice that told her the number was invalid.

"Ugh, Nita, you're losing it! Come on, nah!" she groaned, again feeling miserable, and pulling what was left of her pomegranate Soy Dream from the freezer. She took a big spoon from the silverware drawer. *This stuff isn't bad*, she thought, looking at the non-dairy dessert. She'd gotten the idea from Rashawn, after having snooped in Rashawn's freezer one of the times she was over at their house. Rashawn was looking dang good these days, and if Juanita wasn't careful, soon Rashawn—*with her biggo Amazon self*—would be looking better than her. So, lately, Juanita had been trying some healthier food choices—*yuck*—and a bit more exercising—*ugh*. Of course, now, that belly dancing wasn't so bad. It was all working; she'd dropped about five or so pounds this month and was looking better than ever. It used to be so much easier when all she had to do was call Chance over. He was always good about at least a three- or four-pound weight loss session between the sheets.

"Ovan Dominguez—hmm," she said aloud, licking the spoon slowly while staring at the card. "You lied to me . . . Why?" Suddenly, she noticed a moving shadow outside the back door. There was no wind cutting through the large tree in the backyard. She gawked harder to make sure she saw what she thought she saw. The shadow moved back from the window. It was indeed a moving shadow—a person. Someone was in her backyard. She screamed loudly before dashing out of the kitchen and up the stairs to her bedroom, locking herself in with the cordless.

"Nine-one-one," the dispatcher answered.

Chapter 21

Roman's curiosity had gotten the best of him. He wanted to see Juanita Duncan. It was like old home week, seeing all the people who had been a part of his dethronement. He chuckled at his thought of being a king. "Just a figure of speech," he mumbled under his breath, reprimanding his alter ego. His brother, Blain, wasn't the only one with a monster inside of him. He too carried another personality—only he could control his. Unlike Blain, who allowed his inner man—Doc—to cause him so many problems and eventually lead to his demise, Roman felt he had his inner man subdued. That had to be the case, or else he would have already taken care of Rashawn Ams. He would have already punished her for her betrayal.

Juanita had betrayed him too. She had promised to keep what they shared a secret. But as soon as it came out that he could possibly have something to do with the drugged girls at the school, she ran to the police with the videotaped therapy sessions. "Well, most of them." He snickered, remembering the couple of times their session had led to a sexual encounter. He licked his lips remembering the young, wild, vivacious woman—Juanita Duncan. She was wet and hot and eager for all he had to offer. At just the thought of her tight body, he fantasized that a return to her house could possibly be a good idea. Craven had awakened an inner urge he'd deadened after becoming so ill in London. But now, being home again, it seemed as though these hometown girls were "bringing the old pecker back to life." He chuckled at the thought.

Standing there in that nightgown, licking that spoon brought back such good memories, nonetheless, ones almost as satisfying as the love he used to make with Rashawn Ams while she lay willing and open . . . and asleep. That thought made him laugh out loud. So many nights he would have her, unconscious, yet responsive to his touch. Their son was young then, and often after making love to Rashawn, Roman would visit with the young Reggie in his room, teaching him about life and his destiny. "And then she took all that away from me!" Roman said, souring on the thought of both women now. After Juanita's bloodcurdling scream he quickly left his plans—

voyeuristically plotted and formed. He drove on to his hotel, forgetting about a return visit to Juanita's place. "I'm not in the mood to fight," he admitted. He thought about using a tranquilizer to subdue her; it wasn't as if he didn't have a nice supply of sedatives with him. "No, I've got bigger fish to fry." Just then, his cell phone rang. It was Hap. He sounded out of breath.

"What's wrong with you?" Roman asked.

"The police . . ."

"What about them?" Roman became alert now but didn't let it show in his voice. Had Ovan won the police over? Had he finally found someone to believe him? Impossible—Ovan was not a believable type—he was a clown. A buffoon. And after the bungling fool he'd made of Ovan in Europe, Roman was surprised Ovan was still on the case—or had a job.

"There was an intruder at Craven's house. I had to . . . I had to knock him out and call the police."

"Okay."

"He was asking questions about you."

"Me?" Roman hissed.

"He had an accent . . ."

"Was he short and very fair . . . like a white man," Roman asked, sighing heavily in his irritation.

"Yeah."

"His name is Ovan Dominguez. He's a pain in my ass. Please kill him next time you see him."

"What?"

Roman hung up the phone. He was furious now. What a major distraction. Ovan was getting too close to what he had nothing to do with. Roman was going to have to dispose of Ovan before he did any more damage or caused any delays to his plan. Surely Ovan was telling the police right then about the great Allen Roman returning from the dead. "As if they would believe him . . . but still, it's not what I planned. I don't want the authorities thinking about me. I don't want them even hearing my name." Roman slapped his steering wheel in growing frustration. "Why was Ovan even at Craven's house, unless . . ." Roman slammed his hands on the steering wheel again. "God, I hate women. They will betray you in a heartbeat!"

Chapter 22

Maravel heard the knocking on her front door and glanced at the clock on the nightstand. It was 3:00 A.M. "Got to be Ovan," she huffed. "Everybody else knows how to tell time," she fussed, slipping into her house shoes and quickly throwing on her robe. When she reached the door there stood a tall black man with a shorter white one. "May I help you?" she asked. The tall black man smiled warmly.

"Dude better be glad you have an accent," he said. "Do you know an Ovan—"

"Dominguez," Maravel said at the same time as he. "Yes, he's my . . . First of all, who are you?"

"Jim Beem," Lawrence introduced. "And I'm Lawrence Miller, homicide. We got a call from the SFPD that your 'partner' or whatever he is was in jail after being found in Dr. Michaels's home without a warrant . . . and without a badge and without—"

"I get where you're going, Officer." Maravel rubbed her head.

"Anyway, Dr. Washburn—Dr. Michaels's former boyfriend—came home—since he lives there—and anyway . . . knocked him out cold," Jim added.

"He knocked Ovan out? Well, that seems impossible. But okay, if you say so. But yes, I'm his partner. So where is he?"

"In the car, ma'am," Lawrence said, turning and pointing. Maravel looked around the large man to see Ovan looking sheepish—well, maybe a little goatish—in the backseat of the unmarked car. She had to chuckle.

"Ah, I see. Well, what were you going to with him had I not known him?" she asked as they talked and walked down the walkway.

"Dump in him the bay," Jim teased. Maravel laughed again, harder this time as she fully understood their feelings about her often pesky partner.

"Glad you all are in such good humor," Ovan huffed, pouting. "Here I am drugged with who the hell knows what, and you're all laughing. I need to be admitted to the hospital. I want to know what that guy put in my arm!"

Unlocking the cuffs, Jim just shook his head. "Look, just admit you got clocked and call it a night," he told him.

"That's what happens when a boyfriend finds you in his dead girlfriend's home," Lawrence added.

"Look, that guy is no more her boyfriend I am . . . was. He was over there looking for something, and when he found it he stuck me in the arm with a knockout drug."

"Come on, guy, maybe you can play your James Bond stuff back home, but over here people shoot people with guns and burglars don't burgle their own pads," Lawrence fussed, still not wanting to believe that Ovan had been stabbed with a syringe. He wanted to believe that Ovan had just been knocked out by Washburn's fist. Lawrence didn't want to believe that Jim was interested enough in this guy to come in from vacation a day early just to see what was what and get in on the possible action. But when Lawrence had told him about the chief coming out of her office cheesing like a virgin on the morning after her wedding, Jim had rushed back.

"That's not his house! Listen to me, that Dr. Washburn is an in interloper. He's no more a doctor than I am! He's up to something big—something that involves Allen Roman."

"Oh, yeah . . . the dead guy," Jim snickered.

Ovan swagged his head back and forth in sarcasm. "Yeah, the not-so-dead guy." Ovan's words took on an irritated tone. "Anyway, Craven was trying to tell me something about what they were up to. She, Hap Washburn, and Allen Roman . . . it was big. So big that Washburn or Roman—haven't figured out which yet—killed her."

"Killed her. Come on, guy, she died of a heart attack!" Jim all but shouted. "What are you now, forensics?"

"No, but Maravel here is," Ovan said. "Before I borrowed Her Majesty's Coroner's office for the Southern District of Greater London—boring bit a business there—she was wasting her talents for forensics on old people who died from too much pudding. No mystery there, eh, love?" Ovan said, grinning broadly at Maravel, who again blushed. "Now she works with me." Both police officers turned to look at Maravel, who shyly wiggled her fingers at them in a coquettish wave. "Have any of your people done any blood work on her? Checked for drugs? If he stabbed me—which he did," Ovan snapped at Lawrence, "he might have stabbed her with the same thing. I could be dying right now."

"Or he could have stabbed her with something a bit more deadly," Maravel added, helping him from the car. "Because, um, she'd a bit deader than you," Maravel teased.

"Come to think about it, the autopsy report didn't show the normal indications for a heart attack. No pre-existing heart condition . . . nothing," Lawrence said almost under his breath, as if in deep thought.

"What were you doing in the autopsy report? Don't tell me this guy has you curious?" Jim bashed playfully. "Or maybe it's just your dreams of being a PI again, huh? Maybe you should stick with real police work."

Lawrence's eyes widened and his mouth dropped open. "You nincompoop, this is police work! And if you weren't curious you'da stayed on vacation."

"Look, bubs, can we all go inside? I'm all but naked," Maravel admitted. Jim and Ovan gave her a once-over glance.

Lawrence rolled his eyes in disgust at the two men. "Can't you see she's freezing?"

"Sure can," Jim teased, pointing at her hardened nipple protruding through her flannel gown. She quickly folded her arms over her chest and ran back into her apartment.

Chapter 23

"So she unloaded a .45 into the guy and he survived?" Jim asked.

"No, he didn't, but he was the wrong guy to be dead. The guy Rashawn Ams killed is not who we're talking about," Ovan explained, showing his frustration at the lack of the detective's understanding of the case.

"I thought you said she killed her rapist?"

"No, the man she thought had raped her, but he wasn't. He was the wrong man—however, he was closely connected to the rapist," Maravel explained.

"But closely connected to a rapist doesn't warrant taking a rapist's bullets. I mean, that's taking the buddy system a bit far, don't cha think?" Jim asked.

"You're not listening. Allen Roman was the man who did indeed attack Rashawn Ams—but he set up the man who Rashawn ended up killing, basically framed him, by leading Rashawn to believe that Blain Tollome was her rapist and father of her child."

"How'd he do that? If he was the one who attacked her and got her pregnant, then the kid would look like him . . . not the other guy."

"Not if they were related." Ovan groaned as if tired of the entire discussion.

"What?" Jim asked.

"Roman and Doc," Ovan said the name as if it tasted bad in his mouth, "Blain Tollome–Doc . . . were brothers. Half brothers."

"No shit! Wow, man, I would have loved to be on that case!"

"No, you wouldn't have," Ovan said, digging himself out of Maravel's plush chair and heading into her kitchen.

Lawrence noticed his foul mood and whispered to Maravel, "Why is he so . . . ?"

"Because Allen Roman got away," Maravel whispered, tightening her robe around her.

"So? That happens sometimes," Jim admitted. "I mean, we do our best but sometimes the bad guy gets away."

"I understand that, but Ovan has a personal issue with this case," Maravel explained, keeping her voice low. "And with Allen Roman still alive it just adds insult to the injuries already there. Sure, Roman has been involved with many other things since then but it's that case that Ovan was particularly involved in."

"That case is closed. Dude was deported. I mean, sure, he's managed to—if indeed he did—he managed to get out of Jamaica, which was probably illegal, but that case, that Ams case, was closed."

"Not in Ovan's books. It's the root of his obsession with Allen Roman. I'm not completely sure why but he's in deep."

"So how is he allowed to work a case he's personally involved with?" Jim asked.

"Not sure . . . don't care. I'm just doing my job trying to find the Mad Doctor Roman who's running from authorities."

"So what is your actual job?"

"We're international bou—" Noticing Ovan coming back, Maravel placed her finger to her lips.

"Okay, blokes, so where do we go with this? Are you all going to help us catch this fiend or not?" Ovan asked, coming back into the living room with a cup of hot tea. Jim noticed that Maravel had clammed up.

"Well, bloke," Jim said, sounding a little sarcastic, "providing we believe you, and I'm not saying we do."

"We don't even know who you are. You could be some vigilante," Lawrence explained, not having gotten totally into Maravel and Jim's conversation.

"Nah, he's no vigilante, he dresses far too dapper. Oh, I know, he's Maxwell Smart and she's his Agent 99," Jim retorted with a chuckle. Lawrence fanned his hand as if no longer wanting to hear Jim's voice. Maravel blushed slightly. Ovan showed nothing but frustration and irritation.

"Roman is an international killer. He's been conducting illegal and deadly experiments around the globe. He's here to commit a murder . . . so either you're going to help us prevent it, or run around in circles afterward attempting to figure out why he did it. My people had been keeping tabs on Roman for years. Apparently a doctor in Jamaica—where your government deported him—claimed he died." Ovan snapped his fingers, remembering the name. "Dr. Ghifle—that was his name. To continue." He cleared his throat. "Then as if the good doctor changes his mind he calls our main office, in Johannesburg, to tell us that no, Roman is not dead but planning to visit Johannesburg, however, before anyone can get move a team in any direction, Ghifle dies unexpectedly of a heart attack. Immediately it is deduced that Roman is still alive and had cleared out of Jamaica."

"And this is deduced how?" Lawrence asked. Ovan cut him a glare for interrupting his diatribe, then continued his story.

"Within minutes, it seems, Roman suddenly appears in London. Enter yours truly." Oven pointed at himself. "He's posed as a physician named Seymour Lipton—later we find that Seymour is another physician he's murdered in South Africa—using the same lethal injection that I'm sure is going to be found in Craven Michaels—and would have been found in Ghifle had we been able to get anywhere near the body."

"The injection must be something untraceable—or the autopsy would have shown that, but causes all the symptoms of a heart attack," Maravel interjected.

"Again, why do you think Allen Roman did it?" Lawrence asked, sounding unconvinced. "So far it just doesn't sound like anything we'd take to the DA."

"We have our reasons as to why he killed Lipton and Ghifle, but they aren't solid. But we figure that they both had something Roman wanted that they wouldn't just 'give' to him . . . so he took it. And now Craven Michaels, another person directly connected with Allen Roman, has died of a heart attack," Ovan explained.

"Well, it sounds rather convincing, actually," Jim admitted.

Lawrence frowned. "Not to me."

"If I can just see the body and if I can prove that that she died due to the same type of injection, would you believe us that Allen Roman is possibly still alive and behind her murder?" Maravel asked Lawrence.

"Hmmm, maybe," Lawrence answered, noticing Jim smiling at Maravel. She smiled back, blushing slightly. There was an obvious connection.

"Wait, I have questions. What is the big connection with doctors? Why not professors or some other profession?" Lawrence asked.

"These doctors obviously were witnesses or unwilling partners in Roman's unethical medical experiences. We are not all together sure but we are certain at one time, he was using human cadavers—which is totally illegal on our side of the world."

"Well, here too!" Jim interjected.

"But, hey, what does that have to do with Rashawn Ams? You were saying yesterday he could be at her door any day now. Why?" Lawrence asked.

"The same reason he was there the first time—control," Ovan answered.

"We believe Allen Roman is planning another experiment. One that again will include human subjects . . . last time here, he used his brother. He basically murdered him for his own purposes. This time we're afraid it's even more personal. We believe Roman is planning to become one of his own subjects, and the other one he's planning to use is his son."

"Kill his own son!"

"Why not, he basically killed his own brother." Ovan frowned.

Chapter 24

"I know you all can't see it at first glance, but if you look really close . . ." Maravel explained, noticing where their eyes were going, ". . . here. Not on her breast, thank you," she said bluntly, drawing the men's attention to where her gloved finger indicted. Jim cleared his throat. ". . . you'll see a little prick mark."

"Aren't you looking the wrong area for a prick mark?" Jim asked, and then shrugged, noticing all eyes were intensely on him. "Sorrrry, couldn't resist."

"Ya know, the more hours I spend with you, the more I like your humor," Ovan admitted, grinning broadly.

"Both of you are sick. Now shut up. Go on Ms . . ." Lawrence began, requesting Maravel's last name. She smiled shyly, again showing her coy side, moving her blond bangs out of her face.

"It's Friggins," she answered, grinning at Lawrence.

"Maravel Friggins?" Jim asked, and then glanced over at Ovan for confirmation.

Ovan shrugged. "Go figure," he remarked rudely, adding to his and Jim's frivolity at such an inappropriate time.

Sam, the forensic doctor, leaned closer to the corpse following Maravel's direction. "Wow, I see it as clear as the nose your face now. I had no idea to even look there!"

"It was just a hunch," Maravel gushed shamelessly.

"Hunch my arse, I've been telling these jokers all day to look closer . . . but no, for my troubles and diligence, I get stabbed, shot at, and all the rest."

"Oh, you haven't been shot at," Maravel teased. "Yet."

"But now, one problem: there are no drugs in this woman's body," Sam insisted.

"There wouldn't be, she died of an embolism," Maravel explained. Sam's head went back with the revelation.

"Ahhhhh," he gasped.

"Ahhh what? What is an embolism?" Lawrence asked.

"Death by air bubble," Sam confirmed. "She's good." He grinned, nodding his approval at Maravel's skill. "I'll have to check it out, but it sounds like a 'done.' "

“Hmmph,” Ovan grunted, sounded as if too full of “hateraide” to even speak. He didn’t like her comment about him not having been shot at yet.

“But now, this under her nails . . . unnoticed by the naked eyes or anyone not looking for murder. I’m going to run a sample, under the scope and have more information for you later today,” Sam informed them.

“Great! I have a sneaking suspicion that you’ll find her killer under there,” Maravel said, sounding proud at her work.

“Well, cats, it’s like, tomorrow already. And so that makes me off . . . again,” Jim announced.

“Didn’t you just have a vacation?” Maravel asked.

“Sorta, kinda,” Jim hedged.

“You find murder, Sam,” Lawrence said, pointing at Sam and then at Maravel. “We’ll find you a murder. Until then, our hands are tied. You can do what you do, but ‘bloke,’ ” Lawrence said, now pointing at Ovan, “you cross our lines and we’re gonna do what we gotta do. Until something points to something other than natural, hands off this Hap guy, and this Allen Roman guy, who I still don’t even believe exists anymore.”

“Fine,” Ovan agreed, raising his hands in mock surrender. “Hap is not on my list of things to do . . . even though he tried to kill me.”

Everyone groaned and headed out of the lab. Reaching the elevator doors, Ovan patted his pockets. “Hang on, gang. I forgot something. Better yet, go on, I’ll catch up,” he told the group, who continued out and into the elevator. He then dashed back in the lab to speak with Sam privately.

Sam looked up from his work. “Did we forget something?” he asked.

“Yeah, umm Sam, how about you give me a call after you run those samples there—the ones from under her nails.” Ovan winked.

“I’d planned on it.”

“No, really, because I’m certain she raked off a bit of my buttocks, tiger that she was, and I’d hate to be thrown in with the batch of suspects.”

“Ohhh you were . . . Ohhh!” Sam gasped twisting up his face a bit. “You slept with her?”

“I was, um . . . collecting a little bit of information and, well, you know, things happen.” He pointed at the lifeless and less-than-beautiful corpse of Craven Michaels. He took a closer look. “But then, somehow, she used to look a little better than this. Ya know.”

Chapter 25

"Roman wants me to take care of his son . . . humph, what am I now, a glorified babysitter?" Hap shook his head in disgust. "I'll take care of that kid all right. One step outta line and . . ." Hap pulled a large syringe from the drawer and held it up threateningly. "Bam! Just like that guy last night. Who was that guy anyway? Why would Roman want him dead? He acts like everyone is disposable. Like Craven I guess. Bastard!" Hap thought about Craven and her sexual appetite. He could only imagine her going for a guy like Roman. Roman and the reputation he'd left behind. Anybody would do whatever to work with a genius like him, and apparently Craven had. Besides the fact that Hap knew he could never satisfy her. Roman's prowess had preceded him as well. It wasn't as if journals weren't written by him while he taught at Moorman and even more interesting articles once he started writing about DNA, heredity, and sex. Yes, yes, the things he'd had done in the name of science—the *Sex Experience* was the biggest, most well read journal out there. It wasn't as if it was reviewed in medical school—no way—but you could get a copy of the piece if you visited the not-so-hallowed halls of students of medicine. There, you could learn all about what Allen Roman had done in the name of science. Mind control, wild sex studies, it was rumored he'd even murdered and gotten away with it, in the name of science. Some believed he was just a power hungry control freak—a criminal who should have been executed by the law. While others believed he was a genius. They believed his work with human participants in studies on human nature was phenomenal. Hap's verdict was now out—now that he'd killed Craven. Why did he have to do that? Craven was a woman out for her own interest and pleasures but surely she didn't deserve to die.

Hap paced his office, thinking about what Allen Roman had told him and what he had implied about Craven and how he would frame him for the murder due to the missing money. Where was the money? It wasn't in her safe—he'd checked that right after that run-in with that crazy guy who had broken in.

Had he been betrayed by Craven? Was she really planning to edge him out of this project and keep the money all to herself? He trusted her and assumed they truly did have something going on—something that went deeper than the physical. Even she had said it—while he was choking her, "we're soulmates."

"It wasn't as if I caused her pain," he said aloud, thinking of what Roman had told him. Suddenly greed shoved regret out of his mind. "Where is that money?" He held up the key to her wall safe where he assumed the money was. "I need to get back over there and look harder."

Just then the receptionist paged him. "Dr. Washburn, there's two homicide detectives here to see you."

"Homicide?" he asked, hoping to hide the instant unnerving in his voice. "Certainly, let them in."

The door opened and homicide detectives Lawrence Miller and Jim Beem walked in and introduced themselves. Jim, a shorter white man with thick blond hair and surfer boy tan began to immediately roam around looking at pictures on his wall. He kept his hands in his pockets. That fact struck Hap as odd. "Hello?" Hap asked nervously.

"Hello, Dr. Washburn, this is just a routine visit. It's common when there's been a unclassified death. Now, you knew Ms. Craven Michaels, correct?"

Hap audibly sighed relief. What a fool. Here he was thinking that these police officers were here about murder. No one was even thinking about murder and besides no one would be able to trace Craven's death back to him, not unless they had reason to suspect him. Allen Roman? Maybe he put on one of his many faces and spilled the beans. Hap instantly grew nervous again. "Unclassifed?" he asked.

No. Roman wouldn't say anything. He himself was supposed to be dead. Why would he come from the dead just to betray and ruin everything they had planned? Why would he tell? He was down to only one surgeon now for this project. Roman wouldn't betray him, not now that Craven was dead. Roman had no choice but to work with him, right? But then . . . who was that guy last night? "Yes, of course. I'm the one who called and reported her murder—I mean, death," Hap stumbled.

"So you suspect murder?" Lawrence asked, refusing to disregard the slip of the tongue.

"No noooo, but you're homicide, I mean, you must suspect something."

"No, actually. This is routine. As we said, her death hasn't been classified. Hey, why don't you have any pictures of her up on your wall? She had plenty pictures up of the two of you," Jim stated, still not taking his hands out of his pockets. "After the break-in, we decided we needed to look around so we got a search warrant . . . it's procedure." Hap didn't believe that, not at all. They suspected something. Hap was getting really nervous now.

"I don't know, maybe it's a girl thing." Hap chuckled.

"Hmm, yeah," Jim said, nodding.

"Had she ever complained of chest pains since you two were in a relationship? Were you aware of any medical problems she was having?"

"No and none, but as you know heart disease is a number one secret killer of women these days," Hap said, sounding as if quoting directly from a manual.

"Uhhuh," Lawrencc mumbled. Hap was starting to sweat. He wanted these men to leave.

"Do you know Allen Roman?" Jim asked abruptly. Hap's stomach flipped.

"I've heard of him. Wasn't he a prominent scientist who apparently got too full of himself and started performing some illegal experiments and got himself deported and then died?"

"You seem know a lot about him," Jim noticed.

"Everybody in the scientific medical community knows about Allen Roman," Hap said, hoping his admiration didn't overshadow his pretense at ignorance. Just then the phone rang. It was Roman. Timing couldn't be worse. He let the phone ring twice.

"You gonna get that?" Lawrence asked.

"Umm . . . sure," Hap said, nervously answering his private line. "Hellllloooo," he called into the phone.

"You sound chipper," Roman said.

"Well, I have company," Hap said, looking at Jim and Lawrence and smiling. He held up his finger and then turned his back to them as if that would grant him privacy.

"Who?"

"The police."

"What do they want?"

"Nothing . . . they are just following up on dear Craven."

"Oh, dear Craven, the woman you killed."

"Well, I wouldn't say that too often," Hap said, glancing over his shoulder at Jim and Lawrence, who seemed again to be busying themselves with the décor.

"Whatever. Get rid of them and call me back. I have a problem I need you to see if you can take care of for me."

"I'm already working on one of your problems so I doubt it," he said, hanging up the phone. "Now, Detectives, is there anything else I can do for you?"

"What's this big project you and Craven were working on? She told Ovan Dominguez that she was working on this big secret project?"

"Ovan Dominguez?"

"You know him. You stabbed him in Craven's home last night."

"Stabbed?" Hap's chest was on fire.

"You know, with the knockout juice?" Jim said, pulling a syringe out of his pocket. "You always walk around with one of these in your pocket?" Ovan had described the needle and it didn't take much for Jim to find one that could possibly resemble it. "Is this what you and Roman use to—"

"I don't know what you're talking about. But that man was in my girlfriend's house trying to steal something. I don't what, but I'm sure it was a robbery. Craven has lots of nice things. I defended myself the best way I knew how."

"You always carry a tranquilizer with you?" Jim asked again.

"No. That was a coincidence. I had been at the lab. He scared me and I just used what I had. I thought he was going to kill me."

"He was unarmed and said he was asking you about Allen Roman."

"Well, he's a liar . . . and that's all I have time to talk to you." Hap rushed over to the door. "I think if you have more questions you can contact my attorney."

The men meandered out. Lawrence then noticed the one photo of Hap and Craven hanging by the door. "Nice cabin," he said, pointing at the two of them. "You two look real cozy."

"That was our love nest. It's just outside Klamath in Oregon. Beautiful place," Hap rambled for a moment.

"Looks lovely, and ya know, I saw this very same picture at Craven's house. It was right in front of an open, empty, safe."

"Empty?" Hap's heart dropped—had he forgotten to shut it? "Look, I've just suffered a great loss so you two need to know that your visit today was heartless," Hap said, shutting the door behind them. Quickly he snatched the picture of him and Craven off the wall. "Ovan Dominguez, huh . . ." Hap said, immediately imagining Craven sexing him too.

"You want this case to turn into murder just as bad as I do," Jim said, holding off his full grin while he and Lawrence climbed back into their sedan. Lawrence said nothing. He just frowned up his lip and furrowed his brow.

"What? So that little twerp can get his chase on?"

"You're just jealous. When you found out who he was, you got stone jealous!" Jim poked.

"No, I didn't. I'm a legitimate cop and I like that about me. I'm legit."

"As opposed to setting your own standards, running the close line between good and evil, catching the bad guys on your own terms," Jim went on, glorifying Ovan's profession.

He and Lawrence and spent the better part of the night hunting down Maravel Friggins. She seemed an easier mark than Ovan Dominguez. She popped up after only two clicks into the back door of the Interpol associate's sub-list. After a little technical dancing around, she came up as one of those working within the ten supporting coroner's offices for Her Majesty's Coroner in Sutton. She'd done a little moving around after leaving there, eventually hooking up with Ovan . . . and finding out any more about that guy stopped there. That bothered Lawrence a lot, but Jim seemed okay with Ovan at least associating with legitimate people. It at least gave him a sense of legitimacy.

"Well, okay, I'll say this much, I'll watch this Hap guy when I have a minute or two, but I'm not crossing any lines until we get some kind of something that he's doing something illegal," Lawrence conceded.

"Deal. But frankly, Hap walks, talks, and smells like a killer."

"Yeah. He does." Lawrence hated to admit it, but Hap acted as guilty as sin. Guilty of what, who knew. All they could do—legally—was wait.

Chapter 26

It was Friday morning; Rashawn was planning to board a plane that afternoon on her way to Phoenix, Arizona. Her thoughts about leaving had been marred by all the drama and bad feelings she was leaving behind in her house. She was stressed to the maximum, and so not leaving was not an option. She knew that. Rashawn wondered if Chance was even still in the house, or maybe he had dressed and left extraordinarily early just to avoid her. Maybe he had gone over to Juanita's to find comfort. "What am I thinking?" she asked herself, slapping her forehead. Rainey was snoring lightly. It was Friday, a day before Rainey would start a two week vacation. Rashawn wondered what she had planned. "Probably reading; what all good girls do," she whispered, smiling at her beautiful daughter. Rainey was nothing like she was at her age. Maybe it was because she had so many sisters—who knew—but there always just seemed to be so much devilment to get into. Sure, Rainey was only twelve, but at twelve Rashawn already had sisters sixteen and seventeen years old. There was already talk of boys in the house and so much more. It would be a long time before Rashawn would dabble into heavy badness, but still it was all around her. Rainey was innocent; sweet and pure. Of this Rashawn was sure. Reaching over, she stroked her daughter's thick hair and smoothed her brow. No, Rainey didn't have a bad bone in her body—unlike Reggie, who couldn't help but be difficult. *It's in his genes . . . it's got to be in his blood,* Rashawn thought, standing, stretching.

Chapter 27

Breakfast was tense and quiet. It had been a long night. There would be no talk about Reggie's college plans, as Rashawn didn't want to hear about it anymore, and by her overt silence she had made that fact known. She didn't care what they were deciding to do—frankly. What was the worst that could happen anyway with Reggie going to look over a college in Oregon with Chance, Rainey, and Junior? She stirred the batter for the hotcakes. She wasn't planning on going into the office today. She decided just to concentrate on leaving town. She figured she could simply e-mail Renee with what she needed done, from the airport.

Reggie and Junior came slowly from the room. They looked none too worn for the wear, considering the night before. Surely Reggie argued with Junior for opening his mouth about the college weekend. Reggie had been thoroughly upset at the thought of taking Junior along. *But ohhhhhh well!* Rashawn thought, but didn't say. "Good morning," she said instead.

"Good morning," Junior answered, but not Reggie. He just grunted and sat down at the table. Just then Rashawn thought about Juanita. She would have to call her today to make sure it was okay for Junior to go to Oregon. *I put her out of the equation when in fact—Junior is her* son. *And probably her son only!* Rashawn thought, again shaking her head at the negative pondering. Yes, this weekend was sorely needed. She needed to get her head back in a peaceful place. Maybe that was why she had been dreaming of Allen Roman. She had no peace of mind. All of the negativity was distancing her from her family and those who loved her. Even her sisters who still lived around her were noticing. Something was off and she hadn't felt this way in a long time. Again she thought about Allen Roman and how "off" he had made her life back when he was drugging her. Each day she got more and more clouded in her thinking, until soon her reasoning was completely gone and only a weak shell of a woman had taken over her life. *But not this time! I'll fight these people,* she mumbled under her breath, speaking about her family—her children, her husband, while noticing Chance slowly headed toward the kitchen. He was dressed for class. Sharp and handsome. But she was trying her best to shine him on. She wasn't going crazy again. Nobody was going to control her mind again. Reggie was trying and maybe Chance too. But they weren't going to get away with it.

"I hope everyone is hungry," Rashawn said, sitting the large platter of hotcakes on the table. Reggie and Junior looked up from where they sat. Their eyes were wide and innocent looking—too innocent looking.

"What are your plans today, Reggie?" she asked.

"I have no plans. I have no life!" he answered dramatically.

"Good," she answered, turning to Junior. "And you."

"Me? Oh, I'm just gonna enjoy this beautiful feast with my family," he answered in his normal quirky way, stabbing at the hotcakes and stacking them on his plate. Chance Sr. cleared his throat after watching him put six on his plate.

"And you, husband of mine?" Rashawn asked, hoping that Chance would open up—maybe even speak his heart over the scrambled eggs and fresh coffee. She needed to know what he was feeling. Had he truly stopped loving her, as Reggie had implied? *Stop it, Rashawn, Reggie didn't imply that. He implied that Chance thinks you're selfish and distant. And well, maybe you are,* she pondered while pouring his coffee.

"You don't have to pretend you're not mad at me," Chance whispered.

"I'm not mad at you," Rashawn lied.

"Sure you are," Chance said, still keeping his voice low.

"I told Reggie that you would take him, Rainey, and Junior to Oregon while I was gone."

"What? I'm not going to Oregon! How could you just make plans for me like that?" Chance blurted.

"Then I guess they aren't either."

"What?" Reggie yelped.

"You all can find something fun to do here, until I get back. Then we'll all fly up there together," Rashawn said calmly, hoisting up the big bowl of grits so that Rainey could serve herself.

"That's so flippin' wrong, Mom! This sucks rocks!" Reggie yelled out, slamming down his fork.

"Heyyy, you need watch yourself there, Reg," Chance intercepted.

"No, I don't have to watch anything. This is foul. My life isn't for you two to play paddle ball with."

"Look, don't get beside ya self son!" Chance spoke with firmness and a command for respect. But Reggie wasn't listening.

"I'm not your son!" Reggie said, jumping up from his seat.

"You're my son just as much as Junior is and Rainey is my daughter and what I say goes around here young man!" Chance stood now too.

"Chance, what are you doing?" Rashawn exclaimed. This was getting out of hand. What had she started?

"I've had it! One minute you want me to be a father, and when I'm doing it, you're asking me what I'm doing. Make up your damn mind! Am I Reggie's father or not?"

Rashawn shook her head vehemently. "Are you having some kind of episode?"

Junior quickly grabbed three biscuits and some bacon. "Better get some food to go," he told Rainey, sounding goofy.

"Put that down! You're not going anywhere!" Rashawn yelled.

"Get what you want, we're getting outta here," Chance said.

"No, you're not. Nobody is leaving this house!"

"So I guess I'm not a father to this son anymore either!"

The front door slammed in Reggie's wake. Chance called out to him but it was too late.

"Stop it! Stop it!" Rainey cried out, covering her face and giving way to loud wailing.

Rashawn immediately ran to Rainey's side. "See what you've done!"

"Junior, get your stuff, I'm taking you home. You're not going to school today." Chance's voice was monotone and filled with anger. His face was reddened. Rashawn had never seen him this upset before.

"Man, this is some serious drama jumping off this morning, huh?" Junior mumbled, chewing steadily on a slice of bacon, while Chance stood staring at him sternly.

Suddenly, as if a new reason to be angry crossed his mind, he snapped his finger at Rainey. "Get your stuff, you're getting dropped off . . . now!" he yelled. Rainey pulled away from her mother, grabbed her backpack, and quickly followed her brother and father out the door to the car.

"Chance," Rashawn called after rushing behind them to the door.

"Go on your vacation, Rashawn. We'll get all this fixed when you get back," he said without looking at her, climbing into the car without saying good-bye. Her heart weighed a ton. How did everything get broken? And how did it all become her fault?

Chapter 28

Just then there was a knock at the door. Thinking it might have been Chance, Juanita scurried to the door, fluffing her wild hair and hoisting up her "not as firm as they once were" breasts. Chance had sounded really upset when he called and so she wanted to be there to comfort him. Junior had told her that Rashawn was stressed out and leaving on vacation today, and so maybe there had been trouble between the lovely couple. "Coming," she sang. Just then, through the stained glass she saw him, handsome in his black turtleneck sweater and grey leather jacket with matching pants. Immediately the juices began to flow and Chance flew out of her mind as she swung open the door. His eyes covered her. "Mr. Dominguez?" She was trying to keep surprise in her voice, although she was hardly surprised. In her mind, she and Mr. Dominguez were truly destined to meet again.

Juanita could spot a freak a mile away and Mr. Dominguez had addict written all over him. When she was diagnosed as a sex addict ten years ago, it hurt . . . it really hurt. That is, until she found so many others like her in her therapy group. Relapses had never been so fun. Closets, backseats of cars, secret meetings . . . any and everywhere they could meet for sex, she and a couple of her group members would do it. She'd even learned a new thing or two during that time. When they were all pronounced rehabilitated they gave a party—an orgy of sorts, complete with togas and baked chicken that they ripped apart with their hands.

Chance was an addict too—although he refused to get therapy or admit it. When he and Rashawn first got married, it was a fight to the finish every time he came over to see the baby. Although he was probably wasn't nearly as sick as she had been back then, she could see the weakness in his eyes when he looked at her—even after all this time there was still a weakness, but suddenly, right at this moment, she only could pray he wasn't on his way over for a setback session.

"Ooooh come innnn," she purred, throwing the door open wide. Just her memories of her past sex life had set her libido in action. Ovan smelled good. Looked good . . . He was sex incarnate.

He strolled in, looking around at her décor—the African prints and animal print throw rugs. He then caught sight of her anklet on the visual downswing. It was a thin row of diamonds—a gift from Chance nearly twenty years earlier. Finding it in an old jewelry box a couple of years back, she'd never taken it off. It was a beautiful piece of jewelry and never failed to catch a glance or two—even from Chance.

"Yes, Ms. Duncan. I needed to talk to you about a former client of yours."

"Client? I thought you wanted to talk about my car."

"No. I'm not interested in your car . . . really. I'd like to discuss Allen Roman."

"Oh my God, Allen. Yes, he was a client of mine when I had my practice. But I haven't done therapy in years. Besides, he's dead."

"Yes, I know. I know a lot about you," he said, causing her stomach to jump in excitement. He was affecting her big time.

"You do? Well, who are you? I mean, you're a cop and all, but—"

"Well, not really a cop as you may think. But I am an enforcer of the law."

"So, you lied," Juanita said, holding onto her charm but with a little more caution.

"No, not really . . . but let me get to the point. I was able to watch several of the video sessions you and . . . May I sit down?" he asked, pointing at her comfy sofa that sat deeper into the living room. She was hoping he would choose that seat. She wanted to sit next to him, smell him . . . take in his aura. He was turning her on so badly she couldn't even think straight.

"Certainly," she coo'd, watching him as he moved through the living room like a runway model. He was dressed nicely, in European designs—down to his shoes, which matched the grey in his leather jacket and pants perfectly. He was a man after her heart—for sure. He was much more fashionable than Chance—but that was not the biggest test she had in store for him to pass. She nearly sat on him while sitting at the same time he did on the sofa. His eyes caught hers in a momentary stare down before he moved over allowing her room.

"Excuse me," she whispered, moving only inches away from him. His eyes diverted back to his notepad, which he had whipped out of his jacket only a moment earlier, before she all but jumped him.

He cleared his throat. "Yes, well, where was I?"

"You were wanting to know everything about me . . ."

"No, I believe I said I knew a lot about you . . . meaning, your former practice." He smiled coquettishly. "I know you had some quite unusual sessions with Dr. Roman."

"He was an unusual man. Where did you get the videos?"

"So did you sleep with many of your clients?" he asked abruptly, getting to the point.

Juanita shot up straight on the sofa in her shock and surprise with his bluntness. "What?" she asked, her voice going from sultry to rigid and high-pitched.

"Well, it's obvious you and Dr. Roman had a romp or two so I was just asking because I found that rather interesting that you continued to treat him for . . . for . . . what were you treating him for?"

Juanita jumped to her feet and began to nervously pace. "Look he was very . . . a very controlling man and as I told the police when I turned those movies over that . . ." Suddenly it dawned on her that she'd never turned over the video leading up to the sexually compromising sessions she'd had with Allen Roman. "Heyyy, how'd you know about that anyway?" she asked then.

"I wasn't sure until now, but I had a strong feeling. There were one or two films missing in the sequence of films. I guess the police weren't truly concerned about that, but I was and so I had to do some math, and read between the lines." He chuckled. "The two of you definitely had chemistry, so it wasn't hard to deduce that there had been something there you didn't want the authorities to know. But as I ask again, why did you continue to see him as a therapist once you started having sex with him?"

"Well, it's not like I knew he was crazy, like, bonkers crazy, and besides, I only saw him maybe once or twice after that . . . professionally speaking, that is."

"What about personally?"

"Please. No, he was too busy sexing Rashawn, my ex's wife."

"Quite an ironic twist don't you think?"

"What?" she asked curiously.

"Him ending up being the father of her son and—"

"What?" Juanita gasped. She never knew that Allen Roman was Reggie's son. Who was this man and how did he know so much about Rashawn's business? Sure it had come out that Roman had been drugging and raping her— that came out in the trial, but as to the paternity of Reggie? No. She had no idea until now.

Just then door opened and Junior walked in with Chance behind him. "Mom! Dad said I don't have to go to school today. Oh, 'cuse me, didn't know you had company."

Ovan stood and immediately marched over to Chance with his hand out. "Hello, Mr. Davis? I'm Ovan Dominguez."

Chance looked him over and then at Juanita. His lips were pursed and tight showing his irritation—probably because he believed he'd walked in on an afternoon tryst. "Mr. Dominguez is a cop," Juanita blurted, sensing what he must have been thinking. "I hit his car yesterday. I mean, he hit me . . ."

"Cop? Cool!" Junior blurted out. "Man I wanna be a cop or FBI or CIA—something like that. I wanna do that. Be a spy."

"Ohh, spyin' ain't for faint heart. Are you tough?" Ovan asked playfully. "You'll have to be tough. Like James Bond kinda tough."

"Yeah, I'm tough. I'll kick your ass right now," Junior blurted in playful response.

"Ohhhh, boy's got cajonies." Ovan laughed.

"Chance, what I tell you about letting him talk like that?" Juanita yelped, her face growing hot with embarrassment—first the arrival of an ex and then the vulgarity of a teenager . . . ugh. This was not a good impression to make on her new man.

"What?" Chance asked, sounding puzzled and looking distracted by the fact that Ovan was a cop. "What is it you need here?" he asked.

"He's here to see me—about my car. Okay, maybe not my car all the way, but coincidently he is asking about my old practice. A patient. I can't talk about it while you're here . . . HIPPA, client privilege, and all that."

"Trust me it's not all that serious," Ovan guaranteed.

Chance noticed Junior getting a little interested in the exchange and shooed him off. "Go to your room or something, boy."

"Nice looking kid," Ovan said, glancing over his shoulder in the direction the big boy galloped. "Looks a lot like . . ." Ovan turned back to Chance. "You?"

Chance said nothing but turned the attention back on Juanita, who cleared her throat this time. "Maybe we should put this off. I mean, Roman is dead and I'm sure whatever you want to know can wait—" she stammered.

"Allen Roman? What the hell you wanna know about Allen Roman?"

"Actually, I was hoping to speak with you too," Ovan stammered awkwardly. ". . . eventually. More so your wife."

"Well, I don't wanna talk about it. And she's *not* gonna talk about it. Who the hell are you anyway?"

"Well, I was mostly hoping to speak with your wife and—"

"I don't want you talking to my wife!"

Juanita stepped up to Chance. "Chance, did you know that Allen Roman is Reggie's father? Did you know that? Ovan just told me."

Ovan sighed heavily. "Perhaps later would be a good time . . ." He glanced at Juanita, nodding as if to say goodbye. "Mrs. Duncan."

"No . . . no, there will be no later. You tell me now what this is all about. And, Juanita, it was none of your business who Reggie's father was and therefore you shouldn't have been told!" Chance blurted as his emotions visibly grew. Juanita had never seen Chance this upset. "How the hell did you know that?" Chance asked Ovan.

"Oh, and it's Davis. I changed it back after Junior was born," Juanita corrected, noticing suddenly that Ovan could care less as he and Chance caught each other up in a death stare. The testosterone-filled fog between them was thick.

"Sorry, Ms. Davis," Ovan said without looking at her. "I guess I missed it in my notes."

"It's okay," she rambled on. She was hoping to ease the tension between Ovan and Chance.

"Allen Roman is not dead. Your wife needs to know that," Ovan said to Chance in a low rumbling tone.

"You're crazy," Chance growled back. "And you're not a cop. Who the hell are you and what do you want?"

"You're right, I'm not a cop, but I'm not crazy and I happen to know he's here in the city and very dangerous."

"How do you know this? And why should we believe you?" Chance asked, pointing at Juanita and then back at himself.

"I'm a special agent working for the British government. Me and small team were assigned to find Allen Roman."

"Say I believe you—which I don't—what the hell does Britain have to do with anything?" Chance was still rumbling as if deciding if he would erupt.

"Roman killed a man there, a doctor. As you know Roman is not a stranger to this type of dastardly deed. We believe his reasons for killing this man led to him killing again—here," Ovan explained.

"And this concerns me and my family how?"

"Anyone related to Roman needs to worry," Ovan said flatly, glancing over at Juanita who fought the urge to squirm.

"Okay, I'm bored in there," Junior said, entering the room right at that time. Juanita looked at his tall stature and dark skin tone, his loose lopping curls and coal black eyes. The men grew immediately quiet as everyone's attention now went to Junior. Juanita could see that Chance's brain was spinning.

"I've got to get outta here," he blurted, rushing out to the car. Ovan and Juanita stood silently in the doorway watching him rip out of the driveway, screeching his tires. Junior then stood, between the both of them.

"Are you my mom's new boyfriend or something because I've never seen my dad so pissed off before," he asked.

Ovan glanced sideways at Juanita who now felt the heat rising up on her cheeks. "Junior, please, it's not the time for jokes. Do you know where Reggie could be?"

"School, probably . . . maybe."

"Maybe?" Juanita asked.

"Well, when he left the house this morning, he was really hacked. Dad and his mom really screwed up his plans to go to Eugene this weekend . . . and, well, I guess mine too, for that matter. But then again, Reggie didn't want me to go with him anyhow."

"Why is Reggie going to Oregon this weekend?" Ovan asked.

"College tour. He got this call from a scout who wants him to come."

"Did your dad know about this?" Ovan asked Junior.

"Yeah, everybody did. Reggie was bragging about it big time. Rashawn said he could go but that he had to go with my dad and Rainey—she's me and Reggie's sister—and take me too. Reggie was hacked but said okay," Junior explained. "I guess if it's the only way he could go he decided, whatever. Then this morning it all hit the fan. Rashawn changed up on him like the weather."

"Do you think he would take off by himself?" Juanita asked.

"Maybe. He said dude had his ticket waiting at the station . . . Oops, I wasn't supposed to tell anybody that. Damn! I mean dang! I'm always doing that." Junior smacked his lips in irritation with himself.

"Dude?" both Ovan and Juanita asked.

"The scout. He was callin' Reg like every night. Reggie said he kinda was creepin' him out but . . ."

Juanita looked at Ovan. "What are you thinking?" she asked, noting his furrowed brow.

He looked up at her. "Nothing." It was a lie, Juanita could tell. "But I think I should get going."

"I'm going with you," Juanita said, sliding her feet into her flats that always sat by the door. She wore them to retrieve the paper when barefoot, like now.

"You don't even know where I'm headed," Ovan said, reaching for the door.

"You're British Intelligence," she glanced at Junior, "and 'that man' is still alive. I'm going with you," Juanita insisted, feeling the urgency coming from him and unable to fight the draw. Urgency was like a drug to her. Perhaps being the addict that she was, it was the pheromones Ovan was suddenly releasing that had her hooked on his vibe but she had to be with him right now. Something big was happening and she needed to be a part of it—besides the fact that it did involve Allen Roman being alive and quiet as kept, she too could have a real issue with that. "Stay here, Junior," Juanita insisted, pointing her finger at him while rushing out behind Ovan. "Lock the door and don't let anybody in!" she called over her shoulder. "If you hear from Reggie—call me."

Chapter 29

Rashawn hung up the phone after cancelling her flight. "What a pretty penny that cost," she groaned. But it didn't matter. She had decided to drive. It wasn't as if the roads would be frozen or deadly. A little rain but she was a good driver. "Besides, I really need to think and an hour just isn't enough. I can't think around Trina," she told her sister Rita after calling and telling her about the change of plans.

Rita was working on her husband, Terrell's, legal files. "Nobody can think around Trina," she said with a chuckle. "Well, drive safely," she added, sounding distracted. "So did you get your house in order?"

"What do you mean?"

"Well, the trip—or no trip. Chance and Juanita in your house together while you're gone . . . stuff like that."

"Chance and Juan—thanks for more things to think about—and no. I want to talk to Reggie one more time before I leave. That's another reason I canceled. Reggie was just furious this morning when he left. I've never seen him like that."

"I'm just sayin' you can't take things for granted. You need to get your house in order, Rashawn. Chance told me about the dreams."

"What?"

"You should have seen somebody. But then again, you should have told Reggie the truth years ago."

"What are you talking about and why are you talking about it now?"

"Well, you gonna be thinkin' for the next several hours, I figured I'd put a few more things on your 'thought' agenda."

Rashawn sat quietly on her end of the phone listening to Rita shuffling papers. She waited a moment before speaking. "Perhaps you are right, but Allen Roman is dead. Juanita and Chance are history. The trip? Reggie is not going. So all of that is non-relative. Ya know, I'm just gonna leave. I'm gonna let everythin' fall where it will and take care of it when I get back. Talking to Reggie now isn't gonna make him less mad or understand my side of things any better. I'll call you along the way." Rashawn hung up. Gathering her bag, she lugged it out to the car and threw it in the back seat. Suddenly a feeling of foreboding came over her. She nearly swooned. She took a deep breath. It had been years since she'd had a panic attack but this feeling was reminiscent of the big ones she used to have—back when the rape was new and the pain was fresh. She could barely breathe sometimes. Even when she left to Atlanta to have Reggie without her family knowing the truth—she would have huge anxiety attacks that left her paralyzed with fear. She was unable to read her mail for fear he was sending secret messages in her bills. She was crazy with the paranoia. Upon coming back—feeling healed after nearly two years—within the week it all started again. That's when Roman started drugging her and violating her again. Life was hell for so long, it was hard to believe that it was all fifteen years ago.

Digging around in her purse, Rashawn didn't notice Reggie's BlackBerry was missing. She only noticed her own and grabbed it tightly, willing Chance to call her— first. Again her pride was fighting her and she refused to call him. He was being mean and uncaring. His funky attitude had angered everyone in the house—well—it had angered her! Her anger momentarily beat out the feeling of panic but as she glanced around again, she was hit with the old feelings.

Once, her sister Ta'Rae, had told her that during the time of her husband's death, when she was the most frightened she would call on their mother and "although it was hard to believe" their dead mother came to her aid, calming her spirit. Rashawn had never tried it, but was hard pressed not to call on the name of Zenobia Ams right now. That's just how scared she was suddenly. "Stop it," she told herself, opening the car door, tossing in the phone and climbing behind the wheel.

"Still so deliberate you are," Roman said, watching her, noticing her hesitation to get in the car. She was still beautiful–to a fault. She had ruined his entire study–and maybe his life–a little bit. "Making me fall in love with you that way–you broke my heart, if that's possible," he snickered. Drugging her just made it easier to have her all to himself–compliant and calm. She had always been such a difficult woman–headstrong and independent. The drug broke her down completely. She became passive and easy to manage ". . . and I can tell that's all changed." He smirked, watching her pull out of the driveway. He'd watched her family leave earlier. It didn't look like too loving a scene. That husband of hers and her other two children. "Nice looking boy–musta taken after you like Reggie did. It's clear that girl got all Chance had to offer," Roman mumbled while slowly pulling off behind her. Rashawn had cost him so much and despite how much he loved her, he hated her with the same amount of passion. He had promised to pay her back one day for her betrayal he just didn't quite know how. Killing her hadn't been on his agenda at first, but as the years went by and his health went south, he knew it would come to this. There was no way she would just give him Reggie. "Not even to keep me alive—she's just that hateful!" he growled, again justifying his feelings and intentions. "So, yeah . . . You're gonna get paid back for all you have done and all I'm not going to give you a chance to do." She entered the freeway going south. He followed her.

Chapter 30

Chance pulled into the high school parking lot. He halfway thought maybe Reggie might have come to school on his own. He just needed to talk to him. No more consulting with Rashawn on everything. He needed to talk to Reggie about who his father was and why things were going the way they were right now. "Rashawn should have told him years ago. Roman can't hurt him—but not knowing that Roman was his father can. And for all I know, Roman could be alive. The guy is like evil walking. I need to find Reggie, and then find out who the hell that cat was. Hell, for all I know Juanita could be in danger too!"

Stepping out of his car, several young girls noticed him. "Hi, Mr. Davis."

"Hey there, have any of you seen Reggie today?"

"No, I was just going to ask you the same thing," the tallest, prettiest of the girls said, swinging her long braids over her shoulder.

"Oh, okay thanks," Chance answered, attempting to keep the panic out of his voice. He headed to the office to check with the attendance clerk.

"No, he's been marked absent in his first and second periods, Mr. Davis."

"Dammit," Chance mumbled under his breath. "What about his friend, Francisco."

"Mr. Davis, Francisco is here." She flipped through the logs. "Jackson is here, too."

She noticed his growing despair. "Problem?"

"Yes, and I need you to please call my cell number if he shows up today . . . please," Chance said, rushing out. Climbing behind the wheel, Chance rushed to several different BART stations, just in case he might see Reggie sitting here—trying to get somewhere. His mind was spinning, only momentarily landing on the information Ovan had given him. "Allen Roman alive?" he said aloud, instantly feeling the sharp pain in his side—the pain caused by Doc when kicked his ribs, breaking them. Chance blinked hard hoping to erase the pictures that now began to flash before him mercilessly. The concrete rushing toward his face, the broom he attempted to protect himself with, used as a weapon—a sword. He'd hit that big man—Doc—fifteen, twenty times, to no avail. He just kept coming! Roman had created a monster in Doc. He'd taken a simple man— maybe even a decent man, Blain Tollome and changed him into a drug addicted maniac everyone called Doc—a crazed killer that he could control through hypnotic suggestion. No one really knew why Doc became so obsessed with Rashawn. Only once or twice Rashawn talked about the night she killed Doc. The trial had been hell, and afterward she never really wanted to talk about it, but when she did, she told Chance that Doc had told her he loved her. Chance could only think that despite the control that Roman had on his mind, Doc's heart belonged to Rashawn and that he had stalked her in his efforts to protect her from Allen Roman. That was the part that tore Rashawn up worst of all.

True, Doc had done some terrible things around Moorman campus in his involvement with the deadly Get Ass drug, but as Rashawn had said after it was all over, "I killed an innocent man. He'd never done anything to me. Those bullets belonged to Allen Roman."

Horns honked as Chance sped through the red light. "God! Get your head back here, Chance!" he told himself, catching his heart as it nearly jumped from his body upon realizing he'd nearly been hit by an oncoming car.

Chance had a lot of baggage. He realized that now. He'd buried his pain in order to deal with

Rashawn's. He'd buried his shame in order to deal with Juanita's. But the time had come and now he needed to deal with what he felt—but perhaps this too would wait until later. Right now, he had to find Reggie. Stroking his cell phone, he contemplated calling Rashawn. Surely she was at the airport already. Flying wasn't her favorite thing to do and without a doubt, this would upset her even more. What could she do to fix any of it anyway? Okay, so Roman was alive, it didn't mean he was anywhere near them. He'd done so much to so many people, why would Reggie and Rashawn be the focus of his attention after all this time? "But then, Chance, he is crazy, you know this, right? And if he's here in this city as that guy insinuated—what else is he here for!" Glancing at his watch, Chance realized then he been roaming the streets for over an hour. He headed back to Juanita's. When he arrived no one was home.

Chapter 31

Rashawn had barely cleared the city when she noticed her gas gauge and pulled into the closest gas station to refuel. She hated pumping her own gas. Huffing just a bit, she stepped from the car and pulled out her credit card to slide it into the machine. Again she was hit with the feeling of foreboding, coupled with one of being watched. She glanced around. The black BMW moved slowly through the station. The windows were dark. If she was paranoid, she'd swear the car was circling her. She felt as if it was. Turning her head to and fro, she strained to see the driver but couldn't. She began to pump her gas, watching the car out of the corner of her eye as it pulled over to a parking stall—as if waiting for her to finish up.

Quickly, she climbed in behind the wheel and again thought about calling Chance. "You're being silly," she sighed. "This isn't about Chance. This is about Reggie. Start at the source, Rashawn." Dialing Reggie's phone instead, she suddenly realized that she had it in her purse— or so she thought. Digging around for it she realized it wasn't there. "Shoot, I musta left it in my pocket or in the kitchen . . . dangit." She rubbed her head. Looking around she had to make a decision. She was already pretty far from home but had many miles between there and Arizona. She called Trina only to get her machine.

"You've reached national best-selling author Trina Ams, but then again, if you have this number you must already know that, so what choo want?" the recording said, followed by laughter.

"Trina, this is Shawn, look, I'm having some issues with Reggie—go figure. So, I'm gonna try to deal with them first and then I'ma drive out. So don't expect me until morning. I won't be late for the thing—okay. So just wait for me," Rashawn said before hanging up.

She felt a little better just having said that out loud. Now she could head back to the house and deal with reality before heading off to the land of fiction.

Chapter 32

Chance pulled into the driveway of his home. He noticed immediately that Rashawn's car was missing. "She was supposed to call a cab," he mumbled under his breath. Climbing out of the car he headed over to Rita's house, walking. He knocked on the door. Rita answered. "Rashawn drove somewhere?" he asked.

"You didn't know? God, my sister is losing it." Rita shook her head. "Chance, she decided to drive to Arizona. Why in the hell does she do stuff like this?"

"What?"

"She said she just had too much on her mind to fly. She wanted some time," Rita made quotation marks around the word "time."

"Dammit!" Chance blurted, catching Rita off guard. "Allen Roman isn't dead," Chance blurted.

"What?"

"I know. I know. It's crazy . . . and I don't even know who to call for verification. I guess somebody in Jamaica. But first I have to find Reggie. I can't even relax until I find Reggie—then I'll deal with this."

Rita's eyes widened. "Reggie? Where is Reggie?"

Just then Ovan and Juanita pulled up in Ovan's sports car. Juanita's window rolled down. Her face was reddened and her eyes wide and crazed. "Is Junior with you?" she asked.

"What is wrong with her?" Rita asked regarding Juanita's expression. But Chance's tightened stomach was the only answer he could muster.

Juanita jumped out of the car and flew into Chance's arms. "Tell me he's with you. I went with Ovan to look at the Amtrak for Reggie and we came back and Junior was gone."

Ovan stepped out of the car. "There was indeed a ticket at the station in Reggie's name."

"What? I didn't get him a ticket!" Chance barked.

"My guess is Allen Roman did . . . the purchaser's name was a Dr. Lipton . . . and well, Dr. Lipton is dead," Ovan explained, sounding a bit casual, which Chance could only figure was his way of attempting to keep the situation under control. It wasn't working, though.

Rita clawed Chance's arm. "Junior? Junior was here a little while ago. What's going on Chance? Where is Reggie? Oh my God!"

"Junior was at the house?"

"Yes, a little bit ago. He went in and came out with a couple of backpacks. Hell, I didn't know I was supposed to stop him. If folks would tell me stuff and quit . . . !" Rita's voice trailed off as she went back into the house, only to return within a millisecond with her jacket on.

"Rita, stay home. Don't leave. Rashawn may call you. We need someone to stay and you know it can't be me." Chance moved from Juanita's embrace and headed toward Ovan. "Now what, Mr. FBI, or British Intelligence or whoever you are." Chance asked him. "You've got my attention. Now, if you don't want my foot up your ass you'll play it straight with me."

"I'm here looking for Allen Roman. My search for him brought me looking for your wife because her son Reggie could be in danger. That's as straight as I can give it to you at this moment."

"Well, that's straight enough. Let's go," Chance blurted heading for his house. Ovan stopped him by grabbing hold of his shoulder.

"Where is your wife?"

"She's on her way to Arizona—driving. She was supposed to be on a plane so if anybody is looking for her, they spent some wasted time at the airport. Do you think he might have been following her?"

"Not likely, but if he managed to figure out she was getting on a plane he figured out she didn't. Roman is a bit more direct I think and if he was following anybody it was Reggie. Junior spoke about a scout calling, do you know anything about this?"

"No, but Rashawn has Reggie's phone. I'll have her check the calls on there," Chance called Rashawn's phone.

Chapter 33

It was official, the BMW was following her. She was freaked out and not sure what to do next. Traffic was picking up on the I-5 as she headed north on her way back home. It was a weekend day around noon—soon she was at a crawl with no way off. Her cell phone rang. Thinking it was Chance she answered it without checking the number.

"Chance," she answered. Her voice was choked and nervous.

"Hello, Rashe. I missed you, my beloved. It's your real husband . . ."

"What? Who is this?"

"You don't know? My myyyy. It's Allen baby," he purred sensually. "The father of your first-born—"

"Allen?" she screeched, dropping the phone. Her head spun madly now, as she searched for the black BMW. Madly she began to weave through the slow traffic taking each and every opening she could find. Her phone rang again, but she refused to look at the number or dare to answer it.

Seeing what appeared to be a sudden break in traffic, she aimed for an exit at top speed without any regard for others on the road. Looking in the rear view mirror, the black BMW was right on her tail. Her phone rang again but her hands were frozen to the wheel. She looked again for the black car that now she was certain contained Allen Roman. Darting off the exit, the BMW rushed up behind her. The next glance in the rear view mirror horrified her. She could see his eyes. She could see his wicked smile before feeling the jerk of her neck caused by his car bumping the back of hers. Speeding up, she attempted to merge with the fast flow of oncoming traffic. Again she noticed Roman rushing up behind her. She pulled, blindly, into the lane without paying any mind to the blaring horn of the semi truck. Roman's evil grin was last thing she would remember before the sounds of metal crushing metal, the screeching and smell of burning brakes filling her senses.

Chapter 34

"She's still not answering?" Juanita asked, noticing Chance's tense expression. He'd called at least a dozen times, on their way to the Amtrak station again.

He hesitated and then shook his head. "No."

Juanita rubbed his back. "She'll answer. She doesn't stay mad long." Chance glared at her and moved over to where Ovan was standing. Alongside him stood his team of one, a small built woman named Maravel. Ovan had been making calls as well—one of them brought Maravel to the station, another was to Homicide. That call nearly sent Chance into a frenzy of redial segments to Rashawn's phone.

"We've got people at every local station now. So if they try to get on a train, we've got them . . . no worries," Ovan assured Chance, no doubt sensing his despair.

"Are they going to stop them?"

"No."

"No? What the hell . . ." Chance blurted. Ovan held out his hand.

"They are not going to stop them. They are going to follow them. It doesn't help to stop them if in fact Allen Roman is following them. We need to catch Roman—not two boys on their way to Oregon. Do you understand?"

Chance slammed his phone deep into his pocket. "No, no I don't. I need to talk to a real cop." Chance looked at Maravel. "No offense, lady, but I don't know you either. Do you have kids?"

"No," Maravel answered shyly.

"Then you have no idea how this is killing me. I can't find my wife. I can't find my kids! And I don't know who to trust!"

"I understand, Mr. Davis. The police are looking for your wife right now. Ovan and I are looking for your children—"

"No, no, you're no. You're looking for Allen Roman," Chance snapped before storming off. "We're not on the same page."

"He's got a pretty bad temper," Ovan noticed.

"Well, because of Allen Roman, Chance was almost killed," Juanita told him, watching where Chance was heading.

Ovan's head went back with the revelation. "Hmm . . . well then I guess that will do it. Allen Roman seems to have touched us all pretty personally."

Chapter 35

"Dr. Duncan, I need to ask you about Allen Roman. While you treated him did he ever mention his health," Maravel asked, finding they had time to finally talk. Ovan was on the phone with Homicide Detectives Miller and Beem. Chance was pacing the station like a caged cat.

"His health? You mean his mental health or . . .?" Juanita asked.

Maravel smiled. "No. We already have that answer."

Juanita nodded emphatically. "For sure, he's a fuckin' loony. God, if he hurts my son . . ."

"Why would you worry about your son?" Maravel asked. "Juanita, tell me the truth. If you just say it, it will be easier for all of us to get on with this."

Guilt ran across Juanita's face like a ticker tape. "I'm just meaning both boys. I'm sure Junior is with Reggie and if Roman is after Reggie, then," Juanita answered quickly before moving away from Maravel in search of Chance who had stormed out of the station as soon as a bus pulled up in front.

He was on the phone with Rita when she found him. “Has she called?” Juanita asked.

“No,” Chance answered sadly. He looked at his watch. “It’s been hours. She can’t possibly still be mad at me.”

“Maybe there’s no reception, Chance,” Juanita explained. “She should be pretty far south by now.” He looked at her. His eyes were sad and she felt her heart grow heavy. Unable to stand the look, she pulled him into a tight hug, before kissing his cheek softly.

“We’ve got Sprint . . .”

“Juanita, I think we need to talk,” Ovan blurted interrupting their moment. Juanita still holding Chance spoke without looking at Ovan.

“I’m busy, Ovan,” she answered.

“I’m sure you are but I need you to tell me who Junior’s real father is.” Ovan asked, pulling her arm from around Chance’s shoulder. “Since you won’t talk to Maravel you’ll have to talk to me. Who is Reggie’s father . . . and don’t tell me it’s Chance Davis,” he growled.

“Knock it off,” Chance bit, pulling Juanita from Ovan’s tight grip.

"Sorry, Chance, but we have to do what we have to do. Seems Juanita here has a couple of gaps to fill and I mean right now," Ovan began to explain. Chance now stood wide-eyed and confused.

"What did you do?" Juanita screamed.

Before he could answer Juanita struck out at Ovan, but his reflexes were quick and he caught her flying fist. "Stop it. This lie has apparently reached its end, Juanita!" Ovan said, holding her by both forearms.

She was shaking. "I didn't lie," she growled.

Chance just stood there watching. "Talk, Nita!"

"Chance," Juanita began, her face instantly drenched with tears. "Chance I didn't know . . . I don't know . . . I," she stammered.

"I had our friends at Homicide go to both your house and Juanita's. I tested whatever we could find from the boy's room for DNA. We had multiple matches."

Juanita howled like a wounded animal. "Why would you do that. You had no right to do that. They aren't broth-ers—they can't be brothers."

"Are you blind? Good grief, woman, are you and everyone else blind?" Ovan blurted rudely. At that, Juanita reached out for Chance who seemed in total shock. Suddenly his brow furrowed. He stepped back from her and again pushed the button on his cell phone calling Rashawn. It was as if he had shut her down the way someone shuts down and ignores a crazy stranger on the bus.

Chapter 36

Roman laughed again, watching Chance's number coming up on Rashawn's cell phone. The one he'd taken from the scene, along with her wallet. Sure they would eventually find Chance through the license plate on the car, but first things first. She would have to be taken to the ER as an unidentified woman. That would surely buy him a few hours. He was the first on the scene when she swerved to avoid hitting the large truck. Her car then hit the concrete on the opposite wall at top speed, flipping the car over on its top. Other cars came to a halt, slamming on breaks, causing rear-end bumps, crunches—gridlock. He quickly pulled over and acted as caring and concerned as he could as a few dogooders pulled up behind him. "I'm a doctor," he told them, hoping to be allowed more up close time—ordering everyone else to "get back!" Examining Rashawn for a pulse he could see she wasn't dead; that's when he noticed her small phone. He quickly grabbed it and tucked it in his pocket. Her purse had spilled its contents as well and so her wallet was another handy bit of identification he snagged. Soon the roar of the ambulance was heard, and the crowd pushed forward, cars slowed, and people rubbernecked, some too late or unconcerned pressed forward. During all the commotion, he slipped back into his car and left the scene, appearing to be just another rubbernecker.

Now Chance was calling. Allen was tempted to answer Chance's call, but that would spoil all the fun of the game.

Chapter 37

Juanita stood between the two men. Her heart was pounding. "How dare you," she finally growled in Ovan's direction. "How dare you involve yourself in my life like this. You had no right!"

"Junior is not my son?" Chance finally asked. He sounded oddly calm after calling Rashawn's sister Rita. He didn't want to alert the rest—especially Trina. Trina had a flair for the dramatic so he figured he'd leave that one alone. Rita was already near hysteria and had involved the oldest sister, Carlotta, who had called their other sister who was a doctor, Ta'Rae.

"No," Ovan answered.

"Yes," Juanita answered at the same time. "Shut your mouth!" she screamed at Ovan. "Why are you even here? Who are you?"

"Roman is an international fugitive. It's my job to bring him in."

"That didn't answer her question," Chance interjected.

"We're bounty hunters," Maravel said now, ending the inquiry.

"So this is about money?" Chance asked her.

Maravel's face reddened. "No . . . and yes. It's our job," she tried to explain.

"You're ruining my life for money!"

"I didn't ruin your life," Ovan snapped. "I'm trying to save your life . . . and frankly this isn't even about *your* life."

"So," Chance sighed. "How long have you been looking for him?"

"The best part of a year. We just got assigned. Roman has been at this for much, much longer," Maravel explained to Chance. The two of them were much calmer now. Ovan and Juanita were another story. Both of them were literally at each other's throats.

Just then Chance's phone rang. "What's going on?" he screamed into the receiver getting above Ovan and Juanita's volume, his voice hitting an unnatural pitch.

"What is it?" Juanita yelped jumping, slightly startled at his outburst.

"Is she okay? Is she alive? Thank God. Yes, I'll be there." He hung up his phone. "Rashawn has been in a car accident. That was her sister. Rashawn is in the ICU in Monterey. She's in a coma. I've got to go."

"Chance, this is horrible!" Juanita gasped.

"Chance," Ovan grabbed his other arm. "Go see about your wife. That's your duty, just remember, however, if we find the boys, and Roman is anywhere nearby, I'll have to proceed with mine."

Chance glanced at Juanita, who stood still flustered and looking embarrassed; it was clear she was not happy with what had just been discovered. Her second or two of caring about Rashawn passed quickly when Ovan brought up the boys again.

Chance nodded. "Do what you gotta do . . . just make finding our sons a priority—*duty*." He glanced again at Juanita whose expression softened slightly.

Chapter 38

Allen never thought of himself as a murderer, although, now that he reasoned on it, death seemed to always be where he was. From a young age, people always died around him. He thought about his childhood and the day he saw death up close and personal for the very first time. It was a hot day, hot enough for people to take off their shoes and walk about in bare feet. Allen remembered his mother would take off her shoes at any and all opportunities. She never had to have a reason, but today it was hot and so the excuse had been provided. She was a beautiful woman with a big smile and happy face. But this day she looked scared and worried, pacing back and forth in her bare feet while he and his little brother, Blain—the boy with the cursed white skin—busied themselves playing backgammon. Allen enjoyed puzzle games. Blain always lost so it made playing with him fun. Allen remembered now how he would sometimes set Blain up and still he would fall short. Maybe that was part of the reason Allen hated him so much—the other reason came shortly after the white man came.

Allen remembered his mother fussing with the man outside, he tried to listen but only remembered hearing bits and pieces of the conversation. Their father arrived after, not too much longer, he looked angry and he carried his rifle. That made Allen curious and so he ventured outside to see what was going on. Blain followed—of course. He was always tailing him—bugging him, begging to fit into his world.

Father was a tall man, but very lean, whereas their mother was tall and quite thick and broad. It was like watching giants at war when they began to tussle. The smaller white man in the middle tried to defend Allen's mother but to no avail, Father had pushed her to the ground. The white man then took hold of Allen's brother Blain and like a bolt of lightning it hit Allen—Blain looked like him. Their jaw lines and facial features were the same. But that realization came only a moment before Allen heard the blast from the gunshot and saw the blood pour out of the man's mouth. He fell at their feet. Blain screamed and ran toward his father. He was scared—terrified—but instead of comfort, he too found the angry end of that rifle that his father held.

Sitting in his car, Allen jumped slightly at the memory of sounds and pain-filled cries Blain released as he took those blows from the butt of that rifle—again and again until he lay bloody on the ground. When Blain survived, Allen remembered how disappointed he felt. He always felt that Blain's survival made his father's execution for murder a waste. Sure he'd killed Blain's father but that was his right. But if he had killed Blain then, yes, he maybe could have been considered a murderer. As it stood he was executed for trying to return the honor to his home . . . so what was the fault in that? Allen too committed such an act when he realized his wife had been unfaithful. There was no child to rid himself of so he killed his wife and sought to kill her lover. Finding out her lover was none other than Blain, again, raised the bar on the reasons he needed to die.

When Rashawn Ams killed Blain, Allen was relieved in a way, grateful not to have to do it himself. There was something about Blain that, although Allen hated him, seemed untouchable—charmed, jaded. It was almost as if by him not dying at Allen's father's hands, Blain had some kind of Karmastic aura around him. Allen always felt that if he killed him directly, someone would come and take his life in trade. So instead of taking his life, he took his mind instead.

Looking at his phone Allen thought about Reggie and how much alike they were. Allen was an only child of a deceitful, wicked, and beautiful woman and Reggie was too. Allen had a sibling that he despised, and it was clear that Reggie and Chance's children had no real connection. Allen would go so far as to say Reggie hated them—especially that brother. He'd all but said it in one of his conversations with him.

It had been nice talking to Reggie over the last week. It was reminiscent of when Reggie was younger. He was such a trusting, open boy. Allen was quickly taken with him. "And now look! We are destined to be even closer," he said, thinking about what he was planning. Picking up his phone he called Reggie's phone number.

"Hi Reggie, Mr. Smith here—are you all ready to leave tonight? Good. Don't forget to get to the station early to pick up your ticket. Wouldn't want you to miss your train."

Chapter 39

"Nobody is blaming you for anything, Nita," Ovan said, as they sat in the coffee shop at the pier. The train was not scheduled to leave until 8:00 P.M., so they had time but didn't dare leave the area just in case the boys showed up early. They had confirmed earlier that there had been a ticket purchased for Reggie and so it was now just to wait for them to come pick it up. It wasn't hard to assume they would be together. Junior usually hung pretty close to Reggie most of the time and Juanita could only figure that's where he was now. She'd called all of the friends she knew him to have, but it wasn't as if any of Junior's friends had seen him or expected him to show up.

"Junior would have wanted to help Reggie get to Oregon. That's the kinda kid he is . . . He loves Reggie. You'd think they were . . ." Juanita covered her face with her hand before sighing heavily.

Ovan reached over and took her hand from her face. "Why can't you say it? Why is it so horrible for you to face it? You had sex with the man—"

Juanita pulled her hand back from his touch. "He seduced me. He . . . he raped me," she growled.

"No, he didn't, Juanita." Ovan spoke sternly now—almost as if he knew her better than she knew herself. She looked at him. Her eyes were brimming with tears. Ovan was touching spots she'd not exposed in many years, wounds she didn't realize were not completely healed.

Reaching for her again, he touched her face. His hands were much softer than she expected. "Now again, where do Junior and his brother usually go together?"

"Chance's house. They have a lovely home . . . comfortable. And Rashawn cooks really good."

"I bet you cook good too," Ovan said, hoping to lighten her spirits. He had apologized for their earlier argument. He admitted to acting inappropriately:

"I often get out of line," he'd said, to which Maravel whole-heartedly agreed before she left to drive Chance to the hospital since he'd ridden there in Ovan's car.

"Do you know what you're doing?"

"I do. I've been doing this work for many years. I always get my man."

Juanita chuckled. "I used to always say that."

"I bet you did . . . and I bet you did," Ovan said, sounding flirtatious—at least Juanita wanted to hear that. She wanted to hear something that would make her feel the way she liked feeling—carefree and good. "Do you think Roman knows what you know . . . about Junior that is?" Ovan asked them.

"No. How could he?"

"True, even I was guessing, but that was only because I saw the boy up close. Allen hasn't had a reason to closely examine your boy . . . unlike Reggie who he already knew about."

"I feel bad for Reggie. Gosh I never would have even dreamed that he and Rashawn . . ." Juanita shook her head, before taking a sip of coffee. "I didn't realize he was the one who had raped her."

"Well it's not like I could picture the two of you 'willingly together' . . . and don't think I didn't try to fight that visual."

Juanita smiled. "Why? The thought of seeing me naked, even in your mind, disgust you?"

"Hell no," Ovan blurted, before catching himself. They both broke out laughing.

"I'm sorry. I get so preoccupied with sex sometimes . . . especially when I'm stressed," Juanita confessed for the first time. Ovan was so easy to talk to—it just came out.

Ovan's eyes widened with excitement. "Me too!" he exploded as if finally facing something in his own life.

"I mean, I did rehab and all that . . ."

"Oh, that's so unfortunate," he said, bowing his eyes slightly, looking boyish. "Did they reform you?"

"What do you think?"

"I think that if your son weren't off gallivanting at such an inconvenient time and his insane father weren't on the loose, we'd slip under this table and . . ." Ovan raised an eyebrow.

Juanita felt a familiar calm come over her, yet at the same time the sickening pull of resistance. She was fighting the urge to do something sexual with Ovan. His eyes were calling her again . . . begging her.

How wrong could it be?

Rashawn was near death. Reggie was in danger. Junior was missing. It was real wrong—her shoulder angel told her.

But this was all just too much to deal with . . . almost—the devil on the other shoulder convincingly whispered.

No one came to Fisherman's Wharf on a cold day like this—no one except diehard fishermen and those travelling by train—*and the train wasn't due for a minute.* Ovan locked the door to the men's room just as Juanita turned him around, slamming him against the wall. She was backsliding in a big way right now. She knew it, but she could fight it no longer. Six months of being good was out the window. Inappropriate sexual appetite is what is was but . . . *damn it all to bloody hell right now,* she thought as she ripped at Ovan's leather. Leather—another of her weaknesses. Just touching it was taking her further to the edge—fast. She sniffed at the jacket, filling her nose with the masculine scent that came from it—from him. She unhooked the large decorative buckle on his belt.

Zigggggg went the zipper.

He purred and moaned allowing her access to his manhood which was standing strong and ready. He handed her the condom that he pulled from his pocket. She couldn't help but chuckle. Yes, he too had an inappropriate sexual appetite. Sliding the condom on orally she teased his penis with her tongue and mouth. Before turning around and bending over, offering him the bird's eye view of her treasures. Pulling her thong over to the side, roughly he entered her without much delay. Deep and long were his strokes. As both of them seethed and panted he put his hose to work on the fire between her legs.

Juanita wanted to scream, but it was all moving too fast. All she could do was go with the feeling—the good good oooh so good feeling. He held her by her small waist while riding her back like a champion biker. Tighter and tighter she flexed her muscles until she felt his hands move from her waist and rest on her back before he began pushing slightly. "Whoa, baby . . . you're breaking it . . . dammit!" he gasped. Juanita felt the warm juices inside her.

"What happened . . . oh my gosh . . . did it break?" she asked, turning to him. He looked shocked and shaken a little.

"That's never happened to me. I'm . . ." Ovan was visibly shaken. "You're an animal."

Removing the broken condom from her body, Juanita wasn't sure how to take his comment. She felt—strange inside. Never had anyone disliked having sex with her. Never had anyone had a complaint. Ovan seemed just short of disgusted the way his face twisted up. Tears burned her eyes.

"I'm sorry. I . . ." Juanita began.

Ovan shook his head, lifting her off her feet and pulling her into his middle. She wrapped her legs around him as he pulled her onto his uncovered hardness. "You're a flippin' animal. Baby!

You're fantastic!" he growled again taking her for a ride on his rod.

This time he came with intent. Juanita too gave way to a wild orgasm that caused her to squeal with delight.

Chapter 40

Junior called all the numbers in Reggie's phone, looking for him until finally one of his friends confessed that Reggie was there with him. "I've been looking for you all damn day."

"What do you want?" Reggie asked getting on the line.

"Do you still want to go to Oregon?"

"Stupid-ass question."

"Okay, then you need to get to the Emeryville station at nine o'clock. You got about an hour or so."

"Dude called. He thought I was you . . . told you to make sure you got there early. I went to get your ticket but cops were there. They were undercover but I know spies when I see one."

"Spies?"

"Yeah, they're looking for you. This one agent has been snooping around. He was with my mother talking about you . . . I think. But anyway, yeah you're on the lam for sure."

"Junior, you're an idiot."

"I may be, but I know if you want to make it to Oregon, you better get to Emeryville instead of catching a train at the pier. Dude agreed and said he'd take care of changing the ticket."

Reggie sat on his end quietly as if not sure what to ask next. "Thanks," he finally said. "By the way how'd you get my phone?"

"I got it. That's all you need to know."

"Weirdo . . ." was all Junior heard Reggie say as he hung up.

Chapter 41

Ta'Rae smiled weakly, before addressing the group waiting in the family waiting area. "Okay so she's in a coma but her vitals are strong. That's all I really know for sure except that yes . . . she's gonna pull through."

"Thank God!" Carlotta sighed heavily.

Rita squeezed Chance's shoulders. He'd been quiet most of time after arriving. Rainey too had been biting her nails in worry over her mother—and her brothers. "Does Mom know about Reggie and Junior being gone?" Rainey asked quietly. Chance looked up from his hands and over at her.

"I can't tell your mother that and I won't. We're going to find them."

"So you think they are on their way to Shelby's?" Carlotta asked. Chance nodded.

"Then we can't tell her either. She needs to be there when they get there," Carlotta said, taking the lead as the eldest sister. "If we call

Shelby she'll be on the first plane here and, well, we need her to be there so she can get the boys when they arrive, right? She needs to get to them before . . ."

Carlotta held in the rest. "Plus why upset everyone until we know more."

"She's going to be fine," Ta'Rae answered decisively concerning Rashawn. "Don't call Shelby."

"Mr. Davis," the doctor called, noticing Chance waiting along with Rashawn's sisters and Rainey. Chance hugged Rainey tight as if gathering her love to deliver to Rashawn.

"Yes?"

"You're the husband?"

"Yes, please . . . my wife?" Chance asked. The doctor motioned for him to follow, moving him away from the group.

"Please just tell the man about his wife right here so we can know about our sister. Damn!" Carlotta blurted. She then pointed at Ta'Rae, "She's a doctor!" With that comment everyone could tell Carlotta was at her limit of patience. "She already told us about the coma–shit! Tell us what else we need to know."

"They don't care that I'm a doctor, Lotty. Let Chance go see about her. It's HIPPA," Ta'Rae tried to explain.

"Fuck a hippo. She's my sister!" Carlotta cried out.

"She's alive," the doctor said in a low voice.

"Is that the best you can tell me?" Chance asked, feeling his heart growing almost too large for his chest. "Ta'Rae said something about a coma."

"Yes, she had a pretty rough last few hours. She's pretty banged up. But she's come out of the coma in the last few moments, so."

"Can I see her?"

The doctor shook his head. "No. I don't think . . ."

"I'm sorry, did that sound like a question? What I meant to say was, I'm going in to see her," Chance reworded. The doctor glanced over his shoulder at the formidable woman—Carlotta—and apparently rethought the situation.

"For a moment. Her vitals are strong but she's far from stable."

"I have to see her."

"I understand."

The doctor led Chance into the ICU where he donned a mask and medical covering for his street clothing. He could see Rashawn in the distance laying on the bed still. He'd tried not to look before he had to.

Slowly he crept close to the bed, avoiding all the wires hooked into her. His eyes burned as he fought the tears, noticing the bandages covering her head and one of her eyes.

"Rashawn . . . sweetie . . . Shawnie," Chance called in the softest voice he could muster.

The one uncovered eye crept open slowly as if she sensed his closeness, or heard his whispered voice and she turned her head slightly. "Chance," she mouthed.

"Shh, baby, don't speak."

"I have to," she whispered. "Allen Ro . . ." she began to cough.

Chance's chest tightened. "He did this?"

"He . . ." Rashawn began. "Reggie—Reg—" Just then the monitor began to call out her internal distress. Chance was moved aside quickly as the doctors and nurses came to her aid.

"I'm sorry, Mr. Davis. Really I need to you to wait with your family," the doctor demanded, barely holding onto any bedside manner. Chance nodded.

Moving quickly into the hall, he ripped off the medical coverings as he passed Rashawn's sisters who inquired about their sister. He pulled out his cell phone. "Ovan!"

"Yes, Chance," Ovan answered sounding calm and collected. "Did you find them? We've seen nothing here."

"She saw Allen Roman. He did this to her. Somehow he's caused this accident."

"Then that explains why Hap Washburn was here at the station instead of Allen. He purchased a ticket to Oregon—via the Emeryville station."

"Why didn't you grab him?"

"For what? We have no reason to stop Hap Washburn . . . only follow him. The police have my hands tied on that."

"Following him! I'm not following that fool! If he knows where Roman is grab him and beat the shit outta him until he tells us what we need to know. I want Roman . . . and I want him bad."

"I agree, but as I've been trying to tell you, if we stop the boys or grab Hap, Roman won't show himself. I can promise you that.

"Then what do we do?"

"We get our asses on a plane as soon as you get to the airport. We're going to beat those bastards to their destination. We'll be there waiting for them."

"I'll be there as quickly as I can."

"Chance! Chance!" the sisters yelled as Chance burst from the hospital headed out to his car that had been driven to the hospital by one of the sisters.

Chapter 42

Reggie looked around the Emeryville station. He'd had a hefty walk from where he'd been dropped off. One of his friend's dads didn't work far from there, but far enough to make the walk less than convenient but, oh well; he was determined to make that train tonight. He'd had about thirty minutes before it would get there. That was long enough to pick up the ticket that Junior told him was waiting. He was sweaty and hot from the quick hustle but in his mind, he was thinking with all his wits. Darting into the restroom to freshen up, to wipe his face with a wet paper towel, he took a moment to exhale before heading out to the waiting area. Surveying the room to see if perhaps his folks weren't as clueless as he imagined they were–or if maybe Junior was right about the spies–he saw nothing suspicious so he jumped in the line where he would then pick up his ticket. Reaching the glass, he smiled at the black women behind the window who grinned back. She reminded him of Junior's mother, kinda sweet looking with a dimple in her cheek. Yeah, she reminded him of Juanita—short of the bright red dreads Juanita wore. "I have a round trip ticket to Eugene, Oregon waiting," he requested.

"I need your ID, son," she said.

"Okay," he said reaching for his wallet. "Damn!" His wallet was in his backpack and his backpack was home.

"Here," a familiar voice behind him said, while sliding his wallet onto the counter. Reggie turned only to face Junior. Junior wasn't smiling. He looked actually rather pissed off.

"Hey," Reggie greeted with a cheese grin, after showing the ID to the woman.

"Anyway . . ." Junior snapped as Reggie signed the ticket. "Ya tried to ditch me . . . ya motha." Junior said pushing Reggie hard. Reggie stumbled slightly, messing up his signature.

"I did not."

"You did. You have no plans on trying to take me or wait for me. You didn't once even look around for me. You just got here and came for your ticket. I shoulda let your ass go to the Ferry Building and get apprehended," Junior growled under his breath, moving up to the window after Reggie moved aside. "I need a ticket to Eugene too."

"Train is crowded young man. That's going to be one hundred seventeen dollars."

"Ouch," Reggie groaned, looking in his nearly empty wallet.

"I got it." Junior slid the crisp five twenties onto the counter. The woman handed him his ticket to sign, which he did before briskly moving from the window.

Reggie noticed his backpack and shrugged it onto his shoulder. "Junior, wait. Look," he began, hoping no one would notice them arguing. Junior was embarrassing him and he needed to get this settled quickly. "This is my trip, man. I'm going to college. This was important to me."

"Well, you said I could go. And now you need me to go. You don't even have any money."

Reggie smacked his full lips, unable to deny the facts. Clearly Junior had scoped his wallet out.

"I don't have my phone, either."

"I have your phone. It's in my bag. I found it in your mom's panty drawer."

"My mom's what? You lyin' . . ."

Junior laughed, holding up his hand to prevent getting a smack. "Just playin'. It was in the kitchen where she left it. I found it when I went back to get your stuff. I had to move fast 'cause folks were looking for you but I got it."

"Wow, you did that for me?"

"We're brothers man. I had to."

"We're not brothers," Reggie remarked coldly.

"Okay, so we're stepbrothers, whatever," Junior turned to continue out the door to wait for the train. Reggie pulled at this sleeve and held out his hand to shake. Junior looked at it.

"But we are friends . . . okay. I mean, you saved my ass tonight, I mean . . . I'm not even going to beat your ass for touching my mama's panties and shit."

Junior shook his hand before they knocked fists. "Actually, my mother saved your ass and she's gonna kick mine when she finds out how much money I've been embezzling over the last couple of days. I snagged about six hundred bucks."

"Ohhh shit!" Reggie laughed while covering his mouth.

"And I took all the food you guys had out of your kitchen, too," Junior confessed proudly, holding up his huge full overstuff backpack. About that time they heard the train being called. They headed on outside towards the boarding area.

"By the way, how did you get here?"

"I got friends," Junior said. "Even if you don't like me."

"Don't start," Reggie warned playfully.

The boys were not looking one way or another as tonight they were the only two young men on the planet. They were going on a road trip together. They had stolen money, plenty of food and were high on excitement. It was the closet they'd felt in a long time . . . maybe ever.

So excited they were they didn't notice the other passengers. They didn't notice friend or foe this night.

Chapter 43

"Okay so one of my agents spotted them at the Emeryville station and got on the train with them," Ovan said to Chance over the phone.

"Thank God. So they're safe from Roman. For now we can assume he's waiting at the end of the trip, right? They're safe for now, right?" Nita asked excitedly, overhearing the news. Ovan had been trying to keep her out of way but it wasn't working, she was all over everything–including him. He was hoping Maravel hadn't noticed her overt clinginess–or maybe it was he who was acting differently–who knew. But things had changed between him and Juanita Davis/Duncan and he wasn't happy about it. He was distracted now and antsy. He was fighting to keep his thoughts above the belt.

"So what is our next move," Juanita asked, after he hung up the phone.

He rolled his eyes, perhaps mostly to avoid the sparkle he'd caught in hers. She was an outstandingly beautiful woman and he was having a hard time keeping his hands off of her. Inappropriate as it was, he wanted nothing more than to touch her again. He could understand Roman, taking an opportunity to have her. He understood Chance claiming a boy that was no more his son than the man in the moon's to stay connected to her. This woman was clearly more than a simple shag. She had in just those few moments in a cold, public WC done more than shared a few stolen sexual moments from him. She'd touched his heart. She'd gone deep. She'd gotten into his blood. He'd gone flesh to flesh with her. He'd not done that in years . . . since his first love.

Perhaps he understood now what it meant to be "sprung," for he would do anything for Juanita if she were just to ask . . . and maybe she had. She wanted her son back, and he was now more determined than ever to get both boys back home safely.

"My plan, Ms. Duncan—"

"Davis," she corrected. Her eyes were still doe-like and filled with unearned innocence. He liked that about her. She was far from innocent. Yet, so adorable.

"My plan," he continued, ignoring the correction. "is that Chance and I fly up to Portland—the only place a bloody plane can land close enough to Eugene this time of year. Rent a car and drive back to Eugene—Nab Roman, who will probably be waiting when they get off the train."

"I'm going with you," Juanita said, glancing at Maravel who caught her statement but looked away as if not eavesdropping. "Is that your girlfriend?" Juanita then asked concerning her.

"Juanita, now is not the time," Ovan stated flatly, walking toward the car without looking at her.

"I'm just asking. I like to know who I'm working with," she continued, following closely.

"Really? You coulda fooled me earlier today," he smarted off.

"Ouch! That was rude," she snapped back, rushing to keep up with his quick steps.

He turned and stopped abruptly causing her to bump into him. "Woman! My job is dangerous. You can't go. I'm out to capture Allen Roman. He is my only interest here. The boys are my secondary concern—and your safety isn't even on my list," he lied, "because we shouldn't worry ourselves about it, because, you shouldn't be in way." He shrugged nonchalantly. "And right now, you're completely in the way."

"You're lying, and I'm going," she told him. Ovan threw up his hands and stomped off. Juanita went after him again. "I'm going!"

"Nita, come on, it's not safe."

"I don't care," Juanita pleaded.

"Look, love, you could get hurt and I . . . I can't have that," he said, wondering where those words were coming from.

"I don't care. I can't just stand by while you and Chance find my and Rashawn's sons. I know if she were here she'd be fighting us both to get on that plane and trust me, she not as friendly as I am."

Finally Ovan took her by the shoulders and bravely stared into her hypnotic pools of grey. "Nita. Roman is going to butcher Reggie. He's planning to kill him."

Juanita swooned slightly, her eyes fluttering instantly before she seemingly forced herself to regroup. "Why?" she asked. Her voice was weaker now.

"He's got no kidneys. He's going to butcher Reggie and take both of his. We need to stop him before he realizes that Junior is his son as well. He's insane, greedy and feels he's above the law."

"But if he takes both of Reggie's kidneys . . . he'll die?"

"Yes. He will. But guess what? He may not have to now . . . because guess what?"

"Oh my God, Junior is with Reggie."

"Exactly, and if I can figure out Roman is Junior's father just by looking at him closely and verifying my suspicions from a bloody toothbrush, you can only imagine that it won't take long for Hap Washburn—who is a doctor—to find out the same information."

"No!" Juanita gasped. "No!" she repeated louder. "He can't have my son's kidney. He can't do this! Junior is all I have!"

Ovan glanced around as people began to notice her growing hysteria. "Calm down, Nita. We won't let it happen," he whispered.

"Oh God," Juanita said grabbing at her hair. Her mouth hung open and Ovan knew next she would start to scream. He recognized the start of a conniption fit when he saw one. Pulling her into him, he kissed her shoving his tongue in deep. He pulled her by her rump, grinding her body into his while nearly smothering her with his mouth on hers. He could feel her hot tears on his face as he kissed her, while, with all his might he tried to comfort and soothe her. She grabbed at his hair, pulling on the short ends until finally she pushed back from his powerful clutch. "You're a very sick man, Ovan Dominguez," she mumbled with her head still buried in his chest.

"Takes one to know one, Doctor," he replied.

About then Maravel was coming from the station toward them. "Ovan, there's been an anomaly we think you should know about," she said, speaking as if she didn't notice Juanita pull away from him, smoothing down her blouse and fluffing her hair. "I finally got the ticketmaster to give me information regarding Hap's ticket purchase. Nearly took an act of Congress . . . but that nice Detective Beem helped me . . . anyway, Hap bought a ticket true but not to Eugene. He got a ticket from Emeryville to Klamath."

"Okay so again . . . who is Hap Washburn and what does he matter?" Nita asked.

"He's a surgeon working with Allen Roman . . . possibly the one who is going to actually perform the operation," Maravel said flatly, not noticing Ovan slicing his hand under his chin. Juanita again, went into fits.

Chapter 44

The train was crowded but Reggie didn't notice. He was just excited to be there, squeezing his way up the narrow staircase to the upper section. He didn't care that he had to sit next to Junior—for about fourteen hours! The thought, however, did run briefly thru his mind when Junior stumbled on the steps on his way up.

"Come on, Foo', you can't be doing that," he growled giving him a shove from behind.

"It's not like he meant to," he heard a female voice say in Junior's defense. Glancing over his shoulder as much as he could amidst the hustle bustle of passengers packing their carry-ons below and some attempting to come up the stairway with every other possession they owned—and then there was those at the top of the stairs waiting for Junior to get up and out of the way so they could come back down . . . and for what! *Go, sit down already!* Reggie mentally fused, still not able to see the face of who owned the soft voice behind him.

"Well I guess, but if his feet weren't so friggin' big," Reggie joked.

"Yeah, that's for covering the court twice as fast as you, Bro," Junior retorted, grinning broadly. "Oh yeah you play football . . . whatever," Junior teased playfully. Reggie could see how excited he was. It showed on his face. His grin was nearly ear to ear. Reggie couldn't help but smile . . . as much as he fought it back.

"You play football?" the girl asked.

He had to see her, she was sounding too fine for him to resist. Finally, wrestling up the stairs, Junior took their boarding ticket in order to find their seats. *Fine!* Reggic growled internally. Suddenly, feeling the small soft hands against his back, the girl moved past him and headed in the opposite direction of the coach. Her long thick mane hung down her back stopping at her slender waist, which peeked from below her short top. Her skin was milky, a complexion that begged a touch, but Reggie resisted. His hormones had been in overdrive lately—even he had to admit that—but football first—it was a priority, right? *Phhsst Coach is crazy if he thinks football is the only thing on this mind!* Reggie purred unconsciously not realizing the sound escaped his full lips. That's right when Junior smacked his cheek from behind. He was being playful but Reggie didn't take it that way and turned smacked him back a little harder than necessary.

"Shit bro! I'm just fuckin' with you . . . Come on, I found our seats."

Noticing the older woman frowning up at the volume and language Junior had chosen to use he decided to take the lead in acting more mature. "Watch ya mouth," he snapped following him to the seats.

"Yeah whatever," Junior reluctantly acquiesced.

Bumping butts with other passengers, Reggie struggled to put his and Junior's backpacks overhead. Junior's weighed a ton, no doubt full of video games as well as food. "Damn did you bring the kitchen sink, too?" Reggie asked, forcing Junior to pull the ear buds from his bobbing head.

"What?"

"What the hell is in the bag again?" he asked again, pointing upward.

"Snacks," Junior stated matter-of-factly, putting the plugs back in and bobbing his head again, this time singing out loud a bit. " 'Cause I'm the shit," he sang, imitation of Pharrel Williams—his idol—spinning around in the small isle. Reggie shook his head, realizing then that he'd not thought about eating. He'd only thought about getting there. *Eugene, Oregon. One weekend in a dorm. The possibility of moving away from home. College on a full ride scholarship in the fall. Life is all about the adventure that awaits me—fa sho.* Just then he noticed the girl of his dreams headed his way. She strolled like a model on the catwalk. Slow and sensuous—or maybe that's just what he saw. He was grinning before he could control the muscles in his face. Quickly he got a grip. Clearing his throat he stood facing her. Her eyes met his which was uncommon for most of the girls he knew. Surely she was five ten. Five foot ten inches of blended perfection. Her eyes were dark, like pools of that muddy stuff Chance called coffee.

Pointing around him she grinned. "I need to get to my seat," she said, pointing at the two empty ones in front of him. God she had an accent. Surely he'd missed it earlier. *They really do have black folks in England,* he pondered.

Clearing his throat quickly Reggie sat allowing her to pass. "Ohhh. My bad!"

She grinned and slid into her seat only to turn around on her knees over the seat in front of him. All Reggie could see were her breasts and cleavage pressing against the seat while she spoke.

"I hope I don't get some stinky old man sitting next to me," she said, giggling playfully.

"I'll move up there if you want," Junior answered quickly, surprisingly able to hear her without taking out his ear buds this time.

Reggie noticed that right away. "She don't want your stank ass up next to her either," he grumbled.

She giggled. "Maybe I do . . . a stank ass is better than a stank attitude."

"Ohhh, burrrn," Junior said, covering his mouth and raising his knee up while cracking up. The girl laughed too. Just then her cell phone jingled. She dug deep into the pocket of her tight jeans. All Reggie could see was her breasts—bouncing.

"Hey Mommy," she said, tossing her mane over her shoulder. She glanced up at Reggie and Junior. "No, I'm comfortable. I got good seats." She spoke with flirt in her voice. "No Mommy, no man . . . and I really hope one doesn't sit by me. I spoke with the attendant about it and so I hope they remember who I'm supposed to sit next to. Yes, Mommy, yes, I'll be good." She hung up.

"You shouldn't have told Mommy that lie," Reggie flirted.

"Don't know whatever you mean," she smarted off.

Just then a slender, sharply dressed man with fresh clean looking dreads sat across from her. He smiled at her and then at Reggie and Junior. "Train is crowded today," he said, starting conversation. "Lots of kids on here," he added. "Not many parents."

"Well, I'm over eighteen," she answered, as if he had asked a question.

"Just a baby," he said leaning his head back and closing his eyes as if he wanted to tune them out before they even got rolling—which was fine by Reggie.

"I'm on my way to college," she added, settling into her seat, again answering an unasked question.

"Which college?" the man asked her.

"Pardon?" she asked.

He repeated the question.

"University of Oregon," she answered. Reggie's stomach tightened.

"Me too," he yelped, catching the man's attention. He then pointed at Junior. "Us too . . . We're going up to look it over."

"Sweet," the girl joined in.

Reggie grinned now, not even trying to fight it. Junior just leaned back and closed his eyes, letting his music take him away.

"British?" the man asked, again being nosy—in Reggie's opinion.

"No, South African," she answered. Reggie perked up. He'd never really met anyone from Africa before.

"Interesting. What brings you to America?"

"My father's work," she answered. The man nodded and leaned his head back.

The train began moving slowly, on its way to the next stop. The attendant then started through the coach, double checking seating, making sure everyone was where they belonged.

Chapter 45

Juanita rambled from the moment they got their ticket. Chance wasn't sure if she was genuinely concerned about Rashawn, trying to avoid conversation about Junior, or truly just nervous about the puddle jump from SFO to PDX. If forced to admit it, Chance would have to confess he wasn't a big fan of flying either. But first class was something he could definitely get used to. Getting the tickets was nothing for Ovan who flashed his Secret Service badge. Who was this guy? One minute he was a glorified bounty hunter, the next, Super Spy.

From the airport they would have to drive south to catch the train head on. Nonetheless it would be faster than attempting to get through the snow headed north from California.

Chance missed Rashawn like crazy. But the vision of her in ICU, and knowing that Roman was behind it kept him focused. Ta'Rae had called to assure him that Rashawn was doing all right. "She keeps asking for Reggie."

"I'll have Reggie by morning. Promise her that," he committed. "How is Rainey?"

"She's doing okay. Carlotta has her—they left," Ta'Rae told him. "Rita is about to take off too. We're gonna look in one more time and then both of us head home. There is nothing more we can do but wait for her to improve."

"Good."

"Chance, can you tell me what's really going on? We haven't called Shelby and it's driving me nuts to keep her in the dark this way. Can you fill me in?"

"I can't talk about it all right now. It's just . . ." Chance paused to sigh heavily.

"I had a feeling it was bad." Ta'Rae sighed. "Please just let us know immediately if you find Reggie okay. Are the police involved?"

"Yes and no. Look Ta'Rae, just trust me on this and stay close to the situation there with Rasahwn. Let her know I love her and I'm fixing everything. I'm going to find our son."

"She knows that Chance. I know that, hell, we all do."

Hanging up his cell phone, Chance noticed Juanita staring at him. She'd been listening. Her eyes were red and filled with regret. She quickly turned back to Ovan and as quickly as a light switch went back to babbling aimlessly. Chance had to figure it was how she fought her true emotions—by covering them up with empty banter. "So when Chance and I got divorced it was hard to keep my practice at first, you know, I needed to raise our son and have, you know, money, so," Juanita's words brought him back. She was actually talking as if it hadn't come to light that Junior was not his son. He looked around her at Ovan whose eyes were all but glazed over from the information overload he'd been getting dosed with. His expression cleared for a second as they caught each other's eyes. The men's eyes read "total understanding" where Juanita's *crazy behind* was concerned. Ovan then accepted a stiff drink from the flight attendant. They were about to start the taxi and so service had come quickly for first class.

"So how long were you two married," Ovan asked Chance downing his drink in one gulp.

"Together or married," Juanita interrupted the answer. "I mean, we were soooo really good together it's hard to say. When two people just can't get over one another—"

"Nita," Chance said calmly, touching her hand that gripped the arm rest. "Junior is going to be all right. Rashawn is holding her own . . . and we're gonna find the boys. You should close your eyes for the rest of the flight and relax."

"But . . ." she began to protest, only to have Chance run his palm lightly down the front of her face.

"Just close your whole face. I'm sure they are going to come around one more time for service before we take off. I mean, this is first class, order a drink. Check your nerves," Chance said to her.

Juanita's eyes welled up with tears. "See, that's why I love you, Chance. You are such a good man," she simpered, squeezing his arm and then as if undecided on which man she really had feeling for, she suddenly squeezed Ovan's arm too. "You're a good man too . . ." she said before throwing her head back against the seat and tightly closing her eyes. "Oh God!" she cried out. At the moment the men could only see each other, Ovan's eyes widened and then crossed. Chance nodded in full agreement.

Chapter 46

Before long, the girl rose up in the seat again and turned around. Reggie noticed the man across from them eying her. He grew jealous. He had no idea he had such a possessive nature but then again, short of asking Sandy Banks out a couple of times–*Sandy being the most popular girl in school*–his jealous side had not been tested much. "Hey, he doesn't look old enough to be looking at a university." She pointed at Junior who didn't seem to notice her talking.

"He's not, he's only fifteen but we got shanghaied into this little togetherness trip by my mother," Reggie said, making quotation marks around the word "togetherness." "But it's all good. He's a good kid."

"You sound like he's your pet." She giggled, sending Reggie's heart into overdrive. "I don't have any siblings so I don't actually feel your pain but I can only imagine. By the way, my name is Julia," she introduced reaching out her soft hand for Reggie to take hold.

"Nice to meet you," he said.

She grinned. "Say, do you know which way the food coach is?" she asked. Junior, who normally responded to the word "food," continued lay with his head against the seat and his eyes closed.

"Nah, but I'll look for it with you." Reggie started to rise but the nosy mystery man was too quick for him.

"I was just headed that way. What do you want? I'll bring it back." His offering hit Reggie and the girl a bit strangely and they looked at each other, accepting the odd moment that the offering had created.

"Uhhhh, no," she giggled nervously. "I'll just follow you," she agreed. He shrugged, leading the way. Turning back to Reggie she shrugged and let the man lead the way out of the car through the doors that opened with the push of his large hands against the "open" pad. The noise of the locomotion could be heard as they stepped inbetween the cars before the door slid shut. The man was saying something to the girl. Reggie only wished he knew what.

"Better go get ya girl," Junior teased now, slapping Reggie's leg, motioning him to move it so he could get out of the seat. He was planning to dig around in his snack bag.

As much as Reggie knew Junior was just jeering him, he actually did want to follow them. Something about that guy didn't set well with him. "Maybe I will go get a soda or something," Reggie said, pulling himself from the seat.

"No need. If it's really food you want, I gotcha covered, Bro," Junior said, standing up and digging around in the bad, tossing Reggie a juice box. "Got more if ya wanna."

Reggie, unable to come up with another excuse to follow the girl and the weird guy, just sat back and tried to get over it. What was he thinking anyway going after a girl like that? Sure, she was cute but that was all he knew about her. Maybe she dug old guys. There was nothing worse than making a fool of himself over a girl who wasn't even interested. Here he was trying to be gallant and perhaps she was right where she wanted to be.

"Do you think they miss us yet?" Junior asked sliding in over Reggie's long legs with a bag of chips and drink box in his hands, bringing Reggie's mind back to the reality. The reality that they were both technically runaways. Neither boy wore a watch but Reggie could only figure it was about midnight by now. They'd been riding for a long time.

"I'm sure they might have figured it out. Not sure, with Mom gone and your mom kinda . . . you know."

"Yeah, clueless, you can say it."

"Yeah . . . well, Chance would have to be the one to start a ruckus and you know how passive he is. He's probably still just thinking one of us is gonna call in."

"So, you think they won't figure it out for a while yet, huh?"

"Nah, not for a while."

Junior smiled and nodded. His expression bore with it, a little sadness, maybe even some regret. He stared out the window. Reggie felt bad for him suddenly. Junior seemed to want so badly to fit in with him and his family. He wanted to belong—and bring his mom along, too. But that would never work. First of all, his mom hated Juanita, and secondly Chance couldn't possibly be his real father, so in reality there was nothing truly relating Junior with him . . . nothing.

Downing his juice box in one strong suck on the straw, Reggie stuck the empty box in the back of the seat in front of him and laid his head back, closing his eyes.

"Maybe we should call and tell them we're at a friend's," Junior suggested as if on an impulse.

Reggie was glad one of them finally spoke up. He had been kinda thinking on the same lines. "You put my phone in my bag?" "No, it's in mine." "Then forget it. I'm not digging around that bag until we eat it down some." Junior thought about it and then laughed.

Chapter 47

Roman couldn't believe Ovan Dominguez was still so persistent. He's underestimated him. Seeing him at the airport told him as much. But then again, it wasn't as if he'd really shaken him in London, or any of this stops along the way back to America. Ovan was truly becoming an opponent. Ovan was still in pursuit and had gathered an American team to help him. "Peter Pan is growing up—realizing that it takes more than a little magic dust, a pixie, and a fancy car to catch me." Roman then called Hap but got no answer. "All I know is that idiot better have my son with him by now," Roman growled through his gritted teeth thinking of Hap in addition to actually realizing Ovan's new strategy. The time wasted, catching the cab to the airport and then catching it back to his hotel had put him in a foul mood. "And what were Chance Davis and Juanita doing there?" Roman asked. He'd seen Ovan, his partner Maravel—he remembered her from London—a couple of clearly obvious cops and none other than Chance Davis and Juanita Duncan.

"And what does Chance think he's going to do . . . kill me? He should be with his wife!" Roman added, between sips of water. He'd taken his kidney medication. Time was running out. He could feel it. His body was not responding to the medication any more. He needed a new kidney. Dialysis was not the answer for him and Dr. Lipton was a fool for even suggesting it. Perhaps if Rashawn hadn't been in such a hurry to murder Blain he would have had his donor and wouldn't have needed Reggie this way. "So in reality this is your fault, all of it," he said to her picture—the one he carried with him everywhere. She still had his heart, he wanted to deny but he couldn't. In a very sick and disturbing way—he still loved her. Maybe that was why he ran her off the road—if he was to die she would have to die too. They would be together forever, for the better or worse. It was karma . . . their lot . . . their destiny. Sort of like his mother and father's. After his father was executed for killing Blain's father, Roman's mother committed suicide.

Karma.

Roman would have gone to the hospital to be by her side—to watch her die—had it not been for her family being there. “Something is always coming between us my beloved. But nothing can truly keep us apart—not for long, anyway.”

He called the hospital but could get no answers regarding her condition but in that non-answer he got an actual answer . . . she was still alive.

Throwing he picture into his garment bag he loaded his car and started for the hospital. He wanted to see her once more.

Chapter 48

"Why didn't Rashawn call me to tell me that Reggie was coming? What's really going on?" Shelby asked. "Carlotta said, Rashawn decided to drive to Arizona at the last minute. None of this sounds right . . . and how come I can't reach Rashawn by phone?"

Chance held onto his lie. "Nothing is wrong, Shelby. She's on her way to Trina's place for the week and forgot to call."

"My sister would not have forgotten to call. She's too much of a control freak for that."

"Now, now, Shelby, Rashawn is working on that."

"Hmmph. Yeah right." Shelby laughed. "Well I'm still surprised she let the boys come alone, but sure I'll be there tomorrow to pick them up no problem. Around two ya say?"

"Yeah, around two," Chance said, pacing with the cell phone outside of the airport, while Ovan commandeered a rental car. They were about to start their backward trek to meet the train. By putting Shelby on alert they would have her at the Eugene train station just in case the boys actually made it all the way to Eugene. They couldn't take a chance not having all their bases covered.

"So she's at Trina's?" Shelby asked again, sounding suspicious.

"Yes. Yes she is," Chance answered quickly.

"We got the car," Juanita blurted.

"Who is that?" Shelby asked.

Chance covered the mouthpiece quickly and then uncovering it to answer. "Nobody."

"It was somebody—somebody female. And it's what, midnight? Who was that?" Shelby asked, sounding just like Rashawn—suspicious of everything.

"Nobody I know," Chance said, fanning his hand at Juanita to be quiet. "I'm at the all-night market picking up a snack."

"Still don't know why she couldn't call me. But okay Mr. 'Head of the House Taking care of the Business Out in the Middle of the Night Getting Snacks. I'll be there tomorrow."

"Great thanks," he said hanging up quickly.

"Sorry," Juanita said, uncovering her mouth.

"Did you get your sister-in-law to pick them up?" Ovan asked.

"Yeah."

"Good because if we're wrong and they actually go to Eugene, someone will need to be there to meet those boys and thwart Hap and Allen Roman. Your sister-in-law is like a third hand for us."

"Got cha. Oh I need to call Trina. I'm sure Shelby hung up and called her."

"I see they really trust you," Juanita said with a smirk.

"Anyway . . ." Chance moved away from the two of them and called Trina in Arizona. Trina was no doubt fast asleep so Chance left a voicemail explaining that Rashawn was tired and decided to stay overnight at a hotel. So she would be arriving tomorrow afternoon after making a few stops along the way. This way when Shelby called Trina would not tell her the truth about Rashawn. Trina was just too emotional and was not one to stick with a plan like this one. Chance hated not telling Shelby about Rashawn but the Ams sisters were tight-knit and Shelby would have been torn on what to do—rush to her sister's side or wait for Reggie who she had no idea could be in danger. None of it mattered—the decision to leave Trina and Shelby in the dark had been made. Carlotta, Rita and Ta'Rae all agreed it was the best one to make—who was Chance to argue with the Ams' women.

Hanging up, he climbed in the back seat of the rental with Ovan behind the wheel. Chance caught him looking in the rear view mirror. "It's going to be all right," Ovan said.

"And you know this how?" Chance said in response.

Chapter 49

The time seemed snail-like but Reggie refused to dig out his BlackBerry to check the time. He didn't want to know how long Julia and the stranger had been gone. Besides, he was sure his BlackBerry was even deeper in Junior's bag by now, with all the scrounging for food he'd been doing over the last hour. He'd gotten up at least three times.

Finally Julia returned. She was alone but smiling. She slid into her seat and immediately turned around, looking over it at Reggie whose eyes were wide open now. Junior was finally sleeping—or so it appeared. "Hey, wanna talk?" she asked.

"No," Reggie wanted to answer, but he didn't. He had gotten his mind off the pretty girl and gotten it back where it needed to be—his choices for college, his blatant disregard for his mother's wishes—she was on his mind, heavily. He had accepted finally that things would never be the same between them. He'd crossed the line with this one, and had taken Junior along for the ride. This was serious. What if they had called the cops? What if the cops were waiting at the end of the line? He wanted to call her—to apologize, but pride and inconvenience prevented him.

Besides, all that was crazy thinking. His folks had done no such thing. He had no worries and Oregon wasn't his last stop in life. He knew this. It was just the beginning of bigger and better things. Surely his mother had to know that. She had only offered him Moorman and maybe the Art Institute of San Francisco to consider. Both schools meant living at home. With all that craziness going on there . . . *no way am I staying there.*

"That guy," the girl began, bringing Reggie's mind back. "He said he's going to Eugene too. But his seating ticket says Klamath. Isn't that weird to you?"

"Real weird actually. I mean, it seems like a lot of black folks going to one place don't you think?" he answered with less enthusiasm for the sound of her voice as he had earlier. It was clear she and the man had made some kind of connection for her to have all that information on him, and Reggie wasn't up for getting in the middle of that. He'd watched his mother—for years—sitting in the middle of Chance of Juanita's *thing*. Besides, he had college to think about, *right?* Julia giggled, getting his attention again. He looked up at her. She was so pretty. Instantly, he couldn't help but forgive her for the neglect of his feelings.

"Do you trust me?" she then asked.

"Excuse me?"

"Do you like me," she said.

"No, you asked if I trusted you."

She grinned broadly. "I meant . . . Do you like me?"

"Why?" Reggie asked, returning the flirt to his voice. Julia looked around.

"Because I need to talk to you about something, can we go downstairs?"

"You wanna go downstairs?"

"Yeah, and we need to go like now . . ." she said, sounding serious.

Reggie glanced over at Junior who still appeared asleep. "Sure we can talk," he said standing up. He'd heard about things like this—sex on an Amtrak train. Maybe this was gonna be it. Life was getting exciting and maybe it was about to get—really—exciting, for downstairs was nothing but a room full of old people, baggage, and bathrooms. Surely she was planning for them to duck in one. Condoms crossed his mind as she moved into the aisle.

"It's about that guy," she began.

Reggie rolled his eyes. All passion for her—gone. All thoughts about a good time—gone. "Wait a minute. Do I want to hear this?"

"You need to hear it."

"Not sure I do," Reggie balked, thinking he knew what she was going to tell him. He wasn't in the mood to be her buddy. He wasn't up for hearing about her new boyfriend.

Just then . . . *speak of the perv* . . . the man came back to his seat. Julia quickly sat leaving Reggie standing. The man then gathered up his few belongings and pulling the seating tag from above his head, he, with a wide grin on his face, motioned for Julia to move over in her seat—which she did without hesitation. The man put his hat and glasses into the seat while he stood looking at Reggie standing there.

"So, Reggie, you're going to U of O. That's a good school—my alumni school actually. I mean, I'm a doctor now but I'm going there to do a speaking thing . . ." he stammered. ". . . for the students . . . the new students." His towering presence up this close gave Reggie the creeps but he shook them off. "Did Julia tell you about all that?"

"No," Reggie answered bluntly. The man frowned but then quickly changed his expression.

"Well I'm surprised," he asked glancing at Julia. His body language was confident despite his *weirdness*—in Reggie's opinion.

"Look I'm not interested in you or her—especially you. What I wanna know anything about you for?" Reggie asked, noticing that Julia didn't seem concerned about his comment. "My brother . . ." he hesitantly addressed Junior, ". . . we're just minding our own business, and . . ."

"He's your brother?" the man asked. He looked surprised and Reggie tried to read his face but couldn't. The train coach was dark short of a few built-in dim reading lights along the floor and up top of the seats. Reggie looked at the man's hands that rested on his hips. He wore a large pinky ring filled with what looked like diamonds . . . It was too dark to tell.

"Yeah, he's my brother."

"I wasn't aware . . ." the man began and then stopped speaking.

"Well now you know," Reggie said, deciding then would be a good time to hit the restroom. Maybe when he came back up, everyone would be doing their own thing.

Ending the uncomfortable situation, he headed down the narrow stairs to the restroom.

The train chugged on without much more conversation between any of them, although Julia would rise in her seat periodically to look at him. She wanted to talk—Reggie could tell but now, with her seat mate, their "getting to know one another" time was messed up. Reggie could see even from the seat behind that Julia had put her ear buds in and was nodding against the window after pulling on her sweat jacket and the hood of it over her head. They had made it into the mountains. It was cold, uncomfortably cold on the train but Reggie would just do what he could to stay warm. Snuggling next to Julia came to mind but that was not going to happen now.

Standing to raid Junior's snack bag one more time, Reggie could see that the man seemed engrossed in his reading material—a medical journal—from what he could see. Maybe he was legit and not just a pervert, but Reggie wanted no parts of him and the minute he could get Julia alone he was gonna tell her to stay away as well. Dude gave him major bad vibes.

"Hey, Reg," the man said noticing him standing there. "You should get some sleep," he said.

"I know what I should do and when I should do it," Reggie snapped, sitting back in his seat. The man smiled and shook his head. Reggie glanced over the seat at Julia who appeared to be sleeping.

Sitting back and finishing his snack, he reluctantly gave into the night, falling asleep.

Chapter 50

Rashawn could only wish that her eyes would open. But the dream had taken her too deep. The sleep was far too heavy for her to pull out of. "I wonder am I dead?" she asked herself. She remembered the car going over and she remembered Roman's face looking through the window at her. He was upside down, or maybe she was the one on her head. He called her name, just like he was calling to her right now. Was he by her bed? No, he couldn't be. Surely someone would arrest him if he was. He wore a white jacket, the kind doctors wore.

"I'll take good care of Reggie," he was saying.

"Reggie? What are you doing with Reggie? Please leave my son alone," she wanted to say but couldn't. The sedatives were too strong. She closed her eyes. Maybe this was all a dream anyway.

"I found out my kidneys were shot. I guess it was the drug I was taking. You know the drug, the wonderful drug I shared with you. Well, apparently its murder on the kidneys so mine are shot—how did yours do? But then again, I guess I did take it considerably longer. Reggie is surely a match for me and so why take a chance with an anonymous donor. That's what brought me here. Our son. I'm going to take his kidneys. Yes, yes, I know without them he'll die. I'm aware of that chance but listen I'm going to actually give him mine. Here are my thoughts. He's young. With proper care, he'll make mine last a lot longer than I could. And with his . . . Well, needless to say, I'll live a long, long time. Of course I've done this procedure before. Can't say I've seen the results my patients all died. But at least I've seen it done. Besides, I'm no surgeon and well, it's hard to get good help these days. No, I'm not selfish, Rashawn, not at all. As a matter of fact I was just about to say that about you."

At that Rashawn had heard enough. In her dreams she had once had intimate relations with this man. It was obvious that he had the power to affect her deep into her subconscious so deep that she physically reacted to him. Like now.

Her eyes popped open and her hand immediately went for his throat digging her nails in deep with unnatural strength coming from deep in the otherworld she now resided.

"Call the floor doctor, IC-5 is in distress," the on-staff nurse said noting the monitor going off. She had been at her desk reading. Not much usually happened on the ICU floor at this hour of the night. Maybe a code blue, and those weren't too much to worry about as usually the families were already with their loved ones. But IC-5 . . . This one had a woman in there that had been drifting in and out of a coma all day. Her family was on their way back to hang around after hearing about her last drift into never-neverland.

"I thought Doctor . . ." the nurse looked at the file, "Montaq was in there," she said.

"Who the hell is Doctor Montaq?" the first nurse asked.

"He came in about fifteen minutes ago and said he was the patient's private physician," the young nurse whined realizing her error.

"Sorry but no!" the head nurse on duty snapped, picking up the phone to call both the doctor on call as well as security while the other nurse ran to Rashawn's room, along with several others.

During the surge of doctors and nurses bursting into the room, the mysterious Dr. Montaq who had stood behind the door as they entered, was able to slip past them. On his way out he passed security on their way in. Later they would have to report to the police that Dr. Montaq looked like a slightly excited, distinguished looking doctor who appeared by all rights just as concerned as those who were hovering over the unconscious patient—Rashawn Ams.

Chapter 51

Waking up to Junior nudging him, Reggie noticed he appeared to be keenly concentrating on something.

"You hungry?" Reggie asked him, before stretching and moving his legs for Junior to get by. He had just gotten warm and comfy in that seat but oh well. The day was barely breaking—who knew how many stops he had slept through. Junior just shook his head. "What's wrong?" Reggie asked.

Junior said nothing but nodded toward the seat in front of him. Reggie followed his nod and then quietly shrugged a question. "I gotta hit the john. Come with me so I won't get lost," Junior said loudly.

Reggie was puzzled when Junior nodded to the seat in front again. Reggie agreed to join him. The man seemed not too concerned with their movements behind his head but Junior moved quickly down the aisle urging Reggie to follow at the same pace.

Down the narrow stairwell they went. Reggie, realizing his own need, headed for one of the empty bathrooms only to have Junior change his direction dragging him into the largest one with him. "What the hell is wrong with you! I'm not going in here with you!"

Junior ignored him locking them in the lavatory together. Reggie reached for the door only to have Junior stop him. "Foo' . . . how did that Nig 'get your name?"

"My name?" Reggie asked, showing his confusion. He had no idea what wall Junior's question was jumping off of but for now these bathroom walls were not where he wanted to look. Junior put his finger to his own lips instructing him to lower his voice. "How did dude know your name? Last night. I heard you guys talking and he called you Reggie. It took me a while but I had to finally ask myself when did you two get introduced?"

"Julia told him probably."

"And when did you tell her? I haven't been sleep this whole trip. I know you thought I was, but I wasn't. It's my FBI training at work," Junior added. Reggie rolled his eyes. "You're terrible with women and worse with introductions, seriously trust me, unless you guys talked in sign," Junior waved his fingers as if signing words in American Sign Language. "Never once did I hear you tell that girl yo name or mine!"

"Maybe it was on something," Reggie thought aloud. "My bag, my . . ." Junior shook his head. "Oh shit, you're right."

"I know I'm right. How did they know? What's going on, Reg?"

"I don't know, but I'ma go call my mother," Reggie said, sliding back the lock and pulling open the door.

Julia then appeared down the stairs. Her face was strained and she appeared under duress. "Reggie, Junior, we're going to get off this train right now."

"What? No. And how do you know my name?" Reggie asked.

"Don't argue with me . . ."

Just then the man came down. "Wow, you guys *are* close. But then, *brothers* can be like that. What's your excuse Julia?" The man smiled wickedly showing briefly what appeared to be the barrel of a gun. Junior gasped slightly but Reggie who had already grown agitated showed no fear.

"What the hell is going on? Who are you?" He then pointed at Julia. "And who are you?"

"Reggie, he has a gun on us. I don't think we should be asking anything." Junior said sounding like the straight man in a deadpan comedy skit.

Chapter 52

Juanita was at the counter ordering coffee. The men sat at the booth in the back of the café. "So you're telling me you don't know where this cabin is?" Chance snapped.

"No. I'm not telling you that. But that's the fact," Ovan answered calmly. "Thought for sure Maravel would have found it by now but there's nothing listed for a Craven Michaels or a Hap Washburn in all of the state. The cabin must be in someone else's name. She's doing some cross references . . . It's not that easy."

"Do you know how big this state is?" Chance whispered trying not to alert Juanita who was finally calm. He looked up and smiled and waved at her. She smiled back. She looked worried but was covering it over well. He immediately returned to the two-man huddle with Ovan. "She performed illegal surgeries there, I'm positive it's not a cabin she wanted the authorities to find—so how the hell are we supposed to just trip up on it?"

"Yes, I understand your concern but think about it, Chance, it has to be near here. It's got to be on the route they are taking or Roman would not have devised this plan. He would have sent the boy somewhere else and used another doctor. We just need to get Kingsley Field to the Air Guard there, so we can get in the air. I do know how to do what I do."

"And what do you do Ovan?" Chance growled slamming himself back in the seat. They'd stopped at a coffee shop to regroup, and for Ovan to check his computer for updates from Maravel. He'd also printed out the Amtrak map on his portable printer. Glancing at his watch he was sure they'd beat the train by hours. Just then Chance's phone rang. It was Rashawn's number. His stomach jumped. Ovan nodded for him to answer it.

"What do you want, you bastard," Chance growled into the receiver. He knew in his heart Allen Roman was on the other end.

"Wow, is that anyway to address your wife."

"My wife is in the hospital . . ."

"In a coma I might add. She slipped back into one just a little bit ago. Where are you to where you don't know this?"

Chance paused slightly, rubbing his head and pushing up his glasses. He tried to hide his immediate concern behind a tough exterior. "Don't you worry your black ass about me. What are you doing with her phone? Did you take it as a token of your sick success in killing her? I'ma kill you on sight you fucking murderer—I swear it."

Juanita who had just reached the table sat the coffees down and covered her face at the sound of his hateful words. Ovan pulled her into the booth next to him and quickly handed her one of the cups of coffee.

"She's not dead," Roman mumbled.

"How would you know that?"

"I've been to see her."

"You stay away from her."

"I wasn't trying to kill her, Chance, you have to believe me. I just wanted to talk to her about our son."

"Where is Reggie? Do you have him?"

"Not yet."

The call ended. Chance looked around at Ovan and Juanita. Ovan's face was frozen for a second before he finally spoke. "Okay . . ."

"Shouldn't we get the cops involved? GPS and all that . . ."

"Definitely call Miller and Beem and let them know he's made contact with you on your wife's phone. My guess is he'll dispose of it now, but it's worth the call."

Chapter 53

"Well, I'll be damned," Jim exploded, looking through Roman's things. Nothing they could use in this search would be admissible as they'd entered without a warrant. In all truth this call should have been handed over to Theft as it was tantamount to a stolen cell phone. However, Jim and Lawrence both needed the last bit of confirmation that Ovan was not just some wildman chasing a phantom. "Roman," he said watching a DVD that was clearly from his stash of medical meanderings. They'd found many unrelated items in the room—clothing, books, pictures of Rashawn Ams and other beautiful women but the DVD just called Jim to the player that sat under the television in the room.

"Said his name was Smith . . . Dr. Smith . . . had ID and such. I had no reason to question him," the hotel manager explained looking on with Jim and Lawrence at the operation being performed on the DVD. "What the hell is that?" he gasped at the bloody sight.

"Kidney's my guess," Lawrence said, grimacing at the sight before shutting off the TV. Jim pulled out his phone to call Maravel. Maybe she could make some sense out of some of the stuff in this room. Maybe something here would help Ovan and Chance find Reggie and Junior before this maniac preformed the same surgery on them.

Chapter 54

The train pulled into Klamath Falls. It was not the stop they were even planned to notice let alone where they planned detrain. *How did dude get a gun on here? So much for Amtrak security*, Reggie thought, feeling the hard barrel of the gun pressing against his spine as dude pushed him out the door with the others who were scheduled for this top. Dude had moved them though the cars discreetly and up to the car that would be unloading at this stop. No one seemed to notice as they must have appeared to be a nice family out to celebrate Christmas in the snowy mountainous region of the Pacific Northwest.

Reggie glanced over at Julia who stepped off before him, still holding tight to his backpack and Junior whose eyes were red from strain and the fight with emotions. Dude must have figured Reggie would be less of a threat with both his hands free and he was right because had the chance—Reggie would have busted dude's head in with that heavy backpack and then tackled him down for that gun. But no, dude held the gun on him the whole time as if to use him as a warning for the rest, and it was working.

Reggie could tell Junior and Julia were scared, and what was worse—he was scared too.

For the past few hours that they had sat in the observation car, listening to the voice of the man who was no doubt planning to kill them—and for what—Reggie had no clue. For now it just seemed to be no real good reason. Reggie knew he didn't have any money—and neither did Junior. Dude was mistaken if he thought he was kidnapping kids who could pay off. Juanita didn't have a pot to piss in unless Chance had recently given her one . . . and as far as his mom went, she hadn't even pulled down her first pay check yet and even then, this job was all title . . . even he knew that.

And Julia? Who knew why she had gotten caught up in all this, but she seemed to be a victim as well.

"Let's go," Dude said, as they pulled into the Klamath Falls station. He'd not even made a phone call to anyone. This was all too surreal. But then again, his aunt Trina wrote mysteries for a living and this wasn't any stranger than some of the things she'd come up with—once her story plot had even landed her in jail for being too crazily realistic. She'd written a murder and not to long after her ex had died the same way . . . so, strange things could happen. Reggie's mind drifted on to some of her stranger plots to see if perhaps a kidnapping of teenage kids had ever been tapped by the workings of her twisted mind.

"We're getting off here? It's the middle of nowhere!" Junior finally said, noticing the snow on the ground. His plea brought Reggie's mind back. He had never seen anything like this place outside of photographs. He was a born and raised city boy. Klamath Falls was beautiful and would have been even more so under different circumstances.

"Come on, Roman is waiting," Dude said.

Roman? It was a familiar name. Reggie couldn't place it but he wanted to. He also wanted Junior's backpack. No, he wasn't hungry, he needed his BlackBerry. It was a new one and so surely he'd be able to get a signal—even out here. Surely he'd be able to text a note, even if it went through on a delayed signal—

"I'm hungry," he lied. Julia looked at him with an odd expression.

"What?" she asked, perhaps thinking she didn't hear him right.

"I'm hungry. I need my backpack. I have snacks in there," Reggie continued. Julia looked at him and then at dude, who shook his head.

"No. Not right now. If you're hungry you can just wait. Besides, I'm sure there's more than snacks that you want in that backpack," he growled. "Where's your cell phone?"

"I . . . I . . . " Reggie bluffed. Hap grabbed the backpack from Julia and tore through it, finding Reggie's old cell phone. The one he used only to store his phone numbers. He shoved it deep in his pocket before dropping the backpack on the bench near the entrance of the building. He then ripped open Junior's backpack and saw it filled with goodies. He zipped it up and threw it at Reggie.

"Okay, Mr. Hungry Man, you are now in charge of carrying that heavy-assed snack bag! You need to eat anyway. Keep up our strength. But the cell phone, it's history! Come on," he said, after watching Reggie shrug Junior's backpack on his shoulder. "Don't try anything funny because now the gun is on little brother here."

"They call me Junior," Junior spoke up now. It was as if Junior could tell Reggie was up to something and was willing to play along, no matter how scary it seemed.

"Whatever," Dude answered.

"You gotta name, dude?" Junior asked.

"Sure do . . . We'll get all that out of the way once we get to the cabin."

"Cabin?" Julia asked.

"I told you I had a cabin, sweetie. You were all eager to see it before."

"That's when I thought it was in Eugene. Don't even think I was trying to let you get near me," Julia began, jerking her neck from side to side and swaggin' her finger. British or not, she had all the moves of an angry black woman right now.

"Riiight!" Hap retorted smartly.

They walked toward the lot where a dark SUV was waiting. He pressed the unlock button on his key ring as they approached. "Get in. Julia, you're gonna drive."

"Me?" she asked, nervously. "I don't have a license."

"You don't have your license?" Junior asked sounding almost as if taunting.

"Shut up, Junior," she snapped.

"Hey, I just finished driver's ed . . . and ummm," Junior blew on his nails as if that meant he was all that.

"Then you drive!" Hap snapped showing a loss of patience growing.

"What?" all three kids yelped in unison. Julia rolled her eyes.

"Yeah, you are the only one I have no problem with today . . . matter of fact, I kinda like you . . . Junior. So you drive. You'll be our chance to get away. Chance is your father right? Or do you share a mother . . . must be because you two look just alike. Or is . . ." Hap pondered for a moment and then shook his head. "Can't be."

"No we don't share anything," Junior answered with a smirk. "And yeah, my father is Chance, thus the Junior . . . duh." Chance climbed in behind the wheel of the big vehicle. "Chance to get away . . . ughhh lame. If this is gonna go on all day, I say kill me now!"

Hap laughed. "Yeah I knew I liked this kid."

Julia climbed in the front passenger seat and Reggie and Hap climbed in back. "Let's roll," he ordered. Chance started the roaring engine and off they went, jerking slightly until Chance shifted his weight in the seat and adjusted the mirrors. Reggie would have laughed at his step brother if his life hadn't depended on him at this time.

Chapter 55

Shelby was actually pretty excited about her nephew visiting for a couple of days. If he liked the university there she would offer him a place to live—rent free—while he finished his education and hopefully made the team. She had talked about the opportunity with Chance and it all sounded good earlier in the month. But still this visit seemed so unexpected. So far she'd not been able to reach Rashawn with any of it. Even now, it was strange that Rashawn had been unavailable to talk about it. She'd called her sister a few times but as Chance had told her, Rashawn was not near her phone.

It would be great for him to play some pro ball. Even though she and her husband had made their career in the NBA and WNBA, football was fine for a boy his size—probably a better choice. Besides that, playing a sport wasn't the worse thing he could be doing with his life. So many kids were all methed out right now. Oregon had seen a rough couple of years with the methamphetamine epidemic. More white kids than black ones were drugged out on the junk but that was just because of the demographics . . . per capita the problem was even worse for black kids simply because there just weren't that many there. Reggie's positive presence would make a difference in her day and her nurturing and mentoring would help make a big difference in his life as well.

Shelby was lonely. With her husband always on the road with his team, she was left alone at home to fend for their daughter and herself emotionally. Diversity did not run long in Eugene. She missed her five sisters terribly. She could only imagine her crazy acting ghetto fabulous sisters invading this uptight ultra white city. The thought made her laugh. They were all older now—but still, age had not changed them much. The thought of them all in Eugene made her cringe slightly—but no fear of that— *there's absolutely nothing to bring them here,* she thought.

Shelby glanced at the clock. It was time for the train to come rolling in. She'd called the Amtrak station and the coastline eleven was actually running on time today—the first time in months. Shelby and her daughter often, during season, traveled up to Washington State to watch her husband's basketball team play tournaments in Seattle, so she knew the Amtrak schedule well.

It had been drizzling all morning, so, gathering up her light jacket and umbrella, she and her daughter headed out to the car. They made it downtown in about fifteen minutes, just as the train pulled in. "Good timing, Mom," her daughter complimented. "Will I know him when I see him?" she asked, not having ever seen Reggie in person. Shelby realized then how long she'd been away.

"Yes, you'll know him. He looks like an Ams," she said, knowing the truth of the matter—that actually Reggie looked like his biological father—but nobody would ever want to repeat that one out loud.

Excitedly, Shelby and Stacy climbed out of her car and headed into the station to greet the arrivers. She assumed he'd have bags and Junior too. She'd only met Chance's son Junior a few times, but despite how crazy acting his mother, Juanita was—she'd met Juanita—Shelby was totally fine with Junior being part of the family. As supportive as Rashawn had been, receiving Chance Jr. as if he was her own child, the least Shelby could do was replicate the love.

The people poured into the station, and Stacy grew excited. Her head darted this way and that as she quickly scanned the crowd for her cousin. Shelby had to admit she had thought she too would have spied him by now, as tall as she'd heard he was. The crowd eventually thinned out, with each person unloading, meeting their connections. Shelby felt strange suddenly wondering why amidst all the people there was no sign of a tall handsome young black man—or two. She pulled her cell phone from her bag while heading to the information counter, as the train pulled off. "Where is he?" Stacy asked. Shelby didn't answer but waited for Chance to pick up.

Chapter 56

Thank God for new phones, Reggie thought, feeling the phone vibrating silently in his bag. He'd had it on vibrate before his mother snagged it and apparently she hadn't changed the setting. Good thing too because surely, his phone blasting Lil Wayne or some other rap singer's ringtone, would have been disastrous. It had been vibrating non-stop since clearing the area of no reception. But noting the many turns this weird guy was sending Junior in, Reggie knew there would soon be no signal to be found again.

Junior was doing well behind the wheel and if it had been a driving test he would have passed. Reggie could see him sweating though and he was sitting all up on the steering wheel. When they got to the hills with all the tight turns, and with all that snow on the ground, Reggie had to admit, his forehead began to moisten as well. Julia was as silent as a mouse.

"I have a couple of questions," Junior began as if out of the blue.

"What's that?" the man answered.

"Since we're probably not coming out of this thing alive," Junior went on. Julia groaned. "What is your name?"

"Fair question. It's Hap."

"Hap? Interesting name. Well, Hap," Junior began, "you have three teenagers and I can't believe that this was on your list of things to collect today . . . so my question is this: who were you actually trying to kidnap in this caper?"

"Another good one." Hap chuckled as if absolutely amused by Junior's inquiry and wittiness. "Reggie," he answered flatly.

Reggie turned and looked at him. "Why me?"

"You'll see," Hap answered.

"We'll all see," Julia added.

"Exactly. Turn here," Hap instructed.

Junior made the sharp turn onto a narrow road that ended at a wooded cabin. Snow covered the porch and the cabin looked cold and unlived in. Reggie looked at Hap who now motioned with the gun for him to get out of the car. He obeyed reluctantly, feeling the icy air embracing him.

Junior and Julia climbed out of the car and stood close by each other for warmth. "Let's go!"

Hap barked at them, motioning both of them to walk ahead of Reggie who was now being led by Hap and his gun, up the icy steps. Junior slipped on the ice but quickly regained his footing. They went inside the cabin which was surprisingly just the opposite inside. Inside it was inviting and well lived in with many feminine touches.

"Now, I can tie you all up or trust that you respect Mother Nature—realizing that there is nowhere to go if you run away. You'll die out there." Hap took the keys from Junior's hand and shoved them deep into his pocket.

"Can you please tell me what's going on?" Reggie asked.

"Sure. I'm Dr. Hap Washburn and I'm working for a client who is in need of some medical attention. And you, Reginald Ams, have the cure for what ails him."

"Excuse me?" Reggie asked nearly gasping at what the words implied.

"My patient needs a new part, you could say," Hap stammered as if enjoying the game he was playing with Reggie's emotions.

"New part! And he plans on taking one of mine?" Reggie's voice cracked while pressing his hand splayed out over his chest.

"You plannin' to take something off of him?" Junior yelped.

Reggie stepped forward aggressively. Hap again raised his gun threateningly. "Reggie don't," Julia warned.

"Don't make me shoot you. My client would be furious! Killing you would really put a time crunch on things!"

"You're out your mind! I'm out," Reggie said, breaking for the door. Hap fired the gun over Reggie's head. He froze. Julia screamed.

"Reggie stop!" Junior hollered. "Don't kill him!" Junior begged Hap.

Reggie spun on his heel. His face felt twisted and by the look on Junior's upon seeing his expression, Reggie had to figure he looked unrecognizable. Fear, anger, and growing rage consumed him. "Dead or alive Reggie, it doesn't matter to me. Dead would just make things complicated . . . on one hand." Hap said coolly. "Now just calm down. This will be over tomorrow."

Motioning for Julia to assist him, Hap pointed toward a straightjacket lying on the large dining table. "Get that and put it on Mr. Hulk over there," he told her. Julia picked up the heavy jacket and headed Reggie's way.

"Get away from me!" he growled.

"Reggie, please, he's going to kill you if you don't," Julia tried to reason. "Trust me," she mouthed.

"You're not putting that on me!" he fought, jerking away, pushing Julia so hard she fell flat on her butt. At that Hap aimed the gun at Junior, who quickly raised his hands and closed his eyes wincing in anticipation of the worse. "Don't. Just . . . don't," Reggie said, speaking slowly and determined to be understood while he reached down, helping Julia to her feet and then taking the jacket from her. He began to put it on himself, allowing her then to pull the straps and buckles, tying him in securely.

"Interesting. They say only blood is thicker than water, well, looks like step blood is too." Hap smiled wickedly before instructing Junior to sit in what appeared to be a dental chair and then instructed Julia to clasp Junior's hands in the medical restraints. While she tied him up, Hap moved over to a tray, unveiling an assortment of hypodermic needles, choosing one, while watching Reggie out of one eye. Reggie didn't move an inch. His heart was racing fast, his mind was too cloudy. He'd not thought this completely out so he just stood stiff and ridged, tied up and helpless—for now. But that wasn't to say that before this night was over, he wasn't planning to take this maniac out, some kinda way. There were three of them and one of him . . . Some kinda way they were getting the hell outta there tonight.

Hap called Julia over. "You ever give yourself a shot."

"No," she whimpered.

"It's not hard. Hold the thing up . . . thump it until you see no bubbles. If you get a bubble . . . you could be dead within seconds." He smiled. Julia's eyes widened as if she totally understood what he was saying. "Squeeze the bottom upward until just a little of the juice comes from the top," he explained. "And then . . ." he patted his waistline. "Right there in your belly. It won't hurt as much and it will work faster."

Julia gulped audibly before following the instructions and injecting the fluid into her stomach area. Within moments her eye lids fluttered and she fell to the floor unconscious.

"You're one hell of a babysitter there, Hap," Junior remarked smartly.

Hap laughed. "You know what, Junior, you're one hell of a comedian. You remind me an awful lot of my client."

"Can't wait to meet the guy."

"Oh you're gonna like him . . . a lot."

Chapter 57

Shelby was flustered and confused. Her senses were telling her that something was wrong with this whole thing. She'd called Trina and gotten confirmation that indeed Rashawn was on her way—driving. "Late as hell but maybe she stopped at some malls. Chance said, she was stressed out—but still my thing starts in just a little while."

"Trina have you called Rashawn?"

"No, her phone is off or whatever," Trina told her. "At least that's what Chance said, or something like that."

"Something like that? He told me she left it at home! Doesn't it strike you as weird that she's leaving for there the same time as Reggie is coming here—alone. Well I mean he's coming with Juanita's boy."

"Really." Trina sounded very surprised.

"So you didn't know about that either."

"I'm going to call Carlotta."

"Don't bother, can't reach her nor Ta'Rae . . . Rita either."

"Something sounds raw and I think we're being left in the dark."

"Why us? Let's put our heads together. Rashawn is coming there and Reggie is coming here . . . hmmm."

"I guess we'll know when they both get here and there," Trina had said.

But Reggie hadn't arrived. And now Shelby had a sick feeling that Rashawn wasn't going to make it to Arizona either. She'd lingered just a bit longer around the station hoping that another train would come in—knowing this was the only one. Finally she called Chance from her car. What he told her nearly sent her through the roof. "Chance! I can't believe . . ." Shelby could barely speak. She was beyond flabbergasted.

"Shelby calm down. I had to allow you to go down there to the station. If we had gone, it could have been a disaster. I had to allow you to see if perhaps he would actually make it."

"But he didn't, dammit! My nephew didn't make it. And where in the hell is Rashawn while you're up here running around God's country with Juanita! You should have trusted me Chance. You should have trusted me!"

"I'm not running around with . . ." Chance looked over at Juanita who sat quietly in the passenger seat. Ovan was on his computer in the backseat. "Shelby . . . If I had told you what was going on you would have not been able to do this."

"Why? Where is my sister? Nobody is answering their phones. Where is everybody? I called Trina ya know! Now she's worried too. What's going on Chance? I bet Rashawn is nowhere near Arizona!"

"Shelby . . ." Chance's eyes burned as he held back emotion.

"The National Guard is right up ahead," Ovan said.

"Who the hell was that? Why are you at the National Guard? Where are you?"

"I'm in Oregon. But I'm not in Eugene. We're in Klamath, tracking the Amtrak route. We figured if we missed it or whatever at least you would be at the station, just in case. We've been on the road all day going from station to station. Now we're going off road I guess. We just got some directions on where they could get a plane, maybe."

Shelby began to wail. Chance knew he had to tell her the rest. She was hurting now. He was hurting her.

"Shelby. Listen," Chance began after parking the car. Juanita jumped out and Ovan followed her. "Rashawn has been hurt. She's okay—"

"What! Ooooooh Chance," Shelby cried.

"She's okay. She's had a car accident. She's in ICU and all your sisters are there with her except for Trina. When I get off the phone with you, I'll call Trina. It's my lie, I'll call her. You can hate me if you want, but I had to do it this way. I needed some extra hands and yours and Trina's were the ones I chose," he said, taking sole responsibility for a joint decision. "Reggie sort of ran away and he doesn't know his mother is hurt. We're trying to find him and take him home."

"Chance I can't believe you were a part of this. I will never forgive you for this!" Shelby hung up.

"Dammit!" Chance blurted slamming the cell phone against the steering wheel.

"Chance, come on," Juanita called.

Chance felt so much pent up anger inside. Why was he here? He needed to be with Rashawn. Reggie was not his son and neither was Junior but Rashawn was his wife, his world, the woman he loved. Juanita pulled open the door and tugged at his arm, bringing his thoughts back. "Come on."

"Juanita. Is Roman Junior's father?"

"Come on, Chance. I don't want to talk about that," she said pulling on his arm. He jerked away.

"Was it really Roman? Or maybe Doc. Which one did you screw? Which one!" he screamed. "Did you screw them both? While my wife was being raped and violated did you take a lovely little romp with both of them. Maybe you were just fuckin' Roman while Doc was kicking the shit outta me!" He pushed Juanita back slightly.

Ovan walked back to the car, apparently hearing Chance screaming. "Chance, pull yourself together."

"And you! Who the hell are you? Who? I'm out here running around God's country," he said thinking Shelby's heated words, "with who? Some weirdo from England who isn't even interested in finding my . . ." He couldn't finish the sentence. "Where are Reggie and Junior? What does Roman want with them . . . oh yeah you told me. He wants to *kill them*," Chance screamed.

Chapter 58

Shackled to the chair at the ankles, Reggie was unable to move while Hap took the blood from one of his ankles. He gritted his teeth in pain as Hap took vial after vial with that big needle. "There," he finally said laying the last vial on the tray. He then eyed Junior.

"What?" Junior asked.

"I just can't get over my thoughts," Hap said, rolling up Junior's sleeve.

Junior closed his eyes tight. "Awww shit man . . . come on. I hate needles."

"Me too," Hap said, sounding light-hearted before tying the tourniquet around Junior's arm and thumping the bend of his arm looking for veins. Finding one, he stabbed roughly, drawing blood. "This is sort of silly in a way. I mean, you have the same mother but—"

"No we don't," Reggie coughed out, recovering from his discomfort.

"Ahha! Just as I thought. Who is your mother?" Hap asked Junior.

"Don't tell him shit!" Reggie barked.

"Oh Reggie stop being difficult for no reason," Hap told him.

"Juanita Davis," Junior said.

Hap thought about the name for a moment and then shrugged, "Nope, don't know her but whatever," he said, happily labeling Junior's blood sample.

Chapter 59

Roman was none too happy about the scratches on his neck, no not at all. But if nothing else he knew now not to underestimate his opponents. The years had been strengthening for them whereas he, on the other hand had weakened. He needed to get to Oregon so that he could get Reggie's kidneys. He needed to just do it and leave to maybe South America. He'd already made arrangements to set up a new office somewhere else. He smiled at the thoughts of his globetrotting. He was truly an international celebrity—well at least with the FBI, CIA and now this renegade group of bounty hunters of which Ovan Dominguez was a part.

"Dominguez, what kind of name is that for a Brit?" he asked himself. "But then again, what kind of name was Tollome for a white man," he said, thinking aloud about his stepbrother Blain for the first time in days. His mother had told him that Blain's father was from South Africa . . . Johannesburg. Roman remembered wondering how a white man could be from Africa. "But then again, I didn't know anything back then. Nothing of real value anyway," he corrected.

It was amazing to him how complex and involving these experiments had become. At first when working with only one live patient and one dead one while in Jamaica, it was easier to cover his tracks that way. But in London, where he caught Ovan's tail, he had worked on two live patients—killing them both. As he progressed throughout Europe, all in all the test had been a success. He knew now where he had taken when he should have given and clipped where he should have fused. He'd figured out the magic combination. The ages of the previous victims . . . errr . . . involuntary kidney volunteers, Roman mentally corrected, were too old, he reasoned. He knew the next experiment would have to be perfect—no mistakes, as the next one would be performed on himself—right here in the US. Picking up the phone he called Hap.

"Hello," Hap answered sounding nearly out of breath.

"What are you doing, playing with the children?"

"Funny. Where are you?"

"No, where are you?"

"I'm where I said I would be when I said I would be here."

"You don't sound happy with me," Roman laughed.

"Hey, you didn't tell me I'd have all these people to deal with. And you sure as hell didn't tell me you had another son."

"I don't."

"Don't be so sure about that."

"I'm positive."

"There are two boys here and they are brothers. I've taken blood samples."

"Who is the other one?" Roman asked sounding almost tongue and cheek.

"Junior."

"Junior?"

"Yes."

"That's Chance Davis's boy. The DNA you're seeing is his mother's. They have the same mother."

"No they don't. He said his mother's name is Juanita."

"Juanita has my son? Good job Hap," Roman blurted, his heart was instantly lighter. "This is fabulous news. Now neither boy will die . . . this is fabulous." Roman had just recently pondered the thought of a second donor. He'd thought about using Rashawn's kidney—anything to keep from killing Reggie. But he'd run out of time in that thought process and had just opted for both of Reggie's kidneys—a full transplant. Once his life had been extended he was planning to continue his studies in South America—where the population was a bit more penetrable and where he could blend in a bit easier. He'd planned to take Reggie with him. Why not? They would truly be father and son then. "Father in son and vice versa." Roman smiled.

"Excuse me? These kids are leaving here alive? What about me? I'm not going to prison." Hap's voice brought Roman back from his reverie.

"You kill my children and you won't have to worry about prison."

Roman slammed closed the flip phone he'd picked up from the MetroPCS store before leaving town, and put a bit more speed behind his vehicle. Hap was a lot of things, but crazy wasn't one of the things Roman assumed about him. But now he wasn't so sure.

Chapter 60

"I need to go to the bathroom," Julia called out. It had been hours now. She'd awakened to find herself tied to a chair at the wrist and ankles. Junior was strapped in by the wrist only, with restraints. Reggie was sitting in the straitjacket with his ankles tied now with ropes since Hap found he'd needed more blood samples and the shackles were cutting off a degree of circulation.

Hap came from the backroom. "Fine, I'll take you."

"You're not about to stand there and watch me pee," Julia argued.

"If I don't, you can't go."

"Fine, I'll piss on the floor right here then," Julia growled.

"My that's not very ladylike. What would the queen say?"

"She'd tell me to cut off your balls," Julia spat.

"Sounds interesting. Have you ever even seen a man's balls?"

Reggie jerked at his restraints. "Hey man just take her to the bathroom. Why you gotta humiliate her this way."

"You stay out of it. I'm about tired of you. Frankly, I'm about tired of all of you."

"But I thought we were friends. Well until you started taking my blood like a vampire. Then yeah, I kinda fell out with you too . . ." Junior began.

"Shut up. If I had known you were his kid this whole thing would have gone differently."

"Well I think I told you whose kid I was and—" Junior went on.

"You don't even know what you're talking about. You're both Allen Roman's sons." Hap glared at Reggie who now stared wide-eyed with shock. It was the first time he'd heard the name of his father.

Hap roughly untied Julia, snatching her up from the chair. "Come on," he said, wiping the sweat that quickly appeared on his top lip. "Now I've got this gun. Don't play with me girlie," Hap threatened.

Julia jerked at his grip but could not break it. "You're not much fun anyway."

They disappeared down a hallway that led to the bathroom.

Leaning forward as much as he could, watching them disappear down the hallway, Junior looked at Reggie. "Do you believe him?"

"Believe what?"

"That we're brothers. That that Allen Roman cat—"

"Who is Allen Roman, Junior? Who? He's talking shit to scare us. Your father is Chance Davis. My father—"

"Is Allen Roman," Junior said.

"Just shut up. He's a liar and if he . . ." Reggie stretched his neck to see down the hall, which was impossible.

Suddenly they heard a scuffle. They heard Julia cry out and Hap yell. The sound of a body hitting the wall made Reggie call out for Julia. There was then silence.

"Aww Damn, Julia!" Reggie called again, jerking at the straps.

Julia appeared from the hallway then. She had Hap's gun tucked into the front of her pants before quickly working Junior's restraints. "Come on boys."

Junior's eyes were wide with excitement. "What the hell?"

"Who are you?" Reggie asked while she struggled with the jacket, freeing him. He began loosening the ties on his ankles.

"I guess you realize I'm not a teenager," she said, speaking quickly.

"No shit Sherlock," Junior exploded excitedly.

"Well not quite Sherlock but I guess you could call me a something like that. I'm a bounty hunter—and I'm here to capture your father and take him back to London for trial," she said looking Reggie deep into his eyes.

"Who is Allen Roman?" he asked.

"Look we'll talk on the road. Shit! Where did he put the car keys?" she asked hurriedly searching the small table where she had seen them last. "Go, go get in the car! I'll find them." Reggie and Junior started for the door. "They're probably in his damned pocket," she mumbled.

"No, I'll get them," Reggie insisted stepping back into the cabin.

"No, you boys go. I'm fine," she insisted.

Just then Hap appeared in the doorway. He was bleeding from the mouth and looked worked over. "You want these?" He dangled the keys that he'd pulled from his pocket.

Julia pointed at the gun she was holding on him. "Drop them Hap. Drop them and kick them this way. I'm not here to kill you."

"It doesn't matter bitch, if Roman finds you all gone, he'll do the honors so what the hell," Hap said. "I've got nothing to lose but a lot to gain!"

"Go on boys," Julia instructed, noticing them drifting closer to her.

"No. We won't leave you," Reggie barked. Julia slightly distracted took her eyes off Hap for one second.

Just then Hap charged her. The tussle began. There was a shot and Hap's head went back right before the second shot dropped him to his knees.

Junior ran to get the keys Hap dropped in the doorway before running back over to Julia, that's when he saw Julia bleeding. "Julia!"

"Buggas," she said smiling weakly, stumbling backward.

"I'll get something," Reggie said rushing into the back room where he'd seen Hap going in and out of with the blood samples he'd taken from him and Junior earlier. The room was set up like a hospital room—a surgical room. There were gurneys and stirrups, straps and restraints. There was a tray filled with surgical tools as well. His mind spun with the contemplation of what was to occur here.

"Come on Reggie. She's hurt bad," Junior said, rushing in with his hands covered in blood. Junior froze momentarily as well noticing the chamber of possible horrors.

"Shit!" Reggie grabbed up some bandages and ran to Julia's side. Her belly was bleeding profusely. She was weak. He held the bandages against the wounded area. "Julia, hang in there. Hang in there. Junior, look over there and see if there is anything for pain. She's gonna need something."

"I'm looking. I don't know the names. I . . ." Junior was freaking out. Reggie could tell. He glanced back at Julia who was coughing softly. Her eyes were at half mast. She was fading fast.

"Julia?" Reggie called her. She smiled weakly.

"Leave me," she said.

Reggie shook his head. "No way." His eyes were burning now. He glanced over at Hap, crumpled on the floor. Laying her softly on the floor he ran over to join Junior in his search for painkillers. Just then Reggie heard movement behind them.

Turning, he saw Hap on his knees. He was aiming a dart-like syringe right at Junior. "Die!" he called out letting the syringe fly. Pushing Junior out of the way, Reggie caught the syringe in the shoulder.

"Arrrrg," Reggie cried out in pain, ripping the dart out immediately.

The gunshot was louder than the last one as the bullet entered Hap's back and did not exit. Although blood spilled from his mouth before he fell forward. It was Julia's last brave act before she closed her eyes. "Julia!" Junior screamed, while rushing over to Reggie all at once.

"I'm okay. I'm okay," Reggie growled, trying to hide the pain that the fire in his shoulder had caused. The heat was spreading fast.

"Did he kill you? What was in that?" Junior asked, patting Reggie's arm. Reggie grimaced in pain.

"I don't know. I'm a little numb."

"Julia," Junior gasped, rushing over to Julia now. He lifted her head. "Julia?"

"Come on. We gotta go," Reggie said, sounding full of regret. "She told us to take the car. Let's go."

"We're gonna leave her?"

"We'll get help. We'll come back for her. We gotta get help!"

The boys rushed out of the cabin to the SUV. It was dark now and both knew they had no idea where they were but had to get out. Junior ran around to the passenger seat only to notice Reggie just standing by the driver side. "Come on," Junior yelled.

"I can't open the door man," Reggie confessed. "Shit!"

Chapter 61

Ovan climbed behind the wheel of the chopper, sliding into the previous pilot's headset. "Come on!" he called to Chance who shook his head reluctantly.

"Look fool, I've been fooling with your ass, following you all through God's free county but I refuse to just allow you to take me straight to his doorstep without knowing your real intensions. Something just doesn't feel right about you—about this whole thing."

"He's Ovan Dominguez, Chance! Get in the helicopter now! Quit playin'," Juanita screamed pushing Chance slightly.

At that point, Chance pushed back. "Juanita, stop it! Just stop pushing me. You've pushed me and pushed me and now I want you to stop." Chance raised his hand for a second or two of silence to clear his head. "You don't even know where we're going. Why hasn't that person made contact? You act just as lost as we are." Chance pointed at himself and Juanita. "Why would I allow you to take me any further into this?"

"Chance, now is not the time. You have to get in that chopper and go find your wife's son. You have to find our son . . . my son," Juanita paused. Her eyes welled up with tears. "You have to find my son," she cried pitiably. Chance stood his ground for a moment longer looking at Juanita as she cried. Ugly hot tears streamed her face. He knew she had no one. No one but him. It had always been that way. No matter how many men she'd been through, it always came back to him. Pulling her into his arms he hugged her tight.

"I'm going to find your son." He pulled her hair the way he always did when pulling her head back and looking at her face up close—something he hadn't done in a long time. I'm going to find my sons." He kissed her tenderly. "I'll always love you, Nita . . . but I'm through after this. I'm through with it all."

"So, Chance, are you coming?" Ovan yelled over the sounds of the propellers. He'd not flinched at the questions Chance had fired at him. It was clear he had no intention of answering them right at that moment. Chance, as if accepting that he had no other option, ran around and jumped in the helicopter. Ovan lifted off immediately.

Chapter 62

Trina burst through the hospital doors. “Who the hell is in charge of this place? I need to see my sister!” she bellowed. Carlotta, hearing clear from the waiting room rushed into the lobby. “Trina!” she called. Trina, with a serious expression on her face, marched up to her big sister. “So where is she?”

“She’s still in ICU. She’s not letting go of the coma she drifted into. She was talking a little when she got here, asking for Reggie mostly, but now . . .” Carlotta shook her head. “The doctors don’t understand why she won’t wake up. She had come out of it when Chance was here earlier but she went back in. And then they said there was a disturbance yesterday and they thought she was awake. The monitors read all kinds of brain activity but . . . nothing.”

“What happened? Does anybody even know what happened? I mean, were there other people involved in the accident? I heard nothing on the news.”

"We don't really know," Carlotta began.

"God," Trina sighed.

"Reggie and Junior are missing," she finally blurted.

"Well I know that shit now!" Trina got a little loud slamming her fist on her hip. "Shelby called me she was hysterical. She went to meet Reggie at the train station after Chance tricked her into believing he would be there. But he wasn't there, and then Chance told her that they were missing. They were kidnapped. Who kidnapped them? Do they know?"

"Allen Roman—their father," Rita said, joining in the conversation. She had overheard most of the conversation.

"Their father!" Trina snapped.

"Their father?" Carlotta's eyes widened. "Roman?" Rita nodded. "Roman is alive?"

"Roman is alive and he's Junior's father too. Chance told me right after he found out. I guess he didn't know until now."

"You know, I've always suspected that Junior was not Chance's son," Trina added in. "But Allen Roman!"

"Well the boy doesn't look anything like Chance. Plus Juanita is like . . ." Rita shook her head.

"So was she like dating him while he was torturing our sister! That woman, she needs to be slapped fa sho!" Carlotta jumped in.

"Let's not start on her. She's got a missing child, too. No matter who the father is. She's a mother just like us. It's just . . . Let's not start on her," Ta'Rae said, hoping to end the Juanita bashing before it began.

"It's been so crazy; I guess we all know a little bit of a little bit. Chance came over the house a few years back and was talking about Roman and the possibilities of him being alive—wanted Terrell to do some investigating." Rita went on. "Terrell convinced him that it was fruitless and Chance gave up the thought. He just wanted to raise Reggie in peace I guess."

"And now this." Ta'Rae sighed.

"So, is it kidnapping for Roman to have his own children?" Trina asked.

Carlotta swooned. "Oh Lord, I need to sit down. Does Rashawn know about this?"

"Maybe that's why she's not coming out of the coma!" Trina blurted. "Maybe in her back of her mind she's knowing all this and trying to block it out."

"Hello everyone," the doctor said entering the lobby. "Rashawn is awake again." Trina jumped up from the seat and rushed behind Carlotta to the elevator that would take them to Rashawn's room.

Chapter 63

Junior, white-knuckling the wheel, tried not to pay Reggie's growing moans any mind but it was hard. He sounded wounded and in a lot of pain.

"You okay Bro?" he asked, realizing instantly how true his term was and how much a difference it made in how he felt suddenly. He tried to divert his eyes to look at him but the road curved mercilessly. Reggie had dug round the back pack that was still in the SUV and found the cell phone but here was no signal.

"Yeah, yeah," Reggie groaned. "Watch the road. I'm okay."

"I'm scared Reggie. I'm scared!" Junior confessed. This was no time to joke. There was no humor in this situation at all.

"I know."

Twisting the wheel suddenly Junior followed the quick turning road. "This doesn't feel familiar. I think we're lost! I think we're lost!" Junior panicked.

"We can't be Junior. There's only one road."

"No there isn't. You weren't driving. There were little roads that veered off. I think we veered off!"

"No we didn't!" Reggie growled while attempting to sit up in the seat.

"Shit! I wish I could see," Junior cried out, just as a car with blinding high beams headed straight at them. "Shit!" Junior screamed twisting the wheel sharply to miss the oncoming car. The twist of the wheel caused the large vehicle to head into the shallow soft shoulder. "Oh no! We're stuck!" Junior panicked.

"Don't panic," Reggie said, trying to reach for him with the arm that still worked, but missed. Junior was opening the door. "Stay in here!" Reggie called.

Junior ran around to the front of the car. Reggie could see Junior's wide eyes reflecting off the headlights like a deer frozen in fear from the horrible sight he was seeing. "What?" Reggie called, lowering the window.

"We're so stuck mannn!" Junior lamented, slapping the sides of his head. Reggie then opened the door, dragging himself from the front seat and out of the car. He could see Junior's eyes. They were covering him, noticing his leg dragging. "My God Reggie, your leg . . . your leg is dead man.

You're dying man! Dude killed you!" Junior was freaking out.

"I'm not dying," Reggie hedged. He didn't know for sure if it was fact or not but now was not the time to throw Junior any deeper into already panicked state. "My shit is just asleep. I think Dude just shot me with a tranquilizer . . . like what he gave Julia before . . ."

Both boys suddenly thought about Julia at the same time. Regret caused them both to swallow thick lumps that formed in their throats. "I wish . . ." Reggie began. Junior nodded, knowingly.

"Me too," Junior chimed in.

Just then the car with the lights was headed back. They could see it from far away. Junior ran around to the driver's side and snatched open the door, quickly grabbing the cell phone from off the seat where they had been waiting to get a signal. He stood in the road waving it back and forth, knowing the reflection from the face of it would appear strobe-like—*at least it work for the bus drivers back home.* The car approached quickly seemingly headed toward them.

Pulling up close, the driver pulled over slightly without turning off the motor to the car. The door opened and out stepped a tall dark skinned man. So mirror-like were his features that just the sight of him tightened Reggie's stomach.

Junior too seemed stunned at his powerful appearance, despite his age. As if hit by a brick suddenly both boys knew immediately who this man had to be. "Allen Roman—you bastard," Reggie said just above a whisper. He didn't know this man from the history of him as a rapist. He'd only known that Hap made this man seem to be, a monster, and that Julia had died back at that cabin to keep him from doing something horrible to them. Reggie knew he should fear this man, but he didn't realize at the moment, just how much.

In the silence of the night, his words were clearly heard. "Is that any way to address to your father," Roman said.

Chapter 64

"Juanita isn't a bad woman," Ovan said after many moments of silence between the two of them.

"I never said she was," Chance grumbled.

"She thinks she's wicked."

"How would you know what she thinks?"

"She told me. She thinks you hate her now."

"Well my jury is out on that."

"I know you don't. You could never hate our Nita," Ovan grinned, flying the helicopter, without looking at him. "I could tell by that kiss you could never hate our girl."

"Our girl?"

Ovan just smiled slyly. "She's got something I like in a woman," he admitted.

"Yeah, I'm sure that's what they all thought," Chance said with a smirk, glancing out over the ground below them. He was surprised at how little queasiness he felt. He was actually okay with this. "But if you open that box, you besta believe you about to get all cracked out. Addicted, like a meth head." Chance confessed. Ovan smiled.

"I can handle it."

"Yeah okay," Chance said looking out over the whiteness below.

"So, how are you feeling about all this?"

"Shit, have I had any time to think about all this? I mean, I could get back and my wife could be dead."

"And would it make a difference in how you feel about her lad? Does finding out that Nita was sleeping with Roman change how you feel about Junior?"

"Well, no."

"If Rashawn, heaven forbid, were to pass away, would it change how you feel about Reggie?"

"God no!" Chance balked at the words, the thought of Rashawn dying.

"That's what I thought. You are a father, Chance, and a fuckin' fabulous one, too," Ovan said with a wide grin crossing his lips. "I could only wish my father had been such."

"You had a bad father?"

"Put it like this, my father liked being a father, unfortunately he wasn't careful with whom he fathered children with."

"Aw," Chance nodded understandingly.

"As I've told you, much too many people's mistake I'm not British by birth. I'm from South Africa," Ovan began. "My mother was London born so she took me there when my father . . . well anyway . . . and now I do work in London so . . ." Ovan was sounding as if rambling a little.

"And what do you do for a living there Ovan?" Chance dug. Ovan gave him a side glance and another of his most charming smiles.

"Oh, Chance, that is so not important, but if you must hear it again, I'm an international bounty hunter. I hunt people for money. I hunt people for the government. But in this case, I hunt Allen Roman for my own personal issues with the bastard."

"Tell me more." Chance said, feeling finally as if he was about to hear the truth.

Ovan went on, talking calmly all the while whipping the helicopter through the air. "My father was a traveler—his work took him to many places around the world. He was a minister."

"You're a preacher's son?" Chance asked sounding totally surprised. Ovan continued talking.

"I supposed you could say that. Anyway, my father eventually traveled to Jamaica—without my mother I might add. He absolutely loved the people there. He said the people were very 'receptive.' And clearly so, as he, while there, got involved with a native woman and well, he fathered a child with her so yes . . . He indeed loved it there and clearly had a good reception. It was some years before my mother became painfully aware of why he was actually traveling to Jamaica so often after that first trip."

"To see his son, the one he made in there in Jamaica?"

"And the boy's mother—I'm sure over the years he'd fallen in love with her, despite the fact that strangely enough, the woman was married—and to a black-skinned man at that. Her husband didn't take to kindly to my father's visits and on one occasion he shot and killed him. I supposed I would have too." Just then the snow/rain mix began. "Damn Oregon. I had a feeling we'd catch bad weather. But as they say, wait twenty minutes and it will change," he chuckled.

Chance digested Ovan's story for a moment. "What happened to the boy? He would be your brother . . . right? I mean, wow, that's a tragic story Ovan. I'm sorry."

"Yes. Well he would be my half brother and yes, it's truly tragic."

"What happened to him?"

"Thanks to Allen Roman, your wife killed him."

Chance gasped as he quickly put the story together. Rashawn had killed Allen Roman's half brother, Blain Tollome-known more by his alter ego as Doc. He was a big man, brutish and mad. He loved Rashawn and stalked her mercilessly, driven mostly by the mental control of Allen Roman who fed him drugs and influenced his thoughts through hypnosis. Rashawn thought he had raped her and that he was Reggie's father until it came to light that Blain was sterile due to a childhood trauma. Rashawn had killed Blain Tollome thinking he was Reggie's father, the rapist who had taken her in the parking lot of Moorman University so many years ago, leaving her pregnant. But no, the rapist was indeed Allen Roman. She found out after she'd shot and killed Blain the night he came to tell her the truth about Roman. Blain had his own set of issues but being a rapist wasn't one of them. Rashawn took many years to recover from shooting the wrong man—despite the fact that Blain aka Doc was a wanton and deviant criminal who had been terrorizing the campus with a date rape drug. Roman too had terrorized with the use of the drug but he used the drug on Rashawn for his own purposes and framed Blain who easily looked guilty in Rashawn's eyes. Despite Blain's white skin, the slight family resemblance between Blain and Reggie, Rashawn in her weakened mental capacities due to the drug's grip had believed all she was told by Allen Roman about Blain being guilty of raping her.

"So there you have it. My name is Dominic Tollome . . . well it was. When my mother died, I changed my name hoping it would change my life."

"It's not that easy Ovan," Chance commiserated. "Sometimes life is what it is."

Ovan smiled. "Bloody well said."

Just then Chance spotted a cabin. "Look!"

"That has to be the one. If not, it's a great place to start," Ovan said, aiming for the clearing.

Landing the chopper, both men jumped out and headed for the door. "There's no car, and there's only one light on—look, tire tracks. This doesn't feel right," Ovan explained, holding Chance back with his hand outstretched while pulling out his gun. Chance had a feeling he was carrying a piece but hadn't seen it until now. Chance moved against the side of the cabin while Ovan crept up to the door. Unannounced he kicked it open only to barely miss the gun shots fired continually until the gun clicked empty. Pointing his gun, Ovan slowly looked around the door way only to quickly lower his weapon. "Julia! Aw love—bloody hell!" he gasped rushing in. Chance followed him into the grisly scene. Ovan gathered up the young woman in his arms cradling her not caring that her blood spilled on his clothing and hands.

"Who is she?" Chanced asked.

"She's my partner. She's the one that was on the train." Ovan stroked her face tenderly. "What's happened?"

Chance felt bad now for doubting Ovan earlier about having an actual partner in the field.

"I thought you were Roman. I was going to blow his head off for ya," she whispered. "I killed that prick Hap. He did this to me."

Ovan picked her up. "The boys?" he asked her, waiting for her to catch her breath between painful sounding pants.

"They got away," she finally answered. "They're in a black SUV headed south—I hope."

"Chance, you have to wait here for Roman. I'm going to fly Julia back to the National Guard station. They can help her there. I'll be right back in just a bit," he said without given Chance much opportunity to answer while he tucked Julia's limp body in the helicopter. Chance felt himself nodding but that was all. "You'll need this," he said, handing Chance the gun. The weight was heavier than he thought this being the first time he'd ever held one.

Watching the chopper lift off, Chance realized then he could be the one to kill Allen Roman—or be killed by him—this night. He thought about Rashawn laying there in the hospital. He thought about Reggie and Junior and all the blood in the cabin. How much was theirs? He thought about the dead man laying there next to Julia and realized that no matter how cold it was out there that night he was not going back in that cabin.

In the darkness Chance waited for what felt like hours.

Chapter 65

"Is Allen Roman alive?" Rashawn asked her sisters who gathered around her bed.

"No. You've been hallucinating. The doctors say you passed out behind the wheel and went off the road, hitting an embankment," Ta'Rae lied quickly, speaking softly while stroking Rashawn's hair. She also gave her vitals a once over, Ta'Rae being the family physician. Rashawn had her own private doctor but Ta'Rae did back up for everyone in the family, giving them all that extra attention that their own doctors could not.

"Where is Chance?" Rashawn then asked. The women looked around at each other.

"He's with Rainey," Trina lied. She didn't have all the facts but jumping in with a good whopper when needed was always her specialty.

Rashawn smiled weakly. "Is Reggie on his way home? Chance said he was gonna go get him and bring him home. Or was I dreaming? Where is he?"

"Yes," Rita answered, trying to sound convincing. "Chance is on his way to get Reggie, beat his ass and bring him home."

"Good. Because I had a horrible dream that Allen Roman was alive and said he was going to hurt him. I tried to kill him with my bare hands. I remember thinking, the hell you will. I hate dreaming about Allen that way. It must have been because of me and Reggie's fight. Whenever me and Reggie fight I think about Allen Roman."

"You were just overworked and stressed out. When you get out, you just need to get away."

Rashawn closed her eyes. "Yeah, maybe we'll go visit Shelby in Oregon."

The sisters looked at each other. "Honey, the doctor said we could only stay a minute. We're breaking all kinds of rules. We have to go now," Carlotta said rushing the other's out of the room. Rashawn nodded without opening her eyes past little slits.

Outside the room all of the sisters looked at one another. "Okay, so how long do we keep the lies up?"

"As long as it takes."

"Has anyone heard from Chance?"

"No."

"Is Shelby on her way?"

"You know it. She's probably at the airport now!" Trina blurted. "And if you think I'm mad, you just wait! Why you thought we shoulda been left outta this . . . y'all just insane in the membrane. Our blood is thicker than any of this." Trina fanned her hand around the hall where they stood. "Our sister needs us all together to pull her through! Believe that!"

Chapter 66

Juanita watched the helicopter land and Ovan climb out with the young woman in his arms. He looked so very concerned. The paramedics had met him on the landing strip. They strapped the young girl in the gurney. Juanita had no idea who she was . . . but no matter, she wasn't Junior . . . or Reggie. Juanita tried to fight the negative thoughts she had growing.

"Poor girl," she forced herself to say.

Chance wasn't with him. Where was Chance? Where were the boys? She was overwrought.

Her mind drifted back to Allen Roman. He was so dark and sinister. She couldn't even accept that she actually had found him sexy and seductive at one time. She shook her head in shame thinking about the time she allowed him to have sex with her during their sessions. At first it was a game. He'd teased her about his obsession with a woman he was stalking. He pulled the jealousy out of her with his talk of how he had sexed this other woman. In graphic detail he talked about their encounters until Juanita's passion would nearly drip from the mouth of her womanly cistern. "How could I not know it was Rashawn he was talking about," she said now. "There were so many clues."

Once while sexing her, she could have sworn he called her Rashe. "Rashe . . . Rashawn . . . ugh, Nita." Juanita slapped her head. Allen Roman had an accent that would slip out from time to time. She should have picked up on it . . . and then hiding those videos from the cops and the DA. "That was just plain wrong." Juanita went on browbeating herself. Just showing them those videos could have helped Rashawn's case. Rashawn was acquitted of murder in the case of Blain—receiving only probation for the manslaughter charge that stuck, but surely those videos could have showed everyone how controlling Allen Roman was. And the sessions with Blain confirmed that, maybe they could have put Allen away for good for all the abuse he inflicted on his sick brother Blain Tollome. Juanita had all but burned the sessions she'd had with Blain. He was even worse than Allen. There was no way she wanted them to see her orally pleasing that crazy man and going at it like two animals in all positions. Blain too was masterful and powerful.

Again she shook her head, feeling the heat coming between her legs. Right then she had to realize that what she felt was not want—for she hated Roman more than then anyone could hate anything. What she felt was uncontrollable—just like the doctors had told her she would feel as she reached recovery of her sexual obsession. "I'm gonna get on my medication—I promise God. Please bring my baby back to me," she begged. "I swear I'm doing this." Tears came streaming down her cheek faster than she could wipe them away.

She watched as Ovan jumped back in the helicopter and lifted off. Ovan too was a masterful and determined man. She could only hope he thought of her as more than just a piece of flesh.

Chapter 67

Chance waited in the darkness, each sound more startling than the last. Again, the rain began coming down turning quickly into snow. He thought about Ovan's words now. "Doc was his brother?" he asked himself.

Chance shook his head, as he thought about the role of fathers in the life of their sons. The ironic twist of fate he was now a part of. "Junior is Allen Roman's son," Chance mumbled.

He looked at the gun in his hand and cried out. "Junior is Allen Roman's son! What is happening to my life! How did this one man get into my life this way?"

He thought about the day he met Rashawn. He instantly fell in love with her. She was being stalked by this crazy boyfriend of her best friend. "Ever since I've known her crazy men have desired her . . . Maybe I'm flippin' crazy too." Chance huffed. He then thought about Juanita. He was crazy about her at one time. "That's for damn sure." He laughed. Suddenly he focused on the thoughts in his head. "God I hope my life isn't flashing before my eyes."

"If this man shows up, I don't know what I'ma do. I guess kill him. I'm so angry right now," Chance yelped waving the gun around. "What did I ever do to him? What did I ever do to deserve this?"

Stomping around in the snow, Chance continued his diatribe, airing out his angst and misery over all he'd been through at the hand of Allen Roman.

He'd been beaten, and now cheated out of the one thing he wanted more than anything: a son. Sure he had Rainey, but a son . . . or maybe it was a son with Juanita. "He even took Juanita from me," Chance bellowed. "Was my life too easy?" he asked the heavens, dark and empty of stars. "Was that the problem? Was I taking my life for granted? Was I being pompous? Chance Davis—always the one with the right answers for everybody," he mocked himself. "Well I don't have any answers now. I don't even know where my kids are. There's a dead man in that cabin," he whispered to God, pointing with the gun toward the open door of the cabin.

"When this is over, what will I have? What did you leave me with? Will I even have a wife?"

Thinking of Rashawn, he pulled out his cell phone, foolishly searching for a signal. He was losing control of his senses now and threw the phone into the dirty tracks left by the helicopter. "What if she's dead? What will I have?" he yelled.

Just then the helicopter lights appeared in the darkness. Ovan was on his way back.

Chapter 68

The lights of the helicopter went over their heads. Junior groaned out loud at the sight of it disappearing in the distance. "Yes, that was your rescue. But it's over now," Roman said. "Besides, you're safer with me than anywhere else in the world right now."

"Where are we going anyway?" Reggie asked noticing they were not headed back to the cabin.

"We're sure not going to the cabin. I'm sure if you're out here, Hap is either dead or about to be arrested. I don't want any parts of either of those scenarios."

"You're crazy," Junior barked, cutting him off.

"No crazier than that mother of yours," Roman said stretching his arms over the width of the backseat.

"Don't talk about my mother," Junior yelped.

"It's okay Junior, he's just goading ya," Reggie said. "Don't give into it."

Roman laughed and then playfully slapped Reggie's shoulder. "Oh and don't let me start on that mother of yours. She tried to choke me yesterday."

"You saw my mother? She's in Arizona. How—" Reggie began.

"No she's not. She's in a coma," Roman answered sucking the air through his teeth, sounding cocky and bombastic. "Now see how helpful I've been. Chance isn't here to tell you boys anything you need to know. He's nowhere around when you need a father figure. Where is he? Is he even looking for you? Doubt it."

"I don't believe you. You're lying. My mother is in Arizona," Reggie said, trying to force his body to turn but it was nearly completely lifeless and heavy on one side.

"Believe what you want," Roman said before tossing Rashawn's cell phone cover over the seat and into Reggie's lap. "Would have brought the whole thing but then, hey! They would have found me."

Reggie stared at the ugly floral cell phone cover that Rashawn always thought was so pretty. She covered her phone with it. It was dirty. His lip buckled and his rage grew.

"My dad—" Junior began.

Turning his attention to Junior, Roman's voice lifted in volume. "Let's get this straight! I'm your father! I'm all you've got kid," Roman said, before thumping hard, the back of Junior's head.

"But you're trying to kill us," Junior said, sounding tense, his speed increasing.

"I am not. Who told you that?"

"You were trying to kill me. You were going to take my kidneys both of them. I'm not stupid, I heard Hap talking, and I know you can't live without kidneys," Reggie said squeezing his mother's cover, feeling it crack under his grip. His heart was racing and his mind was soaring. He was not going to let this night happen.

"No. I was going to do nothing of the sort. I would have never left you without any kidneys. I was going to give you mine, but then, when I found out about Junior all that changed. Now I'm just going to take one from each of you. This is actually a great day. I can't understand why you can't see that."

"You're sick mannnnn," Junior said, twisting his face up in growing anger.

"Not for long," Roman said, sounding smug. Reggie had heard enough. No one was taking anything from him or his brother. He had decided. If he and Junior were going to die tonight it was not going to be at the hand of this maniac. Dropping the cover, with his good hand, he reached over and grabbed the wheel firmly.

Chapter 69

The car rolled twice over the embankment and down the one hundred yards of cliff, ending back on its wheels and bouncing with the impact. Reggie fought hard to stay conscious as his head hammered against the window until finally he cracked it. Looking over he saw Junior. He was leaning over in the seat. Reggie shook him hard. "Come on Junior! Come on!" His emotions were at a peak. Junior stirred. "Come on," he begged then in a softer tone. Reaching over and opening the door with his strong arm, he shoved Junior out. Junior stumbled around before falling to his knees. Reggie struggled to pull himself free from the car and made his way around to Junior dragging him to his feet. Junior slowly came to his senses.

"We gotta get outta here," Junior mumbled, realizing he would have to help Reggie walk. Together they held each other up making their way in the darkness. In the cold. In the snow. In the silence of the night, Reggie could hear the door of the wrecked car opening. He could almost hear the man who claimed to be his father stepping into the soggy, wet snowy, marsh that lay beneath his heavy feet.

"I'm not in the mood for this. We don't time for this," his said. His heavy baritone echoing in the night sent a chill of both of the boy's spines.

"Come on, we've got to just keep going," Reggie said moving as quickly as he could through the thick marsh. He was being nearly pulled along by Junior and without Junior he would surely fall. He could feel the man closing in on them from behind. Realizing they were indeed not moving as fast as they could go, he stopped in his tracks. "Go Junior, leave me. You can move faster without me," he told Junior pulling free from his arm.

"No! Are you freakin' crazy? I'm not leaving you," Junior cried.

"Go get help," Reggie demanded.

Suddenly a shot rang out in the night. Junior yelled out a pain-filled cry and dropped to his knees. All Reggie could think was that he was hit by the bullet of Allen Roman's gun. Turning to face the man, Reggie could see his shadow. He became enraged. His weakened limbs became strong as he charged the shadowy figure standing under the reflection of the full moonlight. Tackling him like the star quarterback that he hoped one day to be, they grappled. Reggie pummeled him. "You shot my brother. You hurt my mother. You . . . you . . ." Slugging him hard with hot tears streaming down his face, Reggie cursed him bitterly. "You bastard."

"Reggie!" Junior screamed, distracting him just enough for Roman to get the upper hand pinning Reggie beneath him.

The gun appeared and Reggie knew he had to shoot or be shot. He grabbed at Roman's hand with both of his, twisting at the gun this way and that.

Roman growled and spat as he wrestled with his younger self. He saw his own eyes in the young Reggie's widened orifices. Dark and menacing but with one thing missing . . .

"You're my son!" Roman cried out. "Reggie, you are my son!"

"I could never be your son. I could never have a father as evil as you," Reggie said before feeling his finger on the trigger and pulling it.

Their eyes met for a moment before Roman's closed in death and his lifeless body gave way.

"Reggie!" Junior called again rushing over and shoving Roman's dead body off of Reggie. He pulled Reggie to his feet. "Come on," he screamed.

The skies showed no mercy as the clouds released buckets of snow and rain mixed. The wind took the snow flurries south and then east, blinding them. The weight of their clothes was heavy as they attempted to climb the steep embankment. Junior led with Reggie working hard to keep up. The weakness was returning as the adrenaline was wearing off. "Junior," Reggie called up. "I can't make it. Go on and get help!" he called, his voice, weak against the sounds of the climate burdened trees cracking, snapping and whistling the Oregon winds through their branches.

"No!" Junior screamed, sliding down until he was equal with Reggie. He began unbuckling his belt. "I'm going to put this belt around your leg and mine and when I move you move, okay!"

"You're crazy."

"I ain't crazy . . . I'm your brother," Junior said, smiling weakly while following through on his plan. "Plus I saw it in a spy movie. It's gonna work."

"You're so crazy," Reggie said, allowing a weak smile to cross his lips as well.

Together they started up the hill again.

Chapter 70

"I don't see anything in this snow." Chance said nearly leaning out of the helicopter. They had spied the SUV in the ditch and now searched for Roman's car or worse, the boys' dead bodies.

Circling, Ovan took the helicopter dangerously low. Chance could feel his stomach easing upward but he fought the sensation to vomit.

"Look there," Ovan said pointing to a clearing down below. I think that's a car."

"God! look!" Chance exclaimed seeing what looked like a large animal crumbled on the ground not far from the car. "It's Roman! It's gotta be!"

Just then they saw the boys, waving frantically on the hill side, begging to be rescued.

"There they are! There they are!!" Chance screamed excitedly.

Chapter 71

Spring had taken a while to come in this year. It was still cold and fog hung over the Palemos until nearly noon on most days.

Rashawn didn't mind, as her home was warm and cozy. With the extra time she had now, she'd even gotten around to installing the insert in the fireplace so that they could use it. Normally she was too busy to worry about the little comforts like that but not anymore. She'd taken a year's sabbatical. It was understood by the University's hiring committee; however, her job as dean would not be waiting for her when she returned, if she returned to Moorman. She didn't care. Her body needed time, her family needed time. Reggie needed her time. The counselors said his refusal to talk about the shooting was normal and it may be years before he would be able to face what he'd done.

His physical health had returned for the most part, although there were intermittent nerve spasms from the animal tranquilizer Hap Washburn had stabbed him with. This condition would prevent him from playing professional football for a long time—if ever. But he had other skills. He was an excellent artist. He could work with oils and other medium and was getting better with each portrait or still life.

From the window, Rashawn could see Chance pulling in with Junior behind the wheel. They were talking and Chance was smiling. It was good seeing them both smile again. Rashawn believed in her heart that Junior and Chance had been through the worst of all this. Their innocence was snatched from them and only the worse of realities were left for them to deal with—with no preparation at all. At least she had always felt one day Reggie would have to come to grips with who his father was. She didn't know to what degree and sure she never thought it was be life or death but still she knew the day would come—but not Junior. She knew all along that Reggie had the blood of a madman flowing through him but not Junior. Poor Chance—Rashawn never felt Chance would have to deal with Allen Roman on any level again. It had been beyond traumatic for Chance and Junior to have their lives ripped apart this way.

Rashawn thought about her conversation with Juanita in the hospital—Juanita had come to see her.

"How sorry do I need to be Rashawn?" Juanita said, sitting the flowers on the table by the window. "Because trust me . . . I have enough sorry to cover all the bases. I swear it."

"Not sure what you mean?" Rashawn answered.

"I've lied. I've cheated. I've schemed. I'ma mess," she went on, smiling weakly.

"Juanita, you act like any of that hurt anybody other than yourself," Rashawn told her.

"And my son," she said, squeezing her lips together so that her dimple appeared in her cheek.

"Yes. You've hurt Junior."

"And Chance too," Juanita added. "I tore his world apart. He doesn't love me anymore," she said, sounding truly sad—no act this time. Rashawn remembered feeling sad for Juanita. Realizing then how much she counted on Chance's love and would do anything to keep it.

"Juanita. Chance has always loved you in his own way, and I think he always will. But this is something he's going to have to get over. Junior too. Chance is not his father. You should have told him. Sure he could have guessed or whatever . . . but it was your job to tell him straight out. Even if you didn't know about Allen Roman, you should have said something—given the man some credit."

"I . . ." Juanita stammered but held onto her dignity as much as she could. "I didn't want to lose him."

"Ahh," Rashawn nodded.

"He loves you so much and I didn't want to lose him to you."

"Well . . . I don't know what to say."

"They were so close, Chance and Junior," Juanita sighed. "God I can't believe I let this happen. I know I didn't know about Allen being Junior's father but I could have found out. I had my doubts but I . . ."

Rashawn fanned her hand to silence her. "Juanita, it's okay. Chance is not going to stop loving Junior. He's just not. Just like he never treated Reggie any different even after what happened to him. Chance is the only father those boys know."

"Chance is a big man." Juanita nodded in agreement with her words.

"Yes, he is. And he's a good father."

"Yes, he is. Rainey is a lucky girl."

"Reggie and Junior are lucky boys."

Rashawn reached out for her hand. Jaunita grabbed it tight. "Shawnie, you know we can't be friends, right?"

Juanita smiled in her normal naughty way. She was a vixen and no matter what she would always be one.

Rashawn smiled back and then furrowed her brow playfully. "God no . . . never that."

"Hey Shawnie, what's good to eat?" Junior asked, walking in the house, bringing her mind back to the now.

"Oh man I cooked up a storm. You name it, I cooked it," Rashawn teased, "full moon you know that."

"Oh I love a full moon at your house. Ma just starts howling, at least here there's food." Junior joked. Rashawn snickered. "Where's my brother?"

"In his room painting of course," Rashawn answered watching Junior head down the hall. From behind he looked just like Reggie. Big and bulky. He'd grown a lot in a year and now it was undeniable they were brothers. The resemblance was crystal clear now that everyone allowed themselves to see it.

Chance kissed her lightly on the lips and stared at her a long time. "I love you," he said.

"And you'll just never know how much I love you."

Epilogue

"Juanita. I can't believe this, you're forty-six years old."

"You can't? Oh my God if you only knew how much I didn't want to believe it," Juanita gasped. "Can I do this? I mean physically—can I really do this?"

"I think so. You're a strong woman," he said. "All that taking care of yourself last year paid off. You're strong as a horse."

Staring at the doctor, her eyes burned. It had been over fifteen years since she sat in this seat confused and wondering what to do about her predicament. The last time she was scared and lied about who was responsible. But this time, there would be no need. She had fallen in love with Ovan—with his crazy ass. Domonic Tollome—Blain Tollome's brother. And best of all he had fallen in love with her. Still he traveled all over the world in disguise, lying about his identity—whatever it took to catch a skip. As an international bounty hunter, he was always busy but at least now he had a home to come to when he finished the job. He had told her once that after his brother Blain had been killed he realized he had no one. His mother died not too many years after his father was murdered by Allen Roman's father.

"It's a weird feeling knowing you're not related to anyone," he had told her. "I refused to think that Allen Roman was my only kin . . . ugh God. So when I found out about Reggie and that Roman was actually going to kill him. I had to stop him. Even though we don't share blood—Reggie well, Junior too, they're my family—in a way."

"That's why you said it was a personal matter."

"Quite. I wasn't supposed to even be on the case," he added, biting the grape from the small bunch she held over his head. "Coulda lost my license but . . . didn't care. And now look—again it's all worked out." They'd been lounging all day since he would be leaving the next morning.

"It's kinda weird you 'sorta' being related to my son and now we're . . ." Juanita giggled shyly. He pulled her head in to his and kissed her hungrily.

"How about this, lovey, I'll be 'sorta' related to him and have relations with you, is that all right?" he joked. Juanita laughed not knowing even then, that they would have more than simply relations, now he would truly be blood related. Now with the baby coming, he would be family.

Questions for Discussion

1. What are your thoughts on Juanita?

2. Do you think she is a redeemable character?

3. What are your thoughts on Ovan?

4. Do you think he and Juanita are meant for each other?

5. Why did Chance not find out about Chance Jr.'s, true paternity sooner?

6. Do you think Chance still loved Juanita?

7. Is it possible for a man to love his ex-wife and still be loyal to his current one?

8. Do you feel that Junior is an unusually happy boy or perhaps he's inwardly dark and harboring resentments toward Juanita, Rashawn, and Chance?

9 Do you believe that Reggie will recover from this experience and if so, what will his relationships with his mother, brother, and Chance be like?

10 What was your favorite part of the book?

UPCOMING NOVEL

Back Matter

A Dark Comedy

Introduction

In the world of entertainment, we the public only see what we are shown. Concealed behind fictitious names and events, there's often much truth hidden behind flowery rhetoric and even more behind blatant lies. Frequently, the story heard is not the true story told. Metaphorically speaking, the meaty truth of the tale is sometimes within the written pages of fiction, far from the spine, and sometimes, we can get a glimpse of that truth from what we read on the back cover.

The only problem with that is when one tastes life via this abstract version—this thing called fiction—for so long, after a while one may no longer know what's real and what's made up.

Back Matter is a story about just that.

—Aurora Middleton—

Back Matter

by

Michelle McGriff

Chapter 1

The limousine arrived in front of the elegant hotel. Her heart was pounding but she knew this was the night of nights for her so she would have to do this. There would never be a second chance to make this first impression. The millionaire James Byron Smith would be here tonight, and along with him his entourage of band members, and an assortment of large bodyguards.

Her heart was beating like a wild island drum as her breathing became shallow, so much so that it was more like a panting. This panting caused her ample bosom to rise and fall, her areolas tipping dangerously near the edge of her low-cut designer original—the off-the-shoulder number. She was looking like an Oprah impersonator.

She smoothed down the velvet over her svelte hips and stepped out onto the red carpet strip.

Her diet had worked wonders. She had dropped sixty pounds in ten days. Surely, she looked twenty-five again, instead of forty.

Forty. Who invented such an ugly number?

Against the flashing of the cameras aimed at Mr. Smith, she had to cover her eyes as she walked past him, trying not to stare at the handsome millionaire.

Suddenly he spied her attempting to get through the tight crowd. He saw her trying her best to play coy and shy, and pushed past his protectors.

Again, he had come to this gala without his wife.

"Rebecca!" he called to her, his voice deep and rumbling, just like it sounded on his albums. Just like she remembered it from the last time they were together—back in the days when he was just another poor working stiff. Back when they were in love. James Smith had been her first lover—her true love.

Feeling the heat of his eyes staring at her, she froze.

"Yes, Mr. Smith," she said, her voice just above a peep.

"Rebecca, is it really you? The woman I've loved for so many years. The woman who truly owns my heart? I love you. Tell me you love me and we'll run off," he said, reaching for her hand and pulling it to his well-defined chest.

"Oh Mr. Smith, I love you too," she answered, gasping now for air, leaning her sinuous body towards him.

“Call me James,” he said, his lips sliding into a crooked smile—a sexy smile that had a meaning behind it. “Just say my name and I’ll take you away with me.”

“Jason,” she said before shaking her head noticing the name that came from her lips. She attempted to say the name James and yet found herself unable. Only the name of her control freak boyfriend Jason came out of her mouth, choking her.

She began gasping for air now; it was as if every time she tried to say the name James, Jason, through his wicked controlling power over her, took more of her life from her.

Collapsing, she saw James Smith’s eyes locked on her.

She reached for his hand to save her, only to have it intercepted by the large bodyguard pulling him back.

“Jason? Jason?” Aurora screamed, pressing the backspace key, deleting the name of her ex-husband from the page. “She called the man Jason. Umph Umph Umph. See, you gotta get away from that nut factory or he’s gonna kill all your joy fa sho,” she said, yelling at the character Rebecca that she’d created.

“Girl are you still going crazy in there with that book you call yourself writing,” her sister said, passing by the library where she sat typing away.

"Call myself writing? Samantha, I already told you, I'm the one who wrote Jason's bestseller—not him. He stole my manuscript and made big bucks off my creativity. Now I'm gonna write another book and just do better than him . . . show his ass what real talent looks like."

"Umhmm," her sister chuckled, heading on her way.

Aurora slapped her forehead. She was getting nowhere on this novel. She was totally blocked for sure. At first she was all fired up—anger being her biggest kindling. She was out for payback and this was the only way she figured she could get it. But now—it just wasn't happening.

She had "helped" her ex-husband out with a writing project a couple of years ago that backfired. She'd leant her talents and imagination to his sorry, slow and very dull manuscript landing him a book deal—one that carried with it a tasty movie option. "And with what thanks? None." Jason not only cheated on her but left her pretty much without any recourse or proof that she co-authored the book with him. "Entertainment lawyers and their tricks." Aurora remembered her humiliation while trying to prove she'd written most of the book—if not all. She felt foolish when not even her friends believed she had that much talent. "Why? Because I was fat? Because

I didn't finish high school? Because I never had a real job?" The memory, even now had her tempted to reach for something to shove in her mouth for comfort. She was a mess during that whole thing.

But no sooner than all that started, it ended. The year flew by and before she knew it, Jason was back in her face begging for forgiveness. She gave in. "And now look at me . . . alone again." She shook her head and moved back from the keyboard. The smells wafting from the kitchen were divine. She had to admit her sister may not believe in her talent but she sure was good at taking care of her health. Since recovering from her mini breakdown she'd been living with her big sister. With eating right and exercise—including yoga for stress, she'd lost over one hundred pounds in the last year. Doctors had told her that she was suffering from delusions and grief of her talent dysplasia—or better said she was trying to take Jason's talent for her own because she had none. But she wasn't. And to prove it to herself she wrote—manuscript after manuscript—tucking them away in a hat box in her closet.

About a year later, Jason came back for the second round of "pin the tail on Aurora"—that's what Aurora liked to call it. Still overweight and suffering from low self esteem, she took him back. During that brief stay, he called her his muse, his love, and his forgiveness angel— and then when he left he'd not only taken her heart, he'd stolen her manuscripts.

And this time, not only did he get a book deal but ended up on the *New York Times*. With her book! He'd changed nothing . . . not even the title. Aurora was livid, but this time, she knew better than to try to win him in court. This time she planned to beat him at his own game.

Chapter 2

Looking in the mirror at her naked body, Aurora sighed heavily.

"What's the point with losing all this weight if it all it does is make everything sag?' she asked the reflection. She so dreaded getting old and even more so, with the prospects of getting old alone.

Tomorrow was her birthday. She would be forty.

So far, no one had commented on the event, however, she hadn't gone downstairs. She could tell by the whispered secrets and hush-hush talk, her sisters were planning something horrible—like a party, to rub in and document this terrible moment in life.

"And if Michael shows up with that camcorder his ass is grass," she growled, pointing her finger at the mirror, threatening her brother-in-law. "He knows me. I'll fight 'im," she added, pulling on her heavy robe and slipping her feet into her slippers.

Downstairs, Aurora found her older sister sitting at the table looking over papers. She was deep in thought.

Life had dealt her sister some blows over the last couple of years. Aurora often wondered if her sister was really dealing with things as well as she appeared to be, or was she nearing the breaking point herself. First, Samantha's husband died suddenly in a mountain climbing accident and then she found out he'd left her with a shitload of debt. To add insult to injury she then found out he was having an affair. That was discovered when they recovered his body—along with his lovers at the bottom of that ravine. Aurora felt terrible for her sister's trauma, although, she had to admit, it would make a tremendous storyline in the next book she'd plan to write as soon as she finished this one. She was almost done.

Aurora shook her head at the thought of her sister. Despite her losses, she still took her in and cared for her without asking for a dime. Sure after a while Aurora had gotten a job at the corner convenience store, but that wasn't paying much. But after the publication of her newest novel, she'd make millions, just as Jason had done. Only she would share her wealth with those who loved her.

Writing had been what Aurora had enjoyed for a few years now. It had become a hidden passion that only one person had been made privy to, and unfortunately, he'd taken full advantage of the knowledge, and of her. With a heavy sigh, Aurora shook the thought from her mind and headed to the coffee pot. Aurora didn't want to think about Jason's success, obtained with her words, her thoughts, her manuscript.

"I could just kill him," she mumbled audibly.

"What?" asked Samantha, distant sounding and distracted.

Poor thing, she is a mess, Aurora thought, looking at her sister sitting there, thin and frail—tired and haggard looking. She was vegan and maybe they all looked that way—at least that was what Aurora surmised from Samantha's skinny vegan friends, but for some reason Samantha looked not quite as healthy as they did. Samantha played the flute in a local orchestra. She traveled a little but not enough to wear her out as much as she appeared to be.

"Oh, nothing I was just thinking about Jason again and all this book stuff," Aurora admitted, giving into the realities of it all. Jason and that damned three-figure contract for his second book! *My second book*, she mused.

The first one she had given him freely, as love had motivated her to share of herself this way. But this second book, it was plagiarism, thievery pure and simple. But how could she prove it. She'd written it long hand. There wasn't even a computer trail—nothing.

One night of passion had cost her in a big way.

Aurora thought about it all now. She had tried to resist him, but with Jason's pretty face—soft features, topped off with those light green contacts—honey, he was just too fine to resist.

Aurora squirmed a little now, thinking of his talents between the sheets. He was one who seemed to really get off on oral sex and would often treat her to a little before asking for reciprocation. And then the fun would begin. As big as she was, he easily handled the job, flipping her here and there and over and yarn. "Wow," she whispered, thinking aloud.

"What?" Samantha asked again.

"Oh, nothing," she lied.

"You really need to get Jason off your mind girl. He's gone. It's over," Samantha said, letting her own bitterness show.

"Sweetie what's wrong?" Aurora asked, sensing her sister's need to talk. However, instead of words, Samantha burst into tears. Aurora rushed over to her quickly putting her arm around her shoulder.

"They cut my position from the orchestra. I'm gonna lose the house," she cried.

Aurora stood up straight. "What? Where is your savings?"

"What savings. Douglas left me with so much debt." Samantha sniffed—snorted actually. "I had to use my savings to pay it all off . . . and still I owe so much money," she cried. Her nose was reddening under her smooth brown skin tone.

"Why in the hell did you do that? Why did you pay off Douglas's bills?" Aurora asked, choking out the words. "I wouldn't have paid shit. I would have sent his lover's family an invoice. I mean come on! Half those bills he racked up cheating on you!"

"Aurora stop," Samantha pleaded, sliding from her chair and moving back from the table as if distancing herself from the letter. "There's more."

"More?"

"Douglas and that . . . that woman had a child."

That was too much. Aurora threw up her hands in disgust. This was one too many subplots to this girl's sad tale of despair. *Wow,* Aurora thought. If only she could rewrite her sister's life, how different this would come out for her.

"You're not gonna lose your house I promise you. Once my book gets picked up—"

"Stop, Aurora. This is a real problem here," Samantha snapped, shutting her down with the slice of her hand. "Now stop it. Sure, if you and Jason were together and you could like . . ." Samantha paused as if formulating a plan. "You could borrow some money from him for me, then sure. But all this talk about you writing a book, well I don't want to hear it!"

Aurora was fit to be tied, but something inside kept her from going off. She loved Samantha—maybe that was it. "You're not gonna lose your house." Aurora grabbed her cup of coffee and stormed into the library, slamming the door behind her. She had work to do.

Aurora thought back to when it all started. It took a while to realize Jason had stolen the manuscript as Aurora had gotten busy with all else going on—Douglas's funeral and all that other nonsense. Needless to say, when her former best friend, Jason's then agent and mistress, Stacy, called to tell her about Jason breaking their contract and jumping ship to hook up with another agent, Aurora was a little taken back. "And I care about this why?"

That's when Stacy mentioned Jason's new secret manuscript.

"Jason doesn't have a new manuscript," Aurora had divulged to Stacy, who sighed loudly. "I know this because he was in my bed trying to write one—unsuccessfully I might add. I tried to tell you idiots he didn't write the first one but oooh well. Soon he gave up and made love to me," she said, digging it in that Jason had come back to her.

"Aurora don't be hating," she had said then, attempting slang, which was not her strong suit, being of Minnesota stock.

"I'm telling you, Jason doesn't have a new manuscript. Jason didn't have an old manuscript. So unless he took a class, or stole another one, Jason didn't write anything," Aurora countered, listening to only silence as Stacy's response to her comments.

Aurora hadn't thought to make a contract with Jason over the first book and felt like a fool trusting him to be fair with the advance and royalty installments—the only one who got anything out of that deal besides Jason was Stacy.

"Stacy . . ." Aurora called out. She remembered that feeling in her chest—it was just like the one she had now, thinking about Douglas and all he was putting her sister through—even from the grave. "Stacy, Jason doesn't have a manuscript? Right!"

"And it wasn't even my best work," Aurora scowled now thinking about the manuscript and that conversation with Stacy. "And the fool got a three book deal out of it." Suddenly thinking about Stacy, she started chuckling. "Ohhh Stacy was so pissed. She missed out on a lot of money. Ha! I keep forgetting I wasn't the only woman scorned in that deal. Wonder who Stacy is holding up."

Holding a grudge was one of Stacy's biggest character flaws, Aurora remembered. She'd not heard from Stacy since all that went down. "And good riddance I say," she mumbled, typing the finishing touches on her manuscript. It was the story of a woman who had found an old love but her new lover would not let her go. So she decided to murder the new lover in order to free herself of the spell he had on her. "Dumb sort of, but kinda cool in a way," she thought aloud. She used Jason as the new lover who was in the way of her character finding her way back to her first love. "And now to kill him," she laughed wickedly sitting at her computer and getting down to the dirty business. "Ooooh honey and this is gonna hurt you way more than it's gonna hurt me!" she cackled wickedly.

ORDER FORM
URBAN BOOKS, LLC
78 E. Industry Ct
Deer Park, NY 11729

Name: (please print):_______________

Address:_______________

City/State:_______________

Zip:_______________

QTY	TITLES	PRICE

Shipping and handling-add $3.50 for 1st book, then $1.75 for each additional book.

Please send a check payable to:

Urban Books, LLC

Please allow 4-6 weeks for delivery

ORDER FORM
URBAN BOOKS, LLC
78 E. Industry Ct
Deer Park, NY 11729

Name: (please print):_______________

Address:_______________

City/State:_______________

Zip:_______________

QTY	TITLES	PRICE
	16 On The Block	$14.95
	A Girl From Flint	$14.95
	A Pimp's Life	$14.95
	Baltimore Chronicles	$14.95
	Baltimore Chronicles 2	$14.95
	Betrayal	$14.95
	Black Diamond	$14.95

Shipping and handling-add $3.50 for 1st book, then $1.75 for each additional book.

Please send a check payable to:

Urban Books, LLC

Please allow 4-6 weeks for delivery

ORDER FORM
URBAN BOOKS, LLC
78 E. Industry Ct
Deer Park, NY 11729

Name: (please print):_______________

Address:_______________

City/State:_______________

Zip:_______________

QTY	TITLES	PRICE
	Black Diamond 2	$14.95
	Black Friday	$14.95
	Both Sides Of The Fence	$14.95
	Both Sides Of The Fence 2	$14.95
	California Connection	$14.95
	California Connection 2	$14.95

Shipping and handling-add $3.50 for 1st book, then $1.75 for each additional book.
Please send a check payable to:

Urban Books, LLC

Please allow 4-6 weeks for delivery

ORDER FORM
URBAN BOOKS, LLC
78 E. Industry Ct
Deer Park, NY 11729

Name: (please print):________________

Address:____________________________

City/State:_________________________

Zip:________________________________

QTY	TITLES	PRICE
	Cheesecake And Teardrops	$14.95
	Congratulations	$14.95
	Crazy In Love	$14.95
	Cyber Case	$14.95
	Denim Diaries	$14.95
	Diary Of A Mad First Lady	$14.95
	Diary Of A Stalker	$14.95

Shipping and handling-add $3.50 for 1st book, then $1.75 for each additional book.

Please send a check payable to:

Urban Books, LLC

Please allow 4-6 weeks for delivery